To Mom,
who always likes to be remembered.

Acknowledgments

Many thanks to Larry Segriff of Tekno Books and Shannon Jamieson Vazquez of Berkley Prime Crime, who have so ably shepherded this project along.

And many more thanks to Beth, the wife of the late Dr. Pergola (a very dear high-school friend), for sharing her knowledge of pets . . . and vets.

More praise for

The Big Kitty

"In this debut, Sunny Coolidge, with the able assistance of a 'big kitty' named Shadow, proves she has the skills to make a successful amateur sleuth. Cozy mystery lovers will adore Shadow and pine for many more adventures for him and Sunny."

—Miranda James, *New York Times* bestselling author
of the Cat in the Stacks Mysteries

"Applause for paws—Sunny and Shadow take Best in Show!"

—Susan Wittig Albert, author of *Widow's Tears*

"Deftly combines heartwarming humor and nail-biting suspense for a fun read that leaves you looking forward to Sunny and Shadow's next adventure."

—Ali Brandon, author of *A Novel Way to Die,*
a Black Cat Bookshop Mystery

"A purrfect debut. Four paws up and a tip of the tail."

—Carolyn Hart, author of *Death Comes Silently*

"A charming, witty, exciting new entry in the genre, featuring the best realized and most personable fictional character on four legs. You'll love Shadow. And Sunny's fun, too."

—Parnell Hall, author of *The KenKen Killings*

"A fun amateur-sleuth tale . . . [A] whimsical spin to the light-hearted whodunit."   —*The Mystery Gazette*

"With a deft hand at plotting, an appealing small-town setting, and a determined protagonist, Donally has created a series opener that aficionados of whodunits and felines will find rubs them exactly the right way."   —*The Richmond Times-Dispatch*

"[Sunny and Shadow are] a cute twosome . . . I am looking forward to the next in the series!"   —*Book Dilettante*

"Interesting and engaging . . . [An] enjoyable novel."

—*Genre Go Round Reviews*

Berkley Prime Crime titles by Claire Donally

THE BIG KITTY
CAT NAP

Cat Nap

Claire Donally

BERKLEY PRIME CRIME, NEW YORK

THE BERKLEY PUBLISHING GROUP
Published by the Penguin Group
Penguin Group (USA) Inc.
375 Hudson Street, New York, New York 10014, USA

USA / Canada / UK / Ireland / Australia / New Zealand / India / South Africa / China

Penguin Books Ltd., Registered Offices: 80 Strand, London WC2R 0RL, England
For more information about the Penguin Group, visit penguin.com.

CAT NAP

A Berkley Prime Crime Book / published by arrangement with Tekno Books

Berkley Prime Crime Books are published by The Berkley Publishing Group.
BERKLEY® PRIME CRIME and the PRIME CRIME logo are trademarks of
Penguin Group (USA) Inc.

For information, address: The Berkley Publishing Group,
a division of Penguin Group (USA) Inc.,
375 Hudson Street, New York, New York 10014.

ISBN: 978-0-425-25213-0

PUBLISHING HISTORY
Berkley Prime Crime mass-market edition / May 2013

PRINTED IN THE UNITED STATES OF AMERICA

10 9 8 7 6 5 4 3 2 1

Cover illustration by Mary Ann Lasher.
Cover design by George Long.
Interior text design by Laura K. Corless.

1

The winter morning air was clean and clear as glass—and sharp enough to cut like glass, too. But he didn't mind the cold. After all, he was rested, invigorated . . . and he had a good coat.

He inhaled deeply, closing his eyes against the dawn sunlight. It had been so wonderful this morning, waking up and finding himself lying in bed with Sunny, enjoying the shared body warmth, the closeness, the intoxicating smell of her. And when she'd sighed sleepily and put her arms around him . . . oh, yes, that had been wonderful.

Now he felt badly about the way he'd treated her after they'd gotten up. He'd quietly followed her down the stairs while she blearily bumbled her way to the kitchen to start breakfast. She'd opened the back door and stood there for a moment, sucking in her breath and then retreating with a sneeze when the chilly weather outside invaded the room with a blast of air that seemed to penetrate to every corner.

He'd taken his opportunity while she was distracted, darting out before the door shut. Maybe he should have let her know he was going, but that just seemed like more trouble than he wanted to deal with. What was wrong with going outside for a few moments to enjoy the freshly fallen snow? All his life, he'd found it was better to beg forgiveness than to ask for permission.

He hadn't planned on getting distracted, following a set of squirrel tracks across a neighbor's lawn. When he realized how far he'd gone—and how much time he'd taken—he'd sprinted across several driveways to get back to Sunny's house. But by the time he got there, her big car was gone. That was bad. He had a good thing going here, and now his own thoughtlessness was going to leave him out in the cold. Stupid, stupid, stupid.

Worse still, his foot was beginning to throb with pain. He hadn't paid attention while he was racing back to Sunny. Several times he'd skidded on ice or slush. That hadn't been good. Maybe he'd injured himself on something unpleasant on one of those driveways he'd dashed across.

His pride hurt as much as his foot as he limped, step by unwilling step, around to the back door of the little white house. It wouldn't be easy, talking his way back inside. But he'd have to do it. Maybe it was the pain, or moving slowly after his brisk run, but all of a sudden, it felt much colder out here. He took a deep breath and then let it out in the most plaintive tone he could manage: *"MMMMmmmrrrowwwww!!!!!"*

*

Sunny Coolidge leaned back from her computer keyboard with a grin of triumph, pulling loose the pencil she'd used to hold her wild curls in a topknot and out of her face. The hairstyle probably wasn't pretty, but it had been effective—sort of like the job she'd spent the entire day tangling with. Except for the occasional e-mail or phone call, she had devoted all her time today to updating the Internet website for the Maine Adventure X-perience, MAX for short.

It never failed. Whenever she upgraded the system, the components never worked together properly. She had to strip things down to the barest basics and then build the system back up again, finding and resolving whatever conflicts had been introduced via new versions of software. Sometimes that process could take days. But after putting it off all week, today she'd managed to score a personal best in wrestling with recalcitrant computer code.

Sunny looked through the big plate-glass window to the street outside. It had already gone dark, and the traffic was sparse, to put it mildly. Just a few cars passed while she watched. But then, nightfall came early in southern Maine at this time of year. That and the winter cold tended to discourage tourists from flocking to the delights of Kittery Harbor in January, February, and March. The busy season usually came in summer, when people sailed along the rocky coasts, or in the autumn, when they came to see the foliage or engage in traditional pastimes such as apple picking. Add in an unseasonable early winter warm spell, and the winter activity fans had gone out west instead of up north. That warmth looked likely to change now, though. Yesterday had brought a little snow, and a lot of talk from local weather forecasters about the threat of a bigger storm on the horizon.

Not that weather concerns had done much to slow Sunny's tourist business, though. Bargains were something that brought people to the area year-round, and two bus-loads of shopping tourists had simply pushed up their schedules and started trolling the miles of outlet malls to the north of Kittery Harbor tonight instead of tomorrow morning, just in case a blizzard blew in. Nor had the four couples booking rooms in quiet bed-and-breakfast estab-lishments canceled on her. *If we really get a blizzard, they may find their romantic weekends running a little longer than anticipated,* she thought. *But then, being stuck with someone you love couldn't be all that bad, could it?*

Not having anything romantic on the agenda herself, Sunny couldn't say. Oh, there was a guy she was interested in—smart, good-looking, and he carried a gun. But getting Constable Will Price to notice her "that way" made the tough-est systems upgrade seem like child's play in comparison.

For one thing, I'm not sure I can delete all his memory when it comes to Jane Rigsdale, Sunny thought wryly. Jane was a former classmate of hers, and the local vet—not to mention an all-too-successful rival for Will Price's atten-tion. She finished the last of her tests on the website, grinned again at the results, and muttered "TGIF" as she started shutting down her computer. Then the phone rang.

Sunny tensed a little—all too often, she'd catch some disaster just as she was ready to escape from the office. It seemed to go with the territory in the tourist biz.

Hearing her father's voice on the other end of the line

didn't automatically let her relax her shoulders either. She'd come back to Kittery Harbor from New York when Mike Coolidge suffered a heart attack and needed someone to take care of him. It had been a scary time, made a little scarier when the newspaper she'd worked for back in the city had laid her off in absentia from her job as a reporter. Sunny had had to face the challenge of handling an irascible patient while also finding some way to turn her work experience into a paycheck. Ken Howell, the editor of the local paper, couldn't fit a full-time reporter into his small operation. So in the end, she'd wound up at MAX. Her salary was pretty pitiful, but at least she got a chance to do a little writing for the site in between sieges of grunt work.

But now, as she listened to her dad over the phone, he sounded pretty cheerful rather than scared or aggravated. Sunny had to admit, he'd definitely improved over the past few months. Mike had even recently started driving a little on local errands, and had undertaken a walking program— putting in three miles a day of indoor hoofing around the outlet malls.

Still . . .

"Give me the bad news first," Sunny told her dad.

"Nothing exciting," Mike quickly said. "I found your friend Shadow yowling outside the kitchen door this morning. Dunno what happened, but when he came in, he was limping. Now I see that he's still favoring one paw since he got up from his latest nap."

"Did you look—" Sunny began, but her father broke in unceremoniously.

"Uh-uh," Mike objected. "Even on a good day, I don't think that cat would tolerate me poking at him—especially in a place that hurts." He gave a sour chuckle. "And he has the claws to back up a hands-off policy."

Sunny sighed. Her dad had a point. He and Shadow had settled into a sort of wary truce following some friction when the cat had first adopted Sunny. Shadow had since settled pretty comfortably into the Coolidge household in spite of Mike's initial fulminations, and now, having enjoyed a couple of months of peace and quiet, Mike certainly didn't want to get on Shadow's bad side again.

"Did you give Jane Rigsdale a call?" Sunny asked.

"Of course, especially since she promised you that the mangeball gets a free ride whenever he needs it," her dad replied, every inch the thrifty Yankee trader. "She said she'd fit you in at the end of her Saturday hours."

Sometimes it pays to have someone feel she owes you a favor, Sunny thought. Aloud, she asked, "And is there any good news?"

"A little," Mike said. "I thought we might eat out tonight. Picked up a little football pool money on last night's game."

Sunny laughed. "I thought it sounded like you were cheering harder than usual for the Pats."

"Yeah, well," her dad responded. "I thought we might grab a bite at the Redbrick." He hesitated for a second. "Unless you and Will have plans."

I wish, thought Sunny. Why did everything seem to remind her of Will—or rather her lack of success with him? But when she told Mike she was free, his voice grew brighter over the phone line. "So what do you think? Dinner at the Redbrick? We haven't been there in a while."

"Sure, why not?" Sunny replied. "I'm just closing up the office."

"Would you mind coming to get me?" Mike broke off in embarrassment. "I'm still not ready to go driving at night. And besides," he went on, sounding a bit more like his usual self, "we'll save on gas, using only one car."

Sunny calculated the amount of money in her pocket and the amount of gas in her SUV. They'd be awfully close to E on the gas gauge on the way back into town. Maybe some of Mike's ill-gotten gains could finance a fill-up at Sal DiGillio's service station. "I can be home in half an hour," she told him. "With luck, we can get to the Redbrick in time to beat the dinner rush."

Sunny said good-bye, feeling pleased with the plan, but no sooner had she hung up the phone than it started ringing again. One of the romantic couples was having GPS problems and had gotten completely turned around. Sunny stayed on the line, verbally guiding them through winding country roads, until the couple reached their B&B destination. By the time she managed to leave the office, pick up her dad, and get back into town, they couldn't even find a parking spot near the Redbrick Tavern.

Kittery Harbor was an old town, and the oldest part was crammed in around the harbor. The streets were crooked relics of that long bygone time, as were the surviving buildings, constructed in the New England Colonial style of hemlock and spruce, with clapboard siding and shingled roofs. Their destination tonight, though, came from a more recent era, in a neighborhood with slightly wider streets and, as the tavern's name suggested, brick construction. Wider streets didn't necessarily mean better parking, though. Sunny and her father had to walk several blocks to get to the Redbrick, their breath steaming in the night air.

Mike walked along steadily, his face ruddy from the chill, his white curls bobbing. Sunny couldn't help noticing how much his hair had grown out since his Christmas haircut.

Almost without thinking, she raised a hand to her own reddish mane. She'd finally found a hairdresser who could tame her unruly curls, but the price of looking good was constant—and expensive—vigilance.

Mike climbed the steps to the entrance and opened the door. Once inside, they faced a blast of heat and loud, cheerful chatter bouncing off the big room's tin ceiling and brick walls. The hostess warned them that they'd face a wait of nearly half an hour. What else could they expect from a Friday night? The place was jammed with diners.

Mike gave their names, and then he and Sunny found seats at the bar, where he surprised Sunny by ordering a seltzer with lime.

"At least the fruit makes it look like I'm having a real drink," he said with a grin.

Maybe he's finally taking the idea of healthy eating to heart, Sunny thought.

She asked the bartender for a diet cola; it didn't seem fair for her to flaunt a beer under her dad's nose while he sipped a seltzer. She had an instant to enjoy the warm glow of satisfaction at having finally gotten through to him . . . until her dad added, "I'm hoping that being good here might earn me some slack from the food police when I order a hamburger for supper."

"A hamburger—not a bacon cheeseburger." Sunny was willing to bend a little, especially since the Redbrick was famous for its burgers. "And no fries—how about a salad?"

Mike rolled his eyes but agreed.

*

"I guess that blasted foot is really giving Shadow some trouble," Sunny said, trying to change the subject. "He didn't come charging up as usual when I came home. And I didn't like the way he kept licking at his paw. And then, every time I tried to get a look at it, he shied away." The worry in her voice shaded into a hurt tone as she spoke.

Mike patted her arm. "I know, I know, he's usually all over you. Look at it this way—he wouldn't even come near me after he came limping in today." He scowled, looking a little defensive. "I don't even know how he got out."

"My own stupid fault." Sunny took her glass from the bartender and had a sip. "I opened the kitchen door this morning to wake myself up with a blast of fresh air. Shadow must have sneaked out while I was busy shivering." Her tone went from self-accusation back to worry. "I hope Jane won't find something really wrong when I bring Shadow over to see her tomorrow."

"I think that damned cat's indestructible," Mike said, waving away any thoughts of veterinary problems. "I bet Jane thinks so, too. If you want, you can ask her now." He had shifted on his bar stool and nodded at the other side of the room. "She's eating over there."

Sunny turned to look in the direction her father indicated. Even in a crowded room, it was hard to miss someone with Jane Rigsdale's blond good looks. Jane sat facing the bar—and Sunny—but the vet's intense blue eyes seemed focused on the man sitting opposite her.

For a second Sunny's heart sank. Things would be a lot simpler between her and Will Price if it wasn't for Jane.

Jane and Will had been a couple years ago, back when Jane was the teen queen of Kittery Harbor and Will was a college student. They had broken up and gone off to lead separate lives, but like Sunny, both of them had since returned to the old hometown. Given the shortage of decent, unattached male material in the area, Sunny couldn't blame Jane for trying to become Will's once and future girlfriend.

She didn't have to like it, though.

Just as Sunny was lamenting her bad luck in getting invited out by her dad of all people on a night when Jane and Will were on a date, she stopped. *Wait a minute! I don't think that's Will after all.* Sunny looked more carefully at the man seated with Jane. She could only see the back of his head, but that brown hair looked darker than Will's, and it touched the guy's collar. As a cop, Will would never let his hair grow that long, especially since the last time she'd seen him, earlier this week, he'd been waving at her through the window of Harbor Barbers.

Yeah, that can't be Will. The usually hard-edged reporter's voice in the back of Sunny's head suddenly sounded downright cheerful. *Maybe Jane has found herself a new guy. Now, if only they hit it off . . .*

Sunny felt even cheerier when the man reached across the table to take Jane's hand, his thumb gently stroking her soft skin in an obvious caress.

Even better, Sunny thought.

Until Jane snatched her hand back, jumped to her feet, grabbed her wineglass, and flung the contents right in the guy's face.

2

Jane Rigsdale stormed out of the Redbrick, her full lips compressed in a thin line, the skin tight over her strong cheekbones, her pale eyebrows pulled together, and her blue eyes looking straight ahead as she sailed right past the bar. When Sunny's dad got angry, his blue eyes blazed. Sunny used to call it the laser-glare of death. Jane's eyes got very faraway and cold. Her blond bombshell beauty transformed into the mask of a frozen ice goddess—perfectly matching the chilly air she stepped into outside.

Brrrr, Sunny thought. *Got to remember never to get Jane really ticked off at me.*

Mike sat quietly, his gaze following Jane out the door. Then he grinned, taking a more optimistic view of the goings-on. "What do you think?" he asked. "One of those speed dates?"

"I think those end with a bell ringing, not with a wine spritzer to the face." Sunny smiled at her dad.

"You mean, like between the rounds at a prizefight? Well, that guy could sure have used a cornerman and a good towel. I hope he gets a move on. If we're lucky, maybe we'll get the table."

Sunny didn't answer as she watched the guy Mike was joking about, Jane's victim, who now stood up from his seat, mopping his face with a napkin. The man was shorter and somewhat older than Will. But as he wryly glanced at the suddenly silent tables around him, Sunny could see that he was startlingly handsome.

If Jane's throwing away guys like that, what the heck does she want? Sunny wondered. Even covered in wine, this guy could play Prince Charming—or at least Prince Charming's cool uncle. She sighed, and not romantically. Sunny knew what Jane wanted. *She wants Will.*

A mischievous thought pushed that gloomy realization aside. *Maybe I should make a play for* this *guy. It would only be fair. Share and share alike.*

Whatever he'd said to Jane that had gotten him that wine bath, the man certainly had self-confidence; he didn't display a shred of embarrassment even though every eye in the place was on him. He just reached into his wallet, left some money, finished drying off, pulled on a coat, and strolled out the door. Once he was gone, the murmur of whispers quickly ratcheted back up to the usual dull roar that filled the Redbrick.

As it turned out, Sunny and her dad did get the vacated table. Mike ordered his hamburger with gusto. Sunny had a salad with grilled chicken on top, drizzled with the homemade raspberry vinaigrette. As instructed, her dad also eschewed French fries for a side salad, and although his eyebrows rose longingly when the waitress mentioned blue cheese dressing, he went with the vinaigrette, too, avoiding the need for any intervention from the food police.

When their food arrived, Mike smiled broadly. He sprinkled some steak sauce on his burger, piled on the tomato and onion slices, and then replaced the top of the roll. Carefully holding his creation in both hands, he took a bite. "Perfect. Medium-rare." He turned the conversation back to the scene they'd witnessed earlier. "A good meal and a floor show, too. What do you think that was all about between those two?"

"I have no idea," Sunny replied. While she had a half-friendly relationship with Jane, that didn't mean a lot of confidences got shared. "In fact, I don't even know who that was with her. Did you recognize the man?" Besides being tapped into the local gossip network, her dad seemed to know about eighty percent of Kittery Harbor's population by sight.

"I was thinking he looked familiar." Mike took another bite and chewed in thoughtful silence.

Sunny couldn't stand the suspense and spoke up. "From where?"

Mike swallowed and gave her an infuriating shrug. "Dunno. Guess I must have seen him around town—maybe Judson's Market, someplace like that. As I recollect, he was flirting with a girl behind a counter." He frowned, rubbing a knuckle just above his bushy eyebrows as if trying to massage his memory. "I think maybe it was from before I got sick."

"So almost a year ago?"

"Can't say for sure." Annoyed at his forgetfulness, Mike shot her a look. "Why are you cross-examining me about this guy? You're seeing Jane tomorrow. Ask her then."

"I don't think that's a good idea," Sunny said. What was the etiquette on situations like a wine-in-the-face farewell? "There really is such a thing as sticking your nose in where it's not wanted—and maybe getting it bitten off." That seemed very likely, especially considering the expression frozen on Jane's features as she stalked away from her table.

"Hey, you're a reporter," Mike said with a proud smile. "If anyone can figure out a way to worm the story out of her, it'll be you."

*

Shadow awoke from a nap when he heard the sound of Sunny's car pulling up. He leaped to his feet, ready to welcome her, and winced at the sudden throb of pain from his right forepaw.

Even though the paw slowed him up a little, he reached the front door while Sunny was still rattling her keys outside. Shadow's greeting involved a bit less running around than usual. His approach was a bit more careful, especially since the scents he picked up included that sour stuff that made humans act silly. The Old One—Sunny's father—carefully stepped around them while shedding the heavy cloth that the two-legs used instead of growing sensible fur. That was just as well. Shadow would only give him a cursory sniff at the best of times.

Sunny, though, went down on her knees, reaching out

to him. He could feel the outside cold on her coat as he moved to avoid her arms—a little more complicated now, with his sore foot.

She finally gave up and rose, sighing. Shadow gazed up at her. It wasn't that he didn't want to be close and let her carry him around. It was just a bad idea to get that dependent on someone else. Too many times in the past, he'd been turned out of his home and found himself on the street. He didn't think Sunny would do that to him—he really hoped not. But deep inside, Shadow knew he needed to be able to stand on his own four feet—even if one of them hurt. It was the only way he knew to survive.

Sunny took off her coat and joined the Old One in the room with the picture box. It showed people chasing one another and using those things that made loud bangs. Shadow had seen—and heard—those things up close. Frankly, he hadn't liked them. What the pictures didn't show was that, besides being hard on the ears, those bang-bang things made an awful stink.

Normally Shadow would have gone off to find a quiet place to rest and recuperate. Instead, he lay down beside Sunny, resting his head on her thigh to make up for squirming away from her before. After a while, her hand came down to smooth his fur.

Finally the chasing stopped, and a pair of people sitting behind a desk appeared on the box. That was quieter, but boring. Sunny and the Old One talked for a few minutes. Then they rose from their seats and headed upstairs. Shadow didn't follow them—not right away.

Climbing the stairs brought new protests from Shadow's sore paw and slowed him down. By the time he got to the top of the stairway, all the lights were off up there. *Maybe I should have let her carry me,* he thought.

Shadow crouched on the topmost stair, licking at the pads on the underside of his paw where the pain came from. Sometimes, that helped the hurt to go away. Unfortunately, it didn't do much this time. Shrugging with his whole body, he set off down the hallway. Where a two-leg would have blundered around blindly, he easily navigated the route to Sunny's room, even in darkness. She'd left the door slightly open—good.

Slipping a paw inside, he pulled the door open enough to accommodate his shoulders and slipped inside. Shadow made his way to the foot of the bed and leaped up onto the top, ignoring the twinge of pain on landing. Moving as delicately as if he were stalking a suspicious bird, Shadow advanced along the soft comforter, skirting hill that was Sunny's dozing form. Finally, he reached the head of the bed and slipped under the covers, breathing deeply as he took in her scent. When he leaned against her shoulder, she gave a deep, drowsy sigh.

Shadow snuggled closer. What had he been thinking, wandering away from Sunny like that? After so much roaming around and so many homes, he'd found a good place and a loving friend. He'd never, ever go off like that again.

Unless, of course, he actually *saw* a stupid squirrel standing around outside.

*

Sunny awoke the next morning to find Shadow sleeping beside her. "How're you doing, little guy?" she asked.

Shadow stretched and rubbed against her—but then immediately began licking at his front paw.

"We're going to have that looked at in a little while," she promised him.

There was no time for the usual lazy Saturday morning rituals. Jane's office hours ended at noon. So after a quick breakfast, Sunny got out the cat carrier and set it down on the kitchen floor, adding the furry raincoat lining that Shadow had appropriated as a security blanket. She'd heard stories from other cat owners about wild chases and terrible battles trying to get cats off to veterinary appointments. But Shadow was very cool about it. After an exploratory sniff, he strolled right in, and off they went.

The Kittery Harbor Pet Hospital was a short drive away, on the edge of the town's business district. Sunny entered the one-story brick building to find the waiting room empty and Jane's receptionist, Rita Greene, standing behind her desk, pulling on a parka. Rita was in her late forties, her hair slightly tinged with gray. Like most old-line Kittery Harbor types, she didn't fool around trying to color it.

"Dr. Rigsdale is in the back," Rita said, gesturing down the hall to the examining room. "She asked me to hang on until you arrived." Rita was having a little trouble getting the zipper started on her bright green parka; Sunny suspected that was last year's coat, and that Rita had put on a few pounds. "I want to get a start on my grocery shopping today. We've got a storm coming, you know. Got to stock up, just in case it really turns into something and we get snowed in."

Sunny had heard the news radio storm watch hoopla

during breakfast. They'd hit all the main bases—the readiness of the county's plow fleet, the sudden rush for snow shovels at the home improvement places, and of course, the emergency food purchases. The more she heard, the surer Sunny became that this prediction would be a big bust. Still, she thanked Rita and wished her good look on the shopping front. Then, making sure not to bang the cat carrier against the walls, she walked down the corridor to Jane's domain.

Jane looked professional in her white coat, but she aimed a very personal smile at the cat carrier. "Good to see you again, Shadow."

Sunny placed the carrier on the exam table and opened the door. Shadow stepped out onto the metal surface, heading straight for Jane. He sat back on his haunches and extended his injured paw to the vet.

"Pretty smart," Sunny said. "And he certainly trusts you."

Yeah, everybody loves beautiful Jane, that snarky voice from the back of her head piped up. Sunny fought to repress it. She had other things to worry about than old high school jealousies. Had Shadow really hurt himself this time?

"Conditioned reflex," Jane joked. "Lord knows, Shadow's come in here with enough battle wounds and injuries. That's a very adventuresome cat you've got there." She leaned forward and examined the paw, paying special attention to the pads, looking at them through a magnifier.

"Was he outside recently?" she asked, glancing over at Sunny. "Since the snowfall?"

"He snuck out yesterday morning," Sunny replied. "My dad says he came home limping."

"I think someone in your neighborhood had a heavy hand with the ice melt." Jane let go of Shadow's paw. He immediately extended it again. That got a laugh out of Jane, who gently stroked his leg.

"There wasn't all that much snow on the ground when I got up in the morning," Sunny said. "But we have a couple of neighbors who really don't want to find themselves stuck in their driveways."

"It looks as if Shadow might have walked across one of those drives and picked up a few grains of ice melt between his pads. Hey, didn't your dad deliver rock salt back in the day?"

"Oh yeah, he drove truckloads of salt all over New England before his heart attack. In the old days, they shipped the stuff here from India. Now I hear it comes from Chile," Sunny replied.

Jane nodded, her expression grave, but her smile returned as she took Shadow's paw again. "Well, the stuff you get in most stores now is more chemically active than plain old salt. Sometimes it can even crack the pads on a cat or dog's paw. We usually close those up with a bit of superglue, believe it or not."

She looked up at Sunny. "No sign of that here. On the other hand, while the pads on a cat's paw are pretty tough, the flesh between them is more sensitive. Getting this stuff caught in there is like having a pebble in your shoe, except it's not only getting stuck between your toes but burning them, too."

"Is there a way to fix it?" Sunny couldn't keep the anxious tone out of her voice.

"There's a nice, simple home remedy you can try," Jane

said. "Just warm up a little mineral oil and work it in around the pads. I'll show you." She stepped over to a counter, picked up a bottle of mineral oil, and went to the built-in sink, running the hot water.

After holding the bottle under the stream of water for a couple of minutes, Jane opened the bottle, let a drop of oil fall on her wrist, and nodded. "Just right."

She poured a little oil into her hand and returned to the exam table. "Could I see that paw again, Shadow?"

Shadow immediately obliged, and Jane rested his paw in the pool of warm oil she'd collected in her palm.

The cat gave a little mew of surprise and then settled into purring.

"So, that feels better?" Jane said, gently massaging the oil into and between the pads on his paw. She looked over at Sunny. "See what I'm going?"

Sunny nodded. "Looks as if he's really enjoying it."

"Yeah, do this every day for a week, and he should be as good as new." Jane ran her free hand down Shadow's back as he sat quietly, still trustingly giving her his paw. She smiled gently down at the cat. "It's nice that something so simple can help a patient get better. This time on Saturday—well, after office hours—is when folks would bring in their pets to be put to sleep."

Her smiled faded as she looked into Shadow's upturned face. "Sometimes it's necessary, or even merciful. But it's a part of the job I've never enjoyed. There hasn't been one in this office since I went off on my own. When I worked with my ex-husband, Martin, I always let him take care of that side of the business. He didn't mind. Maybe that should have given me a hint of things to come." Jane raised her eyes to look at Sunny. "I saw you over at the bar in the Redbrick last night. You probably saw how things have worked out with Martin these days."

"That was Martin?" Sunny said in surprise. "He's very good-looking." The words came out before Sunny really thought about them. Her teeth clicked together as she shut her mouth a little too late.

Jane's lips quirked as she ran a finger from between Shadow's ears all the way down his back. "Yeah, Martin's a handsome guy, and an excellent vet—but a piss-poor excuse for a human being."

She gave Sunny an embarrassed smile when she looked at her again. "He could charm the pants off anyone, and he certainly did it with me. We were married less than a year after I apprenticed with him. Problem was, Martin also used the same magic on a lot of the women who brought their pets in for treatment."

Jane took her hands off Shadow and leaned against the table, her fingers clenched into fists. Shadow, sensing her distress, rubbed his head against her arm.

"Martin was clever, too," Jane went on. "He always figured he was the smartest person in the room and had all sorts of schemes to rake in piles of money. Problem is, they never worked. He ran the finances on our practice, and we were up to our eyeballs in debt when I finally discovered he was fooling around on me. Worse, he was actually milking some of his better-off lady friends for money."

"Guess I can see why he's your ex." Sunny didn't know what else to say.

"But not before we came up here for a new start." Jane

tried for a light touch, but her voice grew harsh even as she softly petted Shadow. "Martin managed to straighten out and fly right for a couple of months. Then he fell back into his old ways again—and somehow it was worse that he'd do it here, where I grew up!"

"Yikes!" Sunny said.

"There's a difference between running around in wide-open suburbia and doing the same in a small town. I heard about what he was up to pretty quickly," Jane said quietly. "And that was it. I made sure that the practice was in my name, and he couldn't get anything out of it. So after the divorce, Martin set up shop on the other side of the river and did his best to poach as many of my patients as he could. He was pretty successful, with that patented Rigsdale charm."

She gave a tight little laugh, but her face was flaming. "I don't know why I'm telling you this, except that you saw what I did to him at the Redbrick."

And you really don't have anyone else in town to talk to, Sunny realized. "There are a couple of guys I wish I could do that to," she told Jane, thinking of the editor in New York she'd been involved with. The same editor who'd laid her off when things got tough.

"Well, Martin stayed true to form." Jane sighed. "I thought he was being civilized, asking me out to dinner last night. Instead he hit me up for money—foundation money."

Jane had recently wound up running an animal welfare fund with a sizable endowment. She'd put in a lot of work with animal control people throughout the area. With the financial help of the foundation, they established a no-kill policy at the local shelter and stepped up adoption efforts, not just in Kittery Harbor but all through Elmet County. Every week, Sunny saw advertisements with pictures of furry adoption candidates in the *Harbor Crier* and in other local papers. Jane was even trying to get some of the local TV news outlets onto the adopt-a-pet bandwagon, too. She'd made a couple of successful test appearances. With a gorgeous blonde as the spokesperson, stations were quite willing to try it out.

But Jane wasn't trying to get herself on television; she really was trying to help stray and abandoned animals. She took her position seriously, and she certainly wasn't getting a lot in pay.

"The way Martin saw it, I must be rolling in dough, and I ought to spread it around." Jane's voice grew almost jagged, earning her a concerned look from Shadow. "He thought I should bring him in as a consultant, with remuneration in line with all his years of experience. A low six-figure fee would be just fine."

"He sounds like a piece of work," Sunny said quickly, hoping to head off the icy expression congealing on Jane's face. "So, is there anything else I should do for Shadow's foot?"

"Huh?" Jane blinked for a second, her vengeful train of thought obviously derailed. "Oh. No, just try the oil massage for a week. If he doesn't show improvement, then we'll try something more medical."

Anger crept back into her voice. "Martin, of course, would skip to that step right away. He never saw a procedure he didn't like. The more expensive, the better."

"Well, thanks, Jane." Sunny brought the carrier back

onto the table. She wanted to get Shadow out and away from Jane's too tightly clenched hands.

Good thing old Martin isn't around right now, she thought. *If Jane got hold of him in this mood, she'd probably snap his neck like a rotten twig.*

3

Sunny barely got home before the snowstorm the weather forecasters had been hyping came roaring in. She lugged the carrier to the front door of her house through stinging wind-borne snowflakes, let Shadow out in the foyer, and turned to face what looked like a wall of snow suddenly falling outside.

Looks as if I finally get to try out the four-wheel drive on my Wrangler, she thought.

Her father appeared in the arched entranceway into the living room. "So, you're back," he said. "You, too, hairball."

Shadow slipped around him and disappeared into the room.

"How's he doing?" Mike asked.

"Jane suggested a little home therapy." Sunny slipped

the hood of her coat up over the baseball cap she was wearing. "Anything you particularly want from the store, Dad? I figure I'd better get out there before it gets any worse."

"Not a problem," Mike told her. "I took care of it already. Went to the store, got some milk—skim, so don't get excited—and a few other things on the grocery list." He sounded very pleased with himself. "Including the makings for a stew. Figure that would work pretty well with the weather outside."

Sunny agreed, and with plentiful supplies, they spent the weekend hunkered down. The storm was fierce but brief, dropping a few inches of the white stuff before blowing out to sea. Sunny and her dad didn't mind much—except that Mike missed his heart-healthy hike. A neighbor came by with a snowblower to clear their walk and driveway, so neither Sunny nor her dad had to shovel. They had movies to watch, and more than enough ingredients to re-create Mom's famous pressure cooker stew recipe.

And, of course, Sunny had Shadow to play with. He still wasn't running and jumping so much. That eliminated some of their rougher games. But he definitely seemed to be getting around with less pain.

When her dad watched Shadow purring like a motorboat while Sunny did the warm oil massage on Sunday, Mike grumped, "You're coddling that cat."

"Well, I think warm oil beats superglue," she replied, explaining about Jane's treatment for torn pads. "I used to use something similar to close up paper cuts. The stuff stung like blazes."

"Superglue on his paws . . ." Mike's voice trailed off

and his eyes got a bit dreamy, going from Shadow to the living room mantel.

"Don't even think about it," Sunny warned.

"That's easy enough for you to say," Mike said, only half joking. "You've never had him launch a sneak attack when you're heading to the bathroom for a three a.m. pee. Can you blame me for wanting him to stay put sometimes?"

*

By the time Monday morning came around, the roads had been cleared, and Sunny had no excuse to stay home from work. She sat with her dad in the kitchen, listening to more snow nonsense on the radio. The weather forecaster warned that if the latest cold front to the west and tropical low to the south cooperated, they could create really serious weather. *If.* Apparently, everything had to line up just right to create a perfect storm, so the voice on the radio alternated between predicting doom and being vague, offering anything from a foot of snow to a mere dusting.

"Well, that's really helpful," Sunny told Mike. "Maybe it will also hail with a threat of lightning, too."

"You know what they say," he replied with a grin. "Everybody talks about the weather, but nobody ever does anything about it." He leaned back in his seat. "Me, I'll get out early and get my walk done. Then I'll take it easy back here. We're still pretty well supplied from Saturday."

"Yeah—wish me luck in that big, bad world outside." Sunny put her oatmeal bowl in the sink and got her parka. After a fond good-bye to her father and Shadow, she headed out to the maroon Jeep Wrangler already positioned at the end of the driveway.

Sunny drove down to the New Stores—kind of an odd name for a strip of fifty-year-old buildings housing a variety of shops, from Judson's Market to the offices of MAX. The development had been new when Mike was a young man, and the nickname had stuck for all these decades since.

She parked on the street, reasonably clean except for a bit of slush, headed to her office door, and unlocked the place. MAX was pretty much a one-person show unless her boss, Oliver Barnstable, turned up to holler about something. It looked as if Sunny was in luck today. She turned on the lights, shed her coat, and settled behind her desk to see if anything interesting in the way of e-mail had come in. As she scanned her computer screen, she didn't find anything earth-shaking. One of her romantic couples had decided to extend their stay—they didn't say whether it was because of love or snowdrifts. A few long-range planners asked for general information on spring and summer vacations, and another set of eager consumers wanted to set up an orgy of outlet mall shopping.

About an hour into her day, Sunny sat pulling together customized promo packages for some of the computerized tire kickers when the outside door swung open. She found herself looking up at the handsome guy from the Redbrick on Friday—Martin Rigsdale.

At least his face isn't all wet now, she thought. And then, *I hope my mouth isn't hanging open.*

"Ms. Sonata Coolidge." Rigsdale smiled down at her. "May I call you Sunny?"

"You may, Mr. Rigsdale," she replied, "or should that be Dr. Rigsdale?"

"I think Martin would be less formal." His smile *was*

charming. Sunny found herself wondering if he practiced it every morning in the mirror. He certainly knew he was good-looking, and he worked on the rest of the package to make himself attractive. An expensive patterned sweater showed under his waist-length wool jacket—no downscale parkas for Martin Rigsdale. His hair was sleeked back. Close up, Sunny could make out just a touch of gray at the temples. Very distinguished. She also got a whiff of his cologne—a spicy mix with sandalwood prevailing. It didn't smell like any of the men's fragrances she'd encountered before. *He probably has it mixed up to order,* she thought.

Sunny shook her head slightly. *Don't get distracted now.*

"What brings you to our humble office?" she asked. "From what I hear, you've lived in the area for a couple of years. There aren't all that many local attractions. You ought to know them all by now."

"I just learned about a very eye-catching attraction—you," Rigsdale said. "I noticed you at the tavern the other day."

"The Redbrick?" Sunny asked in disbelief.

Martin Rigsdale nodded. "You were hard to miss. Lots of auburn hair, nice cheekbones . . . I tend to pay attention to great-looking women."

"Even when you're getting a glass of wine in the face?" Sunny laughed. "Usually that's *why* a guy gets a glass of wine in the face."

"When one door closes, you can only hope that another may open." Rigsdale's smile grew wider. "I'm hoping for the beginning of a beautiful friendship here—and maybe some help in getting my ex-wife to see reason."

His pale gray eyes twinkled as he gave her a cheerful

shrug. "I was aware that Jane had a friend named Sunny Coolidge. If I'd known you were so attractive, I'd have introduced myself way long ago."

He grabbed a chair and settled in across from her. "Look, Sunny. You saw how my former wife treats me. A whole lot of the trouble between us involved money, and now that she has some, Jane is just being vengeful."

Rigsdale leaned toward Sunny. "If you could persuade her to loosen the purse strings a little—tell her it will get me out of her hair—we could have some fun with that money, you and me."

Now if I had just met this guy, without the lowdown I got on him from Jane, could he have charmed the pants off me? Sunny looked at that confident smile beaming at her. *Maybe. But knowing what I know . . .*

"Sorry, Martin, but I don't think either of those suggestions is a good idea."

Martin Rigsdale's smile slipped a little. "Don't be hasty, Sunny. It could be awfully nice." Translation: *He* could be awfully nice.

"I'm afraid *you* were a little hasty, thinking you could sweet-talk me into doing anything for you."

The sexy smile disappeared as if it had been snapped off. *It probably was,* Sunny thought.

Aloud she said, "Jane has been busting her buns to keep a lot of animals from getting killed. Why should I tell her that any of the money she's using for that job should go into a private slush fund for you?"

Martin stared at her. "I understood that you weren't all that tight with Jane—and that you should have gotten some of that foundation money yourself."

"Arguable, on both counts," Sunny replied. "But that doesn't mean that I'd go out of my way to screw her over, especially when she's using it to do good work." Time to turn the knife a little. "Maybe you're getting a bit old, Martin. Seems like that smile of yours might not have quite the same wattage anymore."

The amorous twist to his lips was definitely gone now. "If you won't talk to Jane for me, maybe you can warn her. We spent a couple of interesting years together, Jane and I. For richer, for poorer, sickness and health, good things and bad things. She should remember that I was around to see her make some mistakes. Stuff she might not want other people to know about, now that she's starting this wonderful new life as Saint Jane of the Animals. Tell her that, Sunny. She may decide that my silence comes cheap, all things considered."

Martin was up and out of the office before Sunny could muster up any sort of comeback. Frankly, she couldn't think of anything to say—at least, not to Martin.

Sighing, Sunny picked up the phone on her desk and punched in the number of the Kittery Harbor Animal Hospital. Jane wouldn't like hearing about this little meeting, but it didn't sound like something a little hot oil could heal.

*

Shadow found himself waking from a pleasant nap, not because of a noise, but because of a smell. He jerked awake, sneezing, and opened his eyes to find the Old One spraying a sickeningly sweet scent into the air. What was this? Had Sunny's father come up with a new way to drive him out of the house?

But no, the Old One headed down the hallway to the kitchen, away from the stink, making beckoning gestures.

Shadow warily trailed along behind to find his bowl almost overflowing with dry food, and on top of that, the contents of one of those cans that Sunny opened only once a week. It would have been nice, except that he'd eaten his fill just before settling down to sleep.

What was going on here? The Old One was pointing to the food, making cajoling noises, when the front doorbell sounded.

The older two-leg swung round and hurried off. Shadow turned from the food and moved silently to the kitchen doorway. He peered around, down the hall, as the Old One opened the door. Oh, now things began to make sense. There was the other Old One, the female. Shadow had seen them get together before—although they'd made it clear they didn't like him watching.

Maybe the Old One wanted to mark the female with that strange scent. Whatever he had in mind, he obviously wanted Shadow busily eating in the kitchen and far away. Shadow quickly pulled his head back into hiding as the female came in. He didn't need to look at them to know what was going on. From the sounds of their voices, the two went into the room with the picture box.

Settling back on his haunches, Shadow ignored the food, giving the pair of two-legs a few moments to get settled. He didn't want either of them stepping back into the hall and finding him sneaking their way.

He heard talk, then silence. They should be sitting down by now. Shadow set off down the hallway at a rapid trot. He paused at the entrance to the room and risked a quick peek.

The Old One and his female friend shared the couch. The Old One looked a little annoyed that they weren't sitting closer. The female had a large bag settled between them.

Her voice was quick and excited as she reached into the bag, bringing out a small, wiggling form. Shadow couldn't believe his eyes. She'd brought a Biscuit Eater—here? What was she thinking?

Shadow should have been able to detect the scent of dog as soon as the female came in with that bag. That stuff in the air must have overpowered his usually keen sense of smell.

Now the female two-leg made cheerful burbling sounds, showing off the little dog to the Old One. The fool animal was even the color of biscuits, a sort of yellowish cream. As the human female settled the little dog in her lap, she suddenly exclaimed, pointing at the doorway. Shadow ducked his head but stood his ground. It was too late to retreat now; he'd been spotted.

Still making happy noises, the female Old One put the young Biscuit Eater on the floor. The stupid creature stared around, emitting a string of excited yips. Then it, too, focused on Shadow. Stumbling over its own paws, the little dog headed for Shadow, its yipping growing even louder.

Wonderful. It sees something its own size and wants to investigate.

On the couch, the female Old One clapped her hands together, distracting Shadow's attention. He glanced over toward her, and then saw the other Old One—*his* Old One—sitting tightly beside her. The human male's face had an odd, pleading expression as his eyes went from the little dog to Shadow.

What does he expect me to do? Shadow thought. *Or is he afraid of what I'll do?*

The little Biscuit Eater continued to bumble its way in Shadow's direction, still piping with excitement. Shadow had faced off against dogs before, sometimes even fighting with them. They were quick to woof—and just as quick to run when claws came out. But this biscuit-colored dog was obviously young as well as foolish.

Was I ever as young as that? Shadow wondered, looking into the puppy's guileless brown eyes. Maybe, but he couldn't remember.

There was no need for claws here. Shadow arched his back and gave the Biscuit Eater an openmouthed hiss.

Whining in distress, the puppy backed away so quickly it tripped over its rear legs. The dumb dog did something else, too. Shadow recognized the sudden sharp reek even through the sweet-smelling cloud that still lingered in the air. Shadow got out of there quickly, as both Old Ones gathered around the little dog, making distressed noises. He'd heard worse when humans discovered cats not using the litter box.

*

Sunny came home at the end of the day, wanting nothing more than supper, a comfortable pair of sweats, and maybe some TV to vegetate in front of. Instead she found her father and a mortified Helena Martinson dabbing at a damp patch on the living room carpet.

"I didn't expect that at all!" Mrs. Martinson's face was pink as she looked up at Sunny. Mike rose to stand behind his lady friend, rolling his eyes as Helena went on. "How could he do that in the middle of the room?"

Well, the neighbor lady wasn't talking about Mike. And the only other male in the house was Shadow. Oh, no! Could he have created that wet spot?

"I'm so sorry, Sunny." Mrs. Martinson picked up a large bag. "I'm afraid this bad little boy made a mess on the rug." She took out a golden retriever pup, who immediately began yipping with excitement at finding a new face in the room.

"How did Shadow react to this lovely surprise?" a worried Sunny asked her dad.

"Hissed in his face and scared the pee out of him," Mike reported succinctly.

"I adopted this cute little guy from the animal shelter when I saw his picture in the *Harbor Crier*," Helena Martinson explained. "Jane Rigsdale is doing such good work to help the animals in town."

Her expression grew rueful. "But I guess I've got a bit to learn about this whole adoption thing. Come on, little fella, let's get you home." She returned the dog to her bag and beat a quick retreat.

Mike Coolidge let out a long-held breath. "She came over straight from the shelter, all excited. Wanted me to suggest a name for the pup."

"Toby," Sunny suggested with a smile.

"Why that name?" Mike asked with a suspicious expression.

"Toby Philpotts was in my grammar school class—he had the weakest bladder in school."

Mike laughed. "With a name like Philpotts, I imagine that would be a pretty embarrassing problem."

"It's just a suggestion," Sunny said, grinning at her dad. "Where's Shadow now?"

"He headed for the back after his warm greeting to the mutt."

Sunny took the hallway into the kitchen, and found Shadow glowering down from atop Mount Refrigerator.

"Hey," Sunny said, extending her hand. Shadow leaned forward, rubbing the side of his face against her fingers.

"Well, now we know how you react to puppies," she told the cat. "Maybe someday we'll get your opinion on kittens."

Gently brushing fingers through his fur, she smiled up at Shadow. "At least you didn't kill him."

She was just beginning to relax when the phone rang. Sunny turned from the refrigerator to pick up the handset. Jane's voice burst into her ear. "After you called me this morning, I rang up Martin, determined to have it out with him. He has late office hours this evening and told me to come over then. So here I am, ready to go, and wouldn't you know it, I've got a flat. I suppose I could call a cab, but any chance you could give me a lift?" Her voice slowed in embarrassment. "I wouldn't mind a little backup when I go to see him."

And like me, she doesn't really have anyone else to ask, Sunny realized. *Sal DiGillio probably just closed his garage, and I know Will is on duty until midnight. At this time in the evening, it should take less than a half hour to get to anywhere in Portsmouth. Jane certainly wouldn't waste time with Martin, and then the drive back—an hour and change should do it.* She put a hand over the receiver. "Hey, Dad?" she called down the hallway. "Would you mind waiting a bit for supper tonight?"

After Mike agreed, Sunny told Jane she'd be there soon and hung up. It was a brief drive to the Kittery Harbor Animal Hospital, where Jane stood pacing beside her disabled BMW. She quickly climbed aboard Sunny's Wrangler, and they took the bridge over the Piscataqua River to Portsmouth.

As she drove across the span, Sunny glanced at Jane. "Remember all the times we'd cross this in a school bus? And when we got to the middle—"

"That was childish," Jane complained.

"Yeah, but it was fun—and you usually led it. Come on."

Jane sighed but nodded. Then both of them chanted, "*Maaaaaaaaaaaaaiiiiiiiiiinnnnnnnnnnne,*" drawing out the word until they reached the sign in the middle of the bridge. Then they shouted "*NewHampshire!*" all in one breath as they crossed the state line.

"Childish," Jane repeated, chuckling.

"It made you laugh, though," Sunny pointed out. *And I think you could use a laugh,* she added silently.

Following Jane's directions, Sunny cut through the downtown district and headed off to the outskirts of Pease Airport, where Martin Rigsdale had set up his office.

The practice was in an old house, large and impressive at first glance. The clapboard siding had a fresh coat of shiny white paint, and the first floor had been renovated as an office for Martin's practice. But the upstairs gutters were old and discolored, and the roof looked a bit saggy in spots. Sunny pulled up on the street near a stand of wild-looking shrubbery, and she and Jane got out of the Jeep. Even on the ride over, the weather had gotten colder and damper.

Hopefully, those overgrown bushes will give the Wrangler some cover if it really starts to storm, Sunny thought. She took in the neighborhood. "Nice, but not many cars parked around the office. Either he doesn't get many patients toward the end of visiting hours, or business could be a lot better."

Jane sighed. "That's probably why he's after me for the foundation money." She squared her shoulders, her face taking on that ice queen expression. "Well, he's not getting any. I don't care what he threatens to drag up. You can take that to the bank."

With Jane in the lead, they headed up the walk to the entrance marked with a discreet bronze plaque: M. RIGS-DALE, VETERINARY MEDICINE.

Jane jabbed a thumb at the doorbell as if she were aiming for Martin's eye. A moment later, they were buzzed in. The reception area looked expensive—blond wood paneling and deep plush chairs—but it didn't match the architecture outside. The receptionist was blond, too, slim but shapely, wearing a white smock that emphasized generous cleavage. She had a pretty but sulky face, with soft features and a pout that she tried to harden into a professional mask. "I'm afraid you don't have an appointment," she said, aiming for coolness, but it came out more snotty than anything else.

"I have personal business with Dr. Rigsdale," Jane said, cutting through the high school mean girl attitude. To tell the truth, Sunny estimated that the receptionist wasn't all that long out of high school. "I'm also Dr. Rigsdale. Martin asked me to come and see him this evening."

As if Mean Girl here didn't know that, Sunny thought. The young woman drew herself up in her seat, and Sunny spotted a name tag on her smock: Dawn.

Judging from the jealous look on Dawn's face, here's another one that Martin charmed the pants off.

Dawn fiddled self-importantly with the computer keyboard on the reception desk, glancing at a screen that neither Sunny nor Jane could see. "As I mentioned, there's nothing listed—"

Jane had had enough, sidestepping Dawn's desk and heading down the hallway. If this followed the typical layout for most medical practices, somewhere along this corridor would be an examination room, a private office, or maybe both.

"You can't go back there!" Dawn's professional composure cracked as badly as her voice.

"Martin!" Jane drowned out Dawn's complaints. "Stop hiding behind this girl. You made threats to get me to come here, but that's all you're getting out of me. Do you hear me, Martin? Martin?"

As she shouted, Jane stomped down the hallway, opening doors. Finally she reached a brightly lit examination room. "Martin!"

Jane froze in the doorway, with Sunny at her heels. It was pretty easy to see why Martin hadn't responded. He lay sprawled across the metal top of the exam table, very, very still.

4

"Oh my God!" Jane rushed into the room, but Sunny grabbed her by the arm.

"If he's the way I think he is," Sunny said, "you'd better not be touching anything."

Jane shook herself loose. "That's a big 'if' right now." She hurried over to Martin Rigsdale's still form. He lay under a bright examination light, facedown. Jane put a finger to his neck and then glanced back at Sunny, shaking her head.

Dawn appeared in the doorway beside Sunny. "What are you doing?" Her voice grew shrill. "What did you do to him?"

"We found him like this," Sunny told the girl. "Better call 911."

"You're damned right I will!" Dawn spun around and rushed back to her desk.

"Come on back here," Sunny called to Jane. "You can't do anything to help, and you may get in the way of the cops."

That earned her a cold look from Jane. "I forgot that you and Will first met at a crime scene. Is that what he told you at the time?"

"On occasion. It's good advice," Sunny told her. "Especially around dead bodies."

Jane grimaced but joined Sunny at the entrance to the room. Moments later, they heard the door buzzer shrill, and then heavy footfalls come down the hallway. A pair of Portsmouth police officers appeared, with Dawn behind them.

"They're in here." The girl sounded as if she was trying to catch her breath. "He was fine until they arrived."

The cops split up, one entering the room, the other closely watching Sunny and Jane.

At least he's not keeping his hand over his holster, Sunny thought.

"Definitely deceased," the cop in the examination room said to his partner. "Got a contusion on the back of his head. Shirt rolled up on the right arm—I think we'd better secure the scene and call the Detective Division."

*

That meant a pair of detectives who arrived about fifteen minutes later. The lead was a big, burly type, grayhaired with a mournful, basset hound face. His partner was shorter and skinny, with pinched features and lips pursed as if he'd never tasted anything good in his life.

"Detective Trumbull." The big man identified himself, displaying a gold badge. "And this is my partner, Detective Fitch."

Fitch was already inside the room, moving with quick nervous steps. He stopped to examine the body. "Guy took a good knock on the head." Then Fitch delicately raised one of Martin's wrists. "No sign of rigor."

"We'll have to let the lab rats see if they can narrow down the time of death." Trumbull turned back to Dawn. "When was the last time you saw the doctor?"

"About an hour and a half ago," Dawn replied. "Then these two came barging in—"

"Thank you," The detective's rumbling voice overrode Dawn's accusations. He looked from Jane to Sunny. "I understand that one of you is the wife of the deceased?"

"Ex-wife," Jane quickly corrected, not noticing Sunny's wince. "We finalized the divorce more than a year ago."

"She killed Martin—Dr. Rigsdale!" Dawn insisted from the background. "She came down here, and the next thing I know, they're telling me he's dead!"

"As you told me at the doorway, Ms. Featherstone." Was that patience or resignation in Trumbull's voice? "Why don't you go wait in the front room with the other officers?" he suggested, turning his concentration back to Jane.

"What was your name again?" he asked her.

"Dr. Jane Rigsdale. I'm a vet, too. Martin and I used to have a practice together."

"You came down here and found Dr. Martin Rigsdale dead?"

Jane nodded. "He was just lying there."

Trumbull turned to Sunny. "And you are?"

"Sonata Coolidge. I gave Jane a lift over here."

"My car had a flat, and I asked Sunny for a ride," Jane explained.

"It's the maroon Jeep Wrangler outside," Sunny said. "I know it's pretty cold out, but if you check, my hood should still be warm. We only got here about half an hour ago. We were barely in the door before we found Martin."

Trumbull glanced at Fitch, who hurried back outside. "Considering the storm they're predicting any moment," the big detective went on, "you must have had urgent business with your ex-husband, Dr. Rigsdale."

That put a dent in Jane's self-confidence. "We had things to discuss." She stepped aside as Fitch returned. "Car's still warm," he confirmed, and then resumed his prowling around the room.

Good luck, Jane, if you think you put an end to that topic of discussion, the tough reporter who lived in the back of Sunny's head silently jeered.

The skinny detective suddenly stopped on the other side of the exam table, bending down and briefly disappearing. "Got something here, Mark," he reported. "Looks like a rubber tube—the kind doctors use to tie off an arm and make the veins pop."

"His sleeve is rolled up on the right side." Trumbull's voice went down to a low rumble. "Seems as if Dr. Rigsdale might've gotten an injection in his right arm."

That rocked Jane a bit. "Martin had his vices. But I don't think he'd turn to drugs." She paused for a second, then went on more slowly. "Besides, he's right-handed. Why would he inject himself with his left hand?"

Fitch impatiently shook his head. "More to the point, where's the hypodermic?" He gestured around the room. "I've looked. Nothing."

"It may still turn up," Trumbull said. "I guess there must be stuff around here to put animals to sleep, right?"

In spite of Sunny's look of warning, Jane opened her mouth again. "Oh, sure. From what he told me, Martin was trying to get in with the horsey set. He'd need a good supply of sodium pentobarbital if he thought he might one day need to euthanize a fifteen-hundred-pound animal."

"Enough to kill a horse," Trumbull said quietly. Fitch just glared at Jane in silent suspicion.

Sunny bit her lip. *I know you came here in a bad mood, Jane, and you've had a shock. But these are cops. If you're as smart as I always thought you were, you'd be shutting up now.*

"Look"—Sunny desperately spoke up—"why don't you check us out? We barely got in here before Dawn joined us, and we haven't been out since. I know that neither of us has that needle. If it left here, it left with somebody else."

Jane endured a quick search in rigid silence, but Sunny figured the indignity was a small price to pay to get off the suspects list. As she expected, the cops came up empty.

"I think we should get you ladies downtown for a statement." Trumbull looked even more morose than he had when he'd entered. "And you, too, Ms. Featherstone," he added over his shoulder.

*

Sunny had seen the Portsmouth city hall, a vaguely Colonial brick building facing the South Mill Pond, but that part of the complex was like the top bar of a capital T. A string of less grandiose civic buildings made up the body of the T. The entrance to the police station, for instance, looked very much like the door to Sunny's MAX office . . . not counting the large sign in the shape of a badge and the pair of globe lamps labeled POLICE on ether side of the entryway.

Sunny, Jane, and Dawn had been split up at the veterinary office and ferried to the station in separate cars. *Guess they didn't want us talking,* she thought. On arrival, Sunny had her fingerprints taken on a gizmo that reminded her of the multipurpose printer/scanner in her bedroom. Then she'd been stuck in an interrogation room for an interminable wait until finally Detective Fitch came in. He leaned way over the table, invading her space, his ferretlike nose twitching as he asked questions.

"What kind of relationship did the Rigsdales have?" He watched Sunny closely.

She took a moment to decide on an answer. "I only saw them together once." Honest, but not too revealing. Considering the way this guy had looked at Jane, Sunny wasn't about to tell him about Jane throwing her wine in Martin's face.

Although they'll probably find out about all that if they ask around, she thought glumly. *Upwards of a hundred people saw that performance, and the gossip was sure to get around.*

~45~

"You only saw the Rigsdales together once?" Fitch pressed, his face full of disbelief. "And yet you're close enough to Mrs. Rigsdale that she asked you to give her a lift to her husband's office?"

"I've only been back in Kittery Harbor for about a year," Sunny told him. "Jane and Martin had split up by the time I came home."

"So what are you saying?" Fitch said. "You knew Mrs. Rigsdale, but not while she was married?"

Sunny sighed. "Pretty much. Jane and I went to school together years ago. But I left town after college, and just came home to take care of my dad when he got sick. It's not as if there's a wide network of expatriates back in town, Detective. Jane and I just sort of wound up back in touch when I took my cat to the vet and was surprised to find her. I'd only known her by her maiden name—Leister."

Fitch looked disappointed but kept probing. "Do you know what the Rigsdales were going to talk about this evening?"

Sunny took a deep breath. "I think it was about money," she said. "From what I understand, Martin Rigsdale had problems in that direction."

"And where did you get that impression?" Fitch asked.

His annoying manner pushed Sunny into a sharper answer than she'd intended. "From Martin himself. He approached me, suggesting that if I persuaded Jane to 'loosen the purse strings,' as he put it, we could have some fun with the proceeds."

Detective Fitch reared back a little, silenced for once.

"I'll admit that I don't know Jane Rigsdale all that well. From when we were kids, I know she's smart. From the way she treats Shadow—my cat—I know she's kind and conscientious. I only met Martin Rigsdale once. But he impressed me as the sort of man who could very easily create all kinds of reasons to get himself killed."

Slowly, Fitch nodded. "Okay, I look forward to reading your statement, Ms. Coolidge. I'm sure you'll do a wonderful job."

"Excuse me?" Sunny said.

"Well, you are a newspaper reporter, aren't you?" the detective replied. "Even though we live on the other side of a state border, we still get the news from Maine. Somebody gave me a copy of the *Harbor Crier* because they thought I'd be interested in the Spruance case. The piece you wrote was very interesting—very professional. Do you cover a lot of murders?"

Sunny gave Fitch a suspicious look as she took a pen and pad from the detective. Was this part of the interrogation?

"I was a general assignment reporter in New York City," she said carefully. "That meant writing about whatever they threw at you."

Fitch nodded eagerly. Oh, wonderful. She had a fan. He just happened to be a fan who looked like a bad-tempered ferret, and who was trying to trip her up with this statement. She'd have to get this story down very carefully indeed, because she had no doubt that Fitch was after Jane, as well.

*

When Sunny finally emerged from her tête-à-tête with Detective Fitch, she found Jane waiting for her. Even with her hair pulled back in a casual ponytail, Jane looked elegant and slim in boots and riding breeches—and one of those Barbour coats that repelled all weather and cost a serious bundle. Sunny felt frumpy in the parka she'd gotten at the Eddie Bauer outlet during the summer when prices were cheap, but the selection was limited, to say the least.

Sunny sighed. She'd seen twinzie coats on too many thrift-minded inhabitants of Kittery Harbor. Were Jane's fancy coat and car remnants of her high-living days with Martin? Or had she bought them with money from her more recent windfall?

Even with a reporter's arsenal of questions, there was no polite way to edge up on that subject. Jane was facing away from her, so Sunny stepped forward and tapped her on the shoulder. Jane jumped a little at the contact.

So, no matter how calm and cool she looks on the out-side, inside she's feeling nervous, Sunny thought. Aloud, she said, "Looks like you got out pretty quickly. I guess I got the bad cop. Did you get the good one?"

Jane just shrugged. "More like the bored cop. It seemed pretty cut-and-dried. He was just doing his job, asking about how we found Martin . . ." She made a wry face. "How things were between Martin and me." She led the way to the door and they stepped out onto the covered porch outside. While they'd been answering questions in the windowless interrogation rooms, the snow had been coming down pretty heavily—big, fluffy flakes that had already frosted the parking area with more than an inch or two of accumulation.

"Well, I hope Detective Trumbull will be nice enough

to offer us a ride back to the office. My Wrangler is still there."

"Ummmmmm . . ." Jane sat down on the bench outside the door. "I called for a lift."

"From whom?" Sunny asked.

As if in answer, a black pickup truck pulled up at the entrance and Will Price came jumping out. An open parka revealed that he still wore his blue constable's uniform, and his long face with its well-composed features showed concern instead of his usual detached cop's expression. He rushed over to Jane. "Are you all right?"

The next thing Sunny knew, Jane was off the bench and in Will's arms. "It was pretty bad."

"Well, you're okay now," Will said softly, running a hand over Jane's glorious blond hair. Then he noticed Sunny and quickly brought his hand down. "Sunny! How are you doing?"

Well, I didn't come in and find my *ex-husband dead,* Sunny thought. *So I guess I don't rate the full-body hello.*

"I'm not sure," she said aloud. "The cops came, and Martin's receptionist just about accused us of killing him. I got stuck with a nasty little cop named Fitch, and Jane talked with an older guy named Trumbull."

"It's not a big deal," Jane insisted. "He just took me through what happened, did up a statement, and that was that."

"Trumbull is the best cop in the detective division." Will's face went from sappy to serious. "That's what everybody said when I was on the force here."

"Well, that was a couple of years ago," Jane replied.

"He barely paid attention to me. I think maybe he just wants to play out the string till he retires."

As Jane said that, Sunny spotted Trumbull beyond the station's glass door. Sunny didn't think he was close enough to hear Jane's dismissive comment, but he was close enough that Sunny could see the detective clearly. His hound dog face looked saggier and sadder than ever.

But his eyes were clear, cold, and coplike as he watched Jane in Will's arms.

5

"We'd better get going." Will finally tore himself loose from Jane. "The snow is really coming down, and it's start-ing to stick on the roads."

He led them off the porch and into the open air, where fat, feathery flakes drifted down. They'd already spread a white carpet a couple of inches thick on the concrete of the parking lot and the grassy verges. There was even an inch of accumulation on the windshield of Will's pickup, even though he'd parked just a few minutes before.

They crowded into the cab, Jane cutting Sunny off so that she sat next to Will.

"I figured you'd want to be close to the door, since you'll be getting out first." Jane's voice sounded reasonable enough as she talked over the rumble of the starting engine—or it would have, except for the smug undertone that Sunny picked up.

Just as well Jane isn't by the door, because I'd be kicking her to the curb right about now. For a second, Sunny enjoyed the mental image of Jane skidding along the snowy shoulder of the road.

Will nervously filled the chilly silence with cop stories about Mark Trumbull. "About five years ago, a house burned down, killing the man and woman who lived there. The fire department considered it an accident. There were no accelerants; it appeared to be an electrical fire. But Trumbull suspected arson—and proved it. Turns out the guy's ex-wife had a sideline making rustic lamps—wood base, very nice. She gave one to her husband, wired for low wattage, knowing the guy liked bright lights. Of course, he put in a heavier bulb, and sooner or later the damned thing went up in flames."

In spite of herself, Sunny spoke. "How could Trumbull know that was intentional? More importantly, how could he prove it?"

Will shrugged from behind the wheel. "He kept at it. Figured out the starting point for the fire and traced the lamps. Apparently, it was the only low-wattage one the woman had ever made. She could probably have still claimed it was accidental, but when she saw the case he'd assembled, she confessed. Wound up getting life."

Jane stirred from where she sat cuddled up against Will.

Not the best choice for a bedtime story, Sunny thought, *talking about a vengeful ex-wife to a woman whose former spouse just turned up dead.*

"Look, the guy could have been a regular Inspector

Javert five years ago," Jane said. "But when he was with me, he just looked like a sad old man barely asking any questions at all."

"All I'm saying is, don't be so quick to dismiss him," Will warned. "Trumbull is very, very good. And if he has any reason to suspect you, look forward to being investigated within an inch of your life."

After that, the only conversation was directions from Jane. She was efficient, if short. They soon arrived back at Martin's office, where Sunny had left her Jeep.

"Should we stay?" Will began, but Sunny shook her head.

"Get Jane home," she told him. "Whether she wants to admit it or not, she's had a shock."

Jane opened her mouth to protest and then stopped. "You're probably right." She sighed. "I came here tonight thinking I was prepared for anything Martin could throw at me. Finding him that way was the last thing I'd ever have expected."

Will started up the pickup again, and they drove off. Sunny pulled up the hood of her parka. She still had to clear snow off the Wrangler before she could head home. Digging out the long-handled brush from under the front seat, she set to work on the windshield.

It's not so bad, she thought as she worked. *The shrubs blocked a lot of the snow from coming down here.* She stepped back against the piney brush. *Huh! No snow at all.*

Another step, and she found herself in a little clear area. Sunny looked up to see darkness—or rather, interlocked evergreen branches above her head, holding off the snow. Back in the day, these bushes had probably been a lot shorter, maybe even trimmed into some sort of topiary shapes. But like the old house, they had been neglected, left to grow as they would, both upward and outward.

Then Sunny noticed a break in the evergreen wall around her, a fuzzy white patch located a bit above her eye level. On tiptoe, Sunny peered out into the snowstorm, the flakes illuminated by the lights of Martin Rigsdale's house. She wobbled for a second, clutching at the branches in front of her—and realized that several of them were broken.

It looked like someone had created a peephole to keep an eye on Martin's office.

I suppose this would be a perfect observation post, provided you could get in here unnoticed, she thought.

Yanking off her gloves, Sunny dropped to one knee, feeling around on the damp, freezing ground in the darkness. Her fingers encountered what felt like a small battered cardboard tube. Peering at it in the dark was just hopeless. But as she brought the thing up, she got a pungent odor of tobacco smoke.

Sunny held her prize carefully in her palm as she pushed out of the open spot, hurriedly climbing into her Wrangler. Turning on the dome light, she examined the item she'd found. It was a light cardboard tube, maybe two inches in length, crushed flat. One end held what looked like the burnt-out stub of a cigarette, the source of the sharp tobacco smell.

An image swam up in her brain, memories from a couple of years before, when she'd worked on the *Standard*'s New York City edition. Vanya, one of her fellow reporters, hailed from Brighton Beach, Brooklyn, a neighborhood known as "Little Odessa" because of all the Russian immigrants.

Vanya had taken a group of reporters to a club, a place with crowded tables, loud patrons, and a cloud of cigarette smoke up by the ceiling.

Sunny had remarked on a couple of silver-haired, red-faced men flaunting the municipal smoking ban by puffing away on cigarettes like these, the tubing pinched into a sort of cigarette holder.

Her friend had laughed. "Those guys have to be real old-school—probably mafia. You can only get cigarettes like that from Mother Russia."

Sunny hadn't wanted to know from Russian mafia back then. Now, however, she turned the crumpled cardboard tube over and over in her hands. Wait a second! There was something printed on one side.

She held the lettering up to her light—not that she could figure out what the word was.

"I'd say it was Greek to me," she muttered, carefully straightening out the cardboard, "but I suspect it's Russian."

*

Sunny finished cleaning off her SUV and then called home. Mike sounded as if he'd just woken up, but was jovial enough. "I thought maybe the silver-tongued Martin had persuaded you and Jane to go off with him for dinner and dancing, so I ate a while ago," Mike said.

"Well, that's not going to happen," Sunny told her dad. "He's—oh, I'll tell you all about it when I get home. I hope there are still some leftovers from that stew. I haven't had anything to eat."

She took the bridge back across the Piscataqua, staying

on the interstate till she was past the built-up section of Kittery Harbor. Then she took more winding country roads until she came to Wild Goose Drive and home. Traffic wasn't a problem—there were fewer cars than usual on the road. Which was just as well, given the snow that kept coming down heavily all through her drive.

Sunny left four-inch-deep tire tracks when she pulled into her driveway. The door opened before she was halfway there, Mike standing outlined in the light from the hall.

"I spread some newspapers down for you to put your boots on," he said. "And the stew is in the microwave, ready to be nuked."

Catching her looking around as she removed her wet boots, Mike added, "Your friend is up on top of the refrigerator again."

Shadow came down when he saw Sunny, sniffing around her vigorously but avoiding her hands when she reached for him.

"What's going on in that head of yours, cat?" Sunny asked.

But he just stayed at her feet, his odd, gold-flecked eyes giving her an inscrutable look.

"Suit yourself." Sunny heated up the stew and brought it to the kitchen table. Mike had already set out the utensils and left her a bottle of horseradish to season the stew. Sunny smiled, remembering how Shadow had investigated that horseradish bottle—once. He'd made it abundantly clear that he hadn't liked the contents one little bit.

Mike came in to take the chair opposite hers at the table. "I put on the Weather Chanel to see what they had to say about this snow. As usual, they're talking out of both sides of their mouths," he said sourly, then gave her a sly look. "I'm betting that whatever you have to say about your visit will be more interesting."

"You could say that," Sunny told him. "We got there, Jane bombed past the bimbo receptionist, and then she found Martin lying dead on his examination table."

That got Mike sitting up straight. "Dead?" he echoed.

Sunny nodded and gave him all the details, including Will's story about the relentless Mark Trumbull.

"I know Jane's been giving you a lot of competition for Will's attention." Mike gave her a grin. "Maybe this Trumbull guy will go after her and remove her from the game."

His grin wavered a little. "You were supposed to laugh there, Sunny."

Remembering her view of Jane snuggled next to Will as his pickup pulled away, Sunny didn't feel like laughing. She took a big mouthful of stew—mainly horseradish, unfortunately—and went into a coughing fit.

Mike hastily got her a glass of water. "Don't pay any attention to me. I'm still half asleep." He tried to stifle a yawn and failed. "Might as well go upstairs and back to bed. Good night—or should I say 'good morning'?" He gave Sunny a kiss on the forehead and headed out of the kitchen.

"How about 'sleep well' instead?" Sunny called after him. "I'll be up in a little while." She used her fork and smooshed down the last potato to absorb the stew juices. A few more bites, and the stew was history.

She washed her dish and put it in the drainer, along with her knife and fork. At the kitchen doorway she paused for a second, checking that everything had been put away. A small head butted against her ankle. Sunny glanced down to see Shadow looking up at her.

"How's that paw doing?" she asked, returning to the sink to warm up some oil by running the bottle under hot water. After making sure it wasn't too hot, she poured herself a handful and knelt on the floor. Shadow came to her immediately, dabbing his paw into her palm. "Does it still hurt?" Sunny asked, massaging the oil around his pads. "You seem to be walking all right."

Shadow just looked up at her and purred.

That must be the thing that drives vets crazy, Sunny thought. *Your patients can't tell you how they're really feeling—unless you count them trying to bite you if they really don't like what you're doing to them.*

She got a paper towel to blot away any excess oil on Shadow's paw and then nodded at the doorway. "Come along, little guy," Sunny said. "Keep me company while I try to chill out a little." They headed down the hallway to the living room, where the TV was still on.

Picking up the remote, Sunny abandoned the bad-news weather forecast. But the later late-night talk shows weren't very funny. She clicked along, through the middles of several movies she didn't want to see, reruns of once-successful shows exiled to the wee hours . . . In the end, she found one of those true crime shows where newscasters gave all the facts and plot twists but never really solved anything. On the screen, a local cop gave an impassioned tirade about why the suspect in this case must have committed the crime. Sunny was pretty sure some defense witness would be on with a rebuttal after a couple of commercials.

Like I really need to hear this after being with real cops this evening, she thought.

Sunny turned off the TV, getting down on the floor to play with Shadow. She dug a piece of string out of her pocket and led him a merry chase, the cat clambering all over her as he pounced on his make-believe prey.

As she drew the string across her leg, he climbed across her shins. Suddenly he stopped, audibly sniffing. He remained frozen, poised on three paws (he still favored the injured paw, holding it slightly aloft), and then turned his eyes to hers in an odd stare.

"What are you smelling, Shadow?" Sunny asked. Maybe Shadow had detected the scent of Martin's vet office, or of Martin himself. Who knew? Perhaps he'd caught a whiff of Jane. Or maybe Sunny had brought home a trace of the interrogation room. Sunny was pretty sure that Detective Fitch probably smelled like something a cat would like to kill.

What did it matter? She flipped up the end of the string so it appeared just past her knee, and Shadow dove for it, the smell apparently forgotten.

They played for a little while longer, until Sonny was hit by a yawn that threatened to dislocate her jawbone. Running a hand over Shadow's furry back, she said, "Sorry, cat, I'm turning into a pumpkin."

Sunny headed upstairs, took a quick shower, and changed into a warm pair of pajamas. As she pulled down the comforter and bedding, the door to her room swung open slightly, and Shadow came padding in. He went from a trot to a run to a spring, landing on the mattress and heading for the pillows.

Sunny laughed. "Wait for me!"

She climbed into the bed and pulled up the covers. It was a good night to be under a heavy blanket and an old-fashioned wool comforter. The weather outside had kicked things up a notch or two. The falling snowflakes had gone from large and fluffy to the small, icy variety. They pattered determinedly against her window, driven by a howling wind.

Sunny scrunched herself into a small ball, the covers tight, her body heat creating a comfortable nest quickly invaded by a cat who nuzzled against her.

"Just you and me, Shadow," Sunny murmured fondly. All of a sudden, the image of a black pickup pulling away, Jane's head on Will's shoulder, popped through her head again. "Yeah," she whispered. "I just have to get a shawl, and then I'll have everything I need to be an old maid."

*

Shadow lay quietly in the circle of Sunny's arms, sharing warmth with her. He wasn't exactly sure why, but he knew she needed him close tonight. He'd felt an odd tension in her ever since she'd come home, and even playing with her hadn't made it go away. So he kept cuddled against Sunny until her regular breathing told him she was well and truly asleep. Then he gently squirmed his way free of her clasp and the enveloping covers.

Dropping silently to the floor, Shadow padded to the door, easing out into the gloom of the hallway beyond. He'd be back before Sunny woke up and started the day. Until then, there was a big, dark house to patrol.

6

Sunny awoke to morning dimness, cracking an eye open to peek at the clock radio. Five minutes until her alarm. Not enough time to return to dreamland, especially when the dream was so weird. A human-sized version of Shadow had been driving her Wrangler while Sunny rested her cheek against his furry shoulder.

She sighed, and felt a warm breath on her cheek. Sunny glanced over to find Shadow regarding her, almost nose to nose.

"Might as well get up." Sunny smiled and ran a hand over the top of Shadow's head. "Did you enjoy your drive?"

She killed the alarm, got out of bed, and headed downstairs, catching the smell of brewing coffee about halfway down. So, her dad was up, too, unable to shake the lifetime habit of early rising. He turned from the coffeemaker as

Sunny came into the kitchen. "What are you thinking about for breakfast?"

"I think it's a stick-to-the-ribs kind of morning," Sunny replied. "How about oatmeal?"

She went to the kitchen door and opened it, bracing herself for a blast of cold air. Last night's fluffy carpet of snow had been tamped down and covered with a glaze of ice. She quickly shut the door and retreated, Shadow doing the same right beside her. He moved to a warmer corner of the kitchen and looked suspiciously at the door, licking his injured paw.

"I guess he remembers hurting himself out there in the snow," Mike said.

"Well, maybe he'll be a little less eager to go sneaking out, then." Sunny busied herself at the stove, measuring out water for the oatmeal. She took a double handful of walnuts from a container in the cupboard, put them in a plastic bag on the kitchen counter, then whacked the bag a couple of times with a pan. Then she poured the water into the pan and put it on a burner to boil. While she waited for that, she got a jar of applesauce from the fridge, a container of ground cinnamon, the box of quick-cooking oatmeal, and the kitchen timer.

When the water boiled, she scooped out two servings of oats and poured them in, set the timer for three minutes, and began stirring. The oatmeal was nice, thick, and hot just as the timer began its insistent peeping. Sunny took the pot off the heat, got two bowls, and spooned out the oatmeal, topping it with the applesauce, nuts, and spice.

Mike had cups of coffee and spoons waiting on the kitchen table. They sat down and began eating.

"Y'know, when I was a kid, I really hated oatmeal," Mike said, stirring up the cereal and taking a spoonful. "Of course, it didn't have all this nice stuff in it—just lumps."

"Well, if you had eaten more oatmeal and less bacon and eggs—" Sunny began.

Mike waved a hand. "Okay, okay. Where are my pills?"

She pointed to the big box with separate compartments for a week's worth of medications. "Right in front of you. But you're not supposed to have them until you finish eating."

"I know," Mike said. "Just wanted to be ready."

Sunny took a sip of coffee and came to a decision. "How good is the gossip grapevine around here?" she asked. "Do you think you could find out anything about somebody way off in Portsmouth?"

"Me? Probably not." Mike picked up his cup. "Helena, though . . ." He shrugged, giving Sunny a sly look. "Looking for juicy details about Jane's husband?"

"In a way," Sunny admitted. "It's his office receptionist I'm more interested in—Dawn Featherstone. Young, pretty . . . and she tried to sic the cops on Jane and me, accusing us of killing Martin Rigsdale. I don't think it would hurt to know a little more about her."

Mike quickly put his cup down. "You're not going to get involved in this, are you?"

"As if," Sunny laughed. "Will told us the best detective on the Portsmouth force is investigating. There's nothing I need to do. I'm just . . . curious."

"Remember what curiosity did to the cat," Mike said. Shadow raised his head and looked over at them. "Heck of a lot worse than a sore paw."

"Thanks for reminding me about that paw." Sunny quickly finished her breakfast, warmed up some oil, and brought it over to Shadow. While she massaged the cat's paw, Mike brought the bowls and cups to the sink and cleaned them.

Sunny gave Shadow a final pat on the head and got up. "Now I have to put some clothes on and get to work."

"I bet you're glad of the new truck," her dad said, peering out the window at the snow. "That old Mustang of yours wouldn't have gotten down the driveway without spinning out."

"You're probably right," Sunny admitted, then turned to him. "Do me a favor—promise you won't try to clear the drive."

"I'm not an invalid," Mike argued, and then looked out at the ice-caked expanse of snow again. "I'm also not an idiot. Either McPherson will come by with his snowblower, or a couple of neighborhood kids will turn up with shovels."

Sunny headed upstairs to shower and dress, then came back to kiss her dad good-bye and remind him to speak with Mrs. Martinson. "Dawn Featherstone," she repeated.

"From Portsmouth," Mike replied, nodding.

Pulling on her gray parka, Sunny carefully made her way down the front steps to the driveway, skidding a little on the ice as she headed for her Wrangler. The SUV started up with a rumble, crunching its way through the ice rime as Sunny slowly drove down the driveway.

The plow teams must have been busy all night, because the roads were pretty much clear. That didn't mean there weren't icy spots, though. Sunny cringed a little behind the wheel as she and a lot of morning commuters inched past a car not all that different from her former Mustang, stuck at a crazy angle on the shoulder of the road, its front fender crunched.

She knew how that felt. One of the reasons her little car had been retired was due to a road mishap last winter.

Maybe the Mustang curse still hung over her. Even though she'd specifically set off a little early, the traffic left her arriving at the MAX office several minutes after nine o'clock.

Sunny's heart sank a little when she found the door unlocked and a heavyset figure sitting at her desk. *Of all the days for the boss to come in . . .*

"Morning, Ollie," she said, shrugging out of her coat.

Oliver Barnstable looked from her to his wristwatch, but he didn't say anything. That was atypical behavior for Ollie the Barnacle, a guy who was crustier than most crustaceans. Usually he'd jump on any excuse to browbeat Sunny over the management of the office. For a moment, Sunny debated asking whether he was feeling all right but quickly quashed that idea. No good could come of such a question.

Ollie quickly began reassembling the contents of several file folders he'd spread across her desk. "I'm going to be away for a couple of days," he announced.

"Another vacation?" The words came out before Sunny could stop them. Barnstable had gone down to the Caribbean for two of the mildest winter weeks in Kittery Harbor history. And he'd returned with a sunburn that made his normally florid complexion lobster red.

He winced at the memory, a scowl flitting across his

round face. But his voice was pretty mild when he answered. "No, I'm heading down to New York. I might catch a couple of shows, but it's basically business. Unless something happens, I should be gone for a week."

Ollie looked up at her, back to his normal self. "Don't burn the office down while I'm gone."

"I'll try not to," she promised. "Is there anything I should be aware of?" While MAX was essentially a glorified travel agency, Ollie also used the place as the nerve center for his other business and real estate operations—including a set of locked file cabinets in the back of the office. "And are there any arrangements I should be making for you?"

Ollie the Barnacle shook his head. "All taken care of." He gathered the folders into his battered leather briefcase. "If anything really important comes up, you can get me on my cell phone."

With that good advice, he headed out the door.

"I hope you bring your charger along," Sunny called to his back, but the door had already swung closed.

So, it's the middle of the slow season, and the boss is gone for a few days, Sunny thought. *Let the good times roll.*

About an hour later, things were definitely rolling—downhill.

Will Price came into the office, his face tight and strained. "Did you tell Trumbull about my"—he paused for a second, trying to find the right word—"history with Jane?"

Sunny gave him a look. "No 'Hello'? No 'How are you?'"

"Hello, how are you? Did you tell Trumbull about Jane and me?" Will went quiet again. "Not that there's necessarily anything going on right now," he muttered.

"I didn't say anything about the two of you, past, present, or future," Sunny told him. "Maybe he saw—" Now she broke off. What she wanted to say was, "Maybe he saw Jane all over you," but that might not be helpful under the circumstances. Sunny cleared her throat. "Maybe he saw you and Jane together. I think he passed by the door while we were out on the porch."

"Damn!" Will burst out. "That was the whole reason I told her to wait outside. I didn't want anyone to see me."

"Looks as if that didn't work out so well," Sunny told him with a shrug.

"Ah, man!" He dropped in the chair by Sunny's desk. "Trumbull woke me up at the crack of dawn with a bunch of questions about Jane. He said he was just contacting me informally, since he knew I used to be with the Portsmouth PD."

Sunny frowned. "So why is that a problem for you?"

"It's a kind of quiet blackmail." Will grimaced. "The alternative is that he makes it official . . . and goes through Frank Nesbit."

Frank Nesbit was the sheriff of Elmet County, and technically Will's boss. But a bunch of Kittery Harbor community leaders had persuaded Will to take a job as a town constable. Will was the son of the previous sheriff, and a lot of people—including Sunny's father—hoped that a Price would soon be sheriff again. The political overtones did not make for a smooth working relationship between Will and Frank.

"At the very least, that will put me on Nesbit's radar," Will said. "I won't be able to do anything to help Jane. And I think she's going to need some help. Whatever happened between them last night, Mark Trumbull isn't as disinterested in her as she thinks."

He sat for a moment, looking deflated—and embarrassed. "I know this is . . ."

"Awkward?" she suggested when he went silent.

Will leaned toward her across the desk. "But you're the only one I can talk to who might understand."

Sunny nodded. For just a little while, Frank Nesbit had thought she'd shot two guys. She wouldn't wish a full-scale murder investigation on her worst enemy. And Jane wasn't an enemy exactly. More like a rival.

"So what do you think I can do?" she asked.

"Talk to her," Will urged. "Maybe she'll listen to you." He rose to his feet. "She sure isn't listening to me."

"I'll see what I can do," Sunny promised, following him to the door. She put a hand on his arm. "But Jane's a big girl. She's going to do whatever she wants."

"Oh, yeah." Will went out. "I know."

Sunny returned to her desk, frowning in thought. Jane had made it pretty clear that she didn't take Trumbull all that seriously. How could Sunny even bring the matter up?

Well, it's not going to be a chatty phone call, she decided. Picking up the desk phone, she punched in her home number. Mike answered, sounding a little fuzzy, as if she'd woken him from a nap.

"Could you call the animal hospital and make an appointment for Shadow? They have evening hours tonight.

I'm afraid that will mean a quick supper, though. Soup and sandwiches sound okay?"

*

When she closed the office for the day, Sunny stopped off at Judson's Market, splurging on a half pound of fresh-cooked turkey breast, some of their homemade vinegar and oil coleslaw, and the frozen low-salt minestrone soup her dad liked.

She arrived home to a warm greeting from Shadow and a suspicious one from her father. He turned down the volume on the news as she came into the living room. "Okay, you have a seven o'clock appointment lined up," he said. "You got off the phone pretty quickly, before I could wake up and ask any questions—what's this appointment all about?"

Sighing, Sunny recounted her conversation with Will. "I need a reason to go and talk with Jane, and it can't be something like, 'Oh, I was in the neighborhood, so I thought I'd drop by.'" She shrugged. "Maybe it will still sound pretty lame—"

As if on cue, Shadow leaned down and licked his paw.

"But it's the best I've got to work with."

Sunny headed back to the kitchen, where she put the soup in the microwave to heat up and worked on making the turkey sandwiches. She toasted the bread, then arranged turkey slices and tomato on one side, the coleslaw on the other. A quick squeeze of honey mustard, and the sandwiches were ready.

Mike came in and got the soup bowls while Sunny

brought the sandwiches to the table. She took a spoonful of soup. Well, it was obvious why her dad liked this stuff. Unlike canned soup, the vegetables were crisp, as if they were fresh—you could really taste them.

Mike took a sip from his glass of seltzer. "I talked with Helena about that girl in Portsmouth."

"Oh, you mean Martin's receptionist, Dawn Feather-stone?" Sunny said. "So what did Mrs. Martinson say about her?"

"Well, she didn't know anything right off the bat. But she took it on as a challenge." His expression went a little sour. "Anything to get her mind off that damned dog. So she's—what is it you reporters say? Working her sources?"

Sunny chuckled. "Sounds about right."

"By the way, she liked Toby as a name for the pup," Mike reported. He related some of Mrs. Martinson's stories about new indiscretions by the puppy, so they had something to laugh about as they ate.

By the time they'd finished and washed the plates, it was time to head over to Jane's.

"You gonna rub Shadow's paw for him?" Mike asked, looking at the clock.

Sunny shook her head. "Don't think I can fit it in without making us late."

"Well, maybe if he has a little pain, that will justify your visit," Mike suggested.

Sunny shot Shadow a guilty look as she got out the cat carrier. "You aren't hurting, are you?" she asked. "I'll take care of you as soon as we get home—promise."

*

Shadow was a little surprised when he saw Sunny getting out the box-to-ride-in. They were going out—in the dark and cold? But Sunny got the furry thing from his bed—not real fur, but it felt good and had lots of interesting smells. He rolled around in it, keeping warm as cold air came into the box Sunny carried. Then they were inside her car, driving along.

After a quick trip through cold air, they were inside again. Since he was inside the box, Shadow couldn't see where they were going, but he recognized their destination, even in the dark. This was the place where Gentle Hands lived!

Shadow lay down peacefully while Sunny talked with another two-leg. They sat for a little while, with her looking through the barred front of the box, talking quietly to him.

Then they were on the move, going down a long hallway to the bright room where Gentle Hands took care of him. He wasn't sure why they were here. They'd just visited, and his paw felt fine now. Were they going to play a trick on him and stick him with something? Sometimes Gentle Hands did that, but she always tried to make sure that the hurt was as little as possible.

It hadn't been the same when the other one was here, the human male that Shadow always thought of as Hard Hands. He'd never seemed to mind hurting Shadow or any other animal that came here. Even when he seemed gentle, his hands were just too tight. Shadow always wished he could have bitten him. But Hard Hands always wore heavy gloves.

Sunny opened the door on the box, and Shadow came out onto the metal table. Gentle Hands immediately began to pet him, taking his paw in her fingers. But over his head, Sunny and the other human were talking. It wasn't happy talk. What was making them so upset? He looked around, and suddenly his nostrils caught a whiff of Hard Hands.

Shadow took his paw back and prowled around on the table, looking around the room. Is Hard Hands back? A little snarl came from the back of his throat. *I thought he had gone away!*

7

"**Wow, he doesn't** look happy." Sunny felt a stab of guilt as she watched Shadow pace around the perimeter of Jane Rigsdale's examination table, his tail swishing in annoyance. Should she have been massaging more oil, or doing it more often?

"Is that his paw acting up?" she asked as the cat stopped on the opposite side of the table from her.

"Not from the way he's moving around on it," Jane replied. "And he didn't mind when I started examining his pads." She shot a sharp look at Sunny. "So if his foot isn't the problem, what are you doing here?"

"All right, I confess. I came to see how you were doing." Sunny tried to put as much sincerity as she could into her answer. "Listening to you last night, it sounded to me as if you were pretty deep into denial. So I figured I'd check whether or not this had all caught up with you."

That took some of the starch out of Jane. Her shoulders sagged a little. "I guess it did," she confessed. "At least enough to make me dig out a box of Martin's old stuff." She nodded at a cardboard carton lying open on one of the counter tops, but then broke off, staring at Shadow.

He stood poised on the edge of the exam table closest to the box, making hostile noises.

"I guess he's catching a whiff of Martin's cologne." Jane sounded a little embarrassed.

"Well, it was kind of on the strong side," Sunny said.

But that wasn't what bothered Jane. "Shadow never liked Martin. And looking back on our partnership, I have to wonder. After all, this is a medical practice where the patients can never talk. I don't know what Martin did with them when I wasn't around. It's obvious he made a pretty bad impression with Shadow." She scowled. "Another suggestion that I picked a real winner. When we started out, he had me so that I didn't know up from down."

"I know that feeling." Sunny sighed. "And then comes the letdown."

Jane nodded, her expression not so much "How did this happen?" as "How did I get myself into this mess?" She cleared her throat. "It's things like this that make me wonder—was I intentionally blind to his shortcomings?"

"He still had a hold on your feelings." Sunny remembered the editor back in New York whose divorce had been coming through, coming through . . . but then, when people's jobs were on the chopping block, he'd gotten back with his wife, and not only broke things off with Sunny, but laid her off as well. Even so, on cold, dark nights, Sunny found herself thinking about what might have been.

Jane obviously had a different idea. "I should have burnt that stuff." She directed a venomous glance at the cardboard container. "But I can't now, because that might look like if I was trying to destroy evidence."

She turned back to Sunny, her expression showing the same sort of strain that Will's had when he visited Sunny's office—and for the same reason. "Has Detective Trumbull been in touch with you?"

Sunny shook her head.

"Well, he called three times today, asking for a few little details. Like, was it true that I'd thrown a glass of wine in Martin's face at the Redbrick?" Jane scowled at the memory. "He's like that old detective on TV, the one who was always leaving and asking one more question."

"Columbo?" Sunny said.

Jane nodded. "I used to watch that show when I was a kid, thinking it was pretty funny. Let me tell you, though, it's not so funny when it happens to you in real life. More like death by a thousand cuts."

She went silent, and for a second they watched Shadow move restlessly between them.

"I guess he's picking up my bad vibes." Jane extended a hand to the cat. "Sorry, Shadow. Nothing for you to worry about."

Shadow nuzzled Jane's fingers and then came over to rub against Sunny.

"That's good," Jane said. "You're the person he should go to for comfort."

Sunny drew her hand from between his ears and down

his back. Shadow immediately thrust his head at her for a second helping. Then he went back to Jane, getting a laugh out of her.

"Hey, greedy," she said, rubbing his chin with a finger. "I guess that's the best you can do for me—unless you have an in with the Portsmouth police."

Her hand and voice stopped dead, and she looked over at Sunny. "I didn't mean—"

"I know." Sunny's brain raced, trying to figure out what to say. Had Will talked with Jane? It hadn't seemed so when he came into the office. She decided to play dumb. "If Trumbull found out about what happened in the Redbrick, he probably knows that you and Will have been going out. And if he decides to ask a bunch of official questions . . ."

Jane nodded in comprehension. "That could get sticky, considering how Will and the sheriff get along."

"So I guess you'll have to grit your teeth and get through all the questions. I know that's not much fun." Sunny paused for a second. "Do you have a lawyer you can talk to?"

That brought a spark from Jane. "What do I need a lawyer for? I didn't do anything!"

"When you're in an interrogation room—" Sunny began, when a woman appeared in the exam room entrance to interrupt her.

"Mrs. Dowdey!" Jane's receptionist Rita Greene's voice came down the hallway, sounding upset. "You can't just go walking back there—Dr. Rigsdale is with a patient!"

The woman in the doorway paid no attention, entering and marching straight up to Jane. "The animal shelter told me that my application to adopt a cat had been turned down—and that you're responsible!"

She had a large, round face, with the features sort of squeezed together in the middle. Add in the wispy fringe of hair that was supposed to look sophisticated but just looked wrong, and the overwhelming impression was of a Persian cat—in this case, a very annoyed Persian cat. Incipient jowls quivered with indignation. Sunny figured the lady—which was definitely what this woman would consider herself—was about her father's age or a tad older. She dressed stylishly, maybe too stylishly. The dress under her opened fur coat would have been more in tune for somebody twenty years younger—the royal blue color a little too striking, the skirt too short, and the waist too high.

But what really struck Sunny, aside from the woman's angry-cat expression, was the smell that seemed to emanate from her. It reminded Sunny of the time she'd gone exploring in her grandmother's dresser drawer, found an ancient bottle of perfume stuck in the back, opened it, and—phew!

From the rest of the package, I don't think she'd put on stale perfume, Sunny thought. *Well, her face looks hot enough to cook something on. Maybe it's frying off whatever she's wearing.*

Jane, on the other hand, had hidden her upset behind a cool, almost cold, demeanor. "I simply asked them to refer you to me, Mrs. Dowdey," she said. "You've had two cats with health problems—"

"I give my cats the best of everything!" Mrs. Dowdey's voice got a bit strident. "The best beds, the best toys, the best food—"

"And too much of it," Jane interrupted crisply. "In my years at this practice, you had one cat die from renal complications, and the other become very ill—"

"Mrs. Purrley died, too," Mrs. Dowdey's voice switched to an accusing tone. "Your husband was absolutely no help at all."

Now Jane's voice got a bit loud. "He's not—" She clamped her lips together and took a deep breath.

Yikes, Sunny thought. *Talk about sticking your foot in something!*

But when Jane spoke again, her voice was mild. "I'm sorry to hear about Mrs. Purrley. Since I haven't seen her in more than a year, I certainly can't comment on whatever treatment Martin may have undertaken."

"I had to have her put to sleep." Tears appeared in Mrs. Dowdey's eyes. "It's so lonely in the house now."

"We're trying to set up a class on how to keep a pet healthy," Jane began.

"As if you people care about that." Mrs. Dowdey huffed. "Sick animals are your bread and butter."

Jane's lips compressed again, but once more she managed to keep anger out of her voice. "I think healthy animals are what we all want. If you take the class, I'd be willing to revisit the question of adoption."

"You would?" Mrs. Dowdey sounded surprised but hopeful. "This isn't because you're angry that I went with the other Dr. Rigsdale?"

"Of course not. We'll let you know when the class starts." Jane tried to sound nice, but she clearly wanted this conversation to end. "Rita, will you see Mrs. Dowdey out? Make sure you have her number so we can get in touch with her." Jane turned back to Shadow, who had retreated to the far edge of the table, his nose wrinkling. From now on, Mrs. Dowdey would be Rita's problem.

But Mrs. Dowdey apparently had to have the last word. "Thank you, Doctor. I may have been a bit hasty." She seemed to notice Sunny and Shadow for the first time. "That's a very handsome animal."

"Thanks," said Sunny, struggling to keep her annoyance out of her voice.

Mrs. Dowdey finally allowed Rita to conduct her down the hallway and back to the reception area. After a brief exchange, the voices muffled by distance, the front door closed.

Jane gave Sunny a wry grimace. "So now you've gotten to see behind the scenes in the exciting world of veterinary medicine. Does it make you feel as if you made the wrong choice way back at career day?"

Sunny grinned. "In the newspaper business, people who don't agree with what you write do it in the letters to the editor, not face-to-face."

Jane sighed. "Carolyn Dowdey means well. The problem is, she really didn't know how to take care of her cats. She figured as long as they got the best of everything, they would be fine. And that there was no such thing as 'too much of a good thing.' That's not always true, even if you can afford it."

Her expression darkened. "And because she *could* afford it, I'll bet Martin went for the most expensive treatments he could come up with, even if it meant keeping that poor animal hanging on in agony."

There it is, always coming back to Martin, Sunny

thought. *He still sticks to Jane like a bad smell—even worse than Mrs. Dowdey's perfume.*

She reached out to touch Jane's arm, and Shadow came over to press his head against her, too.

"Take care of yourself," Sunny said.

Jane smiled down at Shadow, combing her fingers through his gray fur. "And you take care of this little guy. I'd say he's pretty well recovered, but keep giving him the oil massage for a few more days." She looked at Sunny. "And if there's any problem—any problem at all—you let me know."

Sunny got Shadow's carrying case. "You've got it, Jane," she promised. "After all, we returnees have to stick together."

*

Usually, Shadow regretted leaving Gentle Hands—she was always so nice to him. But as Sunny opened the box, he just about jumped in there, eager to get away. He burrowed into the fur that wasn't real, inhaling deeply to breathe in the scents trapped in the fibers. Anything to block that awful stench in the air outside.

The loud older human might have gone, but the stink that had surrounded her still hung in the air.

However long Shadow stayed around the two-legs, he'd never understand some of the things they did, especially their attitude when it came to smells. Most of the time, they didn't seem to smell things at all. Oh, sometimes he'd see them sniff the air around cooking food. And if his litter box got too full or his stomach rumbled and a little ripe air escaped, the humans would make sounds of annoyance.

But those things they rode in to go fast, they let out smoke that was a lot riper—it was enough to make a cat gag. And some of the two-legs actually got things that they set on fire so they could breathe in the smoke and breathe it out. He'd seen them do it, and he certainly couldn't fathom why anyone would want to. Sometimes they'd even blow smoke at him, which he didn't like. And the odor of the stuff would cling to their hands and faces—not very nice at all. Sometimes he encountered humans with an unwashed, dirty, musky smell. It might not be the nicest scent, but at least it was natural. Better than that smoke.

But this was the first time he'd ever encountered a human who apparently bathed in a bad smell and then went out to spread it around.

He looked out the barred entrance as Sunny set him on the seat of her car.

I'm glad none of our Old Ones would do anything like that, he thought.

*

Sunny got home in time to give Shadow his promised paw massage and get in a little television viewing and playing with the cat.

Mike looked at her from his usual place on the couch. "You seem awfully quiet tonight."

"I'm thinking," Sunny told him, joking, "in case you were worried that the burning smell was coming from the TV."

"Did you have problems with Jane?"

Sunny shook her head. "She's the one having problems. I think the detective in charge of Martin's case suspects her. But instead of having her mind free to deal with that, she still seems to be dealing with a lot of old crap Martin pulled. The guy's messing her up more now that he's dead than he managed when he was alive."

They went to their beds shortly after that. Sunny awoke the next morning to find that a freak warm front had blown in after the arctic blast.

Mike stood looking out the kitchen window. "If we get enough sun today, we probably wouldn't have needed McPherson to plow out the driveway," he said. "It will all melt away."

When she got into work, Sunny found the warm weather already changing snow to slush. While her duck boots kept the icy water at bay, it quickly soaked into the cuffs of her jeans. She spent the first hour or so sitting as close to the baseboard radiator as she could manage, trying to dry out the damp cloth.

Memo to self, she thought. *Keep a spare pair of pants in the office.*

At last the denim got reasonably dry, and Sunny resumed her usual office routine. She went online to find a couple of e-mails at the MAX website, but no messages on the answering machine. Drafting replies to the e-mails went quickly—she had templates to deal with all but the most off-the-wall requests. In some cases, she pulled together a few information packets. After that, well, it was pretty much downtime until the mail arrived in about an hour and a half.

"Well, if you're going to do it, do it," Sunny muttered to herself. She hadn't mentioned her discovery in front of Martin Rigsdale's office to anyone. Jane was still trying to get her head around how much trouble she was in, and Will was trying to keep himself out of Trumbull's investigation. And of course, there was the thing that Sunny's editors always complained about—once she got on a story, she wanted to make it hers.

Taking a deep breath, Sunny cranked up her local sources database. Dealing with tourists meant providing a surprising array of services for a wide variety of people, including folks from foreign countries . . . and smokers. A lot of those foreign visitors smoked foreign cigarettes, and Sunny had compiled a list of stores specializing in exotic brands.

Whoever had been keeping an eye on Martin Rigsdale's place smoked some sort of Russian cigarettes. Where would he or she find the nearest supply?

She quickly narrowed in with her search. Portsmouth Tobacconists, on the edge of the downtown shopping district, and not all that far from Martin Rigsdale's office.

Sunny sat, looking at the address, until the mail carrier finally arrived. She almost snatched the thin sheaf of letters from the surprised woman's hand, and then said, "Sorry. I was, um, expecting something."

At least it wasn't Andy, the regular guy. He'd have wanted to shoot the breeze for a few minutes. This fill-in carrier merely shrugged her shoulders and continued on her daily round.

Probably happy to get away from the crazy lady, Sunny thought.

Sorting quickly through the few envelopes, Sunny made sure that there was nothing urgent, nothing that couldn't be handled after lunch.

Especially the long lunch she was planning. She locked up the office and got into her Wrangler, heading for the bridge to Portsmouth.

It wasn't hard to find Portsmouth Tobacconists. They had a large black sign with gold letters, and a window display that even included a couple of hookahs.

It wouldn't surprise me to see those down in the East Village back in New York, Sunny thought. *But do people in this neck of the woods really go in for that kind of stuff?*

An old-fashioned bell jingled as she opened the door and stepped into a long, narrow room furnished with all sorts of smoking paraphernalia and memorabilia. Old cigarette ads, a poster of Humphrey Bogart with his trademark cigarette hanging off his lips, cigarette cases, pipes . . .

"How may I help you?" a voice came from the rear of the store.

Sunny tore her eyes from the wild display to look at the young man behind the counter. He was tall and skinny, wearing a black turtleneck that only accentuated his pale skin. Watery blue eyes peered at her through a pair of wire-framed glasses, and the forelock of his long, dark hair dangled down past his eyebrows. He brushed it back with a practiced gesture, smiling at Sunny. "It's a little much, I know. My dad started this place, and it's as much his collection as our sales stock."

"You sell foreign cigarettes?" Sunny asked.

The skinny young man nodded, dropping his forelock into his eyes again. "We have a wide selection, and if need be, we can order almost any brand for you."

Sunny dug out the crumpled cigarette butt she'd kept in a small plastic bag. "Do you have any of these?"

The young man's face lit up with an enthusiast's excitement. "A *papirosa*!" he exclaimed.

"A whoosy-whatsa?" Sunny asked.

"It's an old variety of cigarette that pretty much went out of style after World War Two, except in the Soviet Union. They didn't have filters, and you used the cardboard tube as a sort of cigarette holder, pinching it together here for your fingers . . ."

He held up the butt between his thumb and forefinger and the end of the tube near the tobacco. "And then you pressed it together here for your mouth." With his other hand, he squeezed the cardboard perpendicular to his first hold, creating a sort of mouthpiece. He let go that end of the tube and, grinning, gestured with the cigarette, his fingers making a sort of "okay" gesture with the palm facing him and the remains of the tobacco facing her. "You can almost see this in an old movie. 'Ve haff vays of makink you talk.'"

"Do you have the brand?" she asked.

The young man looked at the Cyrillic letters on the side of the tube. "Oh, Belmorkanal. Sure. Named to commemorate a triumph of Soviet engineering—they cut a canal from the Baltic Sea—"

"Does that mean you have it?" Sunny interrupted. *Geez, this guy doesn't know when to stop talking.*

The clerk turned to a floor-to-ceiling pigeonhole arrangement behind the counter, featuring a huge array of cigarette packs, from American brands that Sunny was familiar with to gaudily colored packets with words and even alphabets she didn't understand.

"I'm sorry, we're out." The skinny young guy glanced

back at Sunny over his shoulder. "Are you sure you want that brand? It's awfully strong."

"It's not for me, it's for a friend—an acquaintance, actually," Sunny quickly amended. "We met at a concert, and I never really got his name. But he left that cigarette at my apartment, and I wondered if he might buy them here."

Let's see if the old Cinderella story gets me anywhere, she thought.

The young clerk frowned dubiously. "We do have one customer who gets Belmorkanals. I'd say he was an Eastern European gentleman, on the older side, but sort of big and burly—"

"That's the guy," Sunny said. Then she let her lips droop in disappointment. "Don't tell me he came in and cleared you out?"

The young man shook his head, forcing him to sweep his hair back again. "He always calls in advance to make sure he can get a full carton."

"Then maybe you can do me a favor." Sunny dug out a business card for MAX and scribbled her cell phone number on the back. Then, trying not to wince, she pulled a twenty from her pocket—a big chunk of her weekly expense money. She slid the card and the bill across the counter to the young man. "When he gives you a call, can you give me a call?"

The clerk stared at Sunny's offering as if it might bite him. "This really isn't about cigarettes, is it?"

Sunny tried to look like a girl in love. "I just want to see him again, that's all." She gave him a bright smile, "Hey, if it works out, you'll have a great story for your customers."

Sighing, the young man took Sunny's card and the twenty. "I can't promise when he'll come," he warned.

"Then I'll just have to hope," Sunny told him. She left the store feeling a bit poorer but with a little thrill in her belly—the way she used to feel when she started pulling on the end of a string that could lead to a big story. Maybe, with luck, she'd get a look at the mystery man who had been staking out Martin Rigsdale—not to mention his possible killer. *Whoa! Slow down,* Sunny told herself. But as usual, when it came to a fight between that reporter's rush and her good sense, the rush won.

She got into her Wrangler and continued down the street instead of turning around for the bridge. A few minutes' drive brought her to Martin's office. In the daylight, the neighborhood wasn't very mysterious. The houses were a little bigger than on Wild Goose Drive, with more space and landscaping between them. The house where Martin had set up his practice still had the look of a work in progress—fine at first glance, but it looked shabbier in the sunshine. Trumbull and the Portsmouth cops hadn't festooned the area with crime scene tape. The only difference Sunny could see was that there was some sort of notice or seal stuck on the office door.

Well, I'm not going in, she told herself. *I just wanted to stop by for a look.*

Sunny pulled out her cell phone, dialed the office, and input a code when she got the answering machine. She sighed in relief. No new messages.

I'll pick up something to eat on this side of the river and go straight back to the office, she decided.

She swung her SUV back the way she'd come, pulling

into the parking lot of a diner she'd passed. Stepping inside, she asked the waitress if they did takeout orders.

The older woman looked distracted. Sunny turned around to find Martin Rigsdale's face on the TV set installed up by the ceiling.

"Huh," the waitress said. "Him."

8

Sunny swung back to the waitress. The woman had about ten years on her, but she still had a good figure, a broad, pleasant face, and a sassy smile.

I'll bet she makes out pretty well on tips, Sunny thought. "You know the guy up there?" she asked, trying not to go too far overboard or get too loud.

"Know him? No." The waitress shrugged and quirked her lips. "But he sure as hell wanted to change that. Used to come in here and try out the old charm on—well, I won't say on everybody. Let's just say anybody who could wear a skirt and looked fairly decent. It got so I had to warn off a couple of the younger kids. I don't know what it is about some guys. They get a thing about waitresses—something about a good-looking babe who brings you food."

She made a face. "And then he made this place his

headquarters. Guess he must have lived or worked someplace nearby. Even so, I don't know why he chose us. Trust me, unless you're hooked on grilled cheese, it ain't the cuisine. And he was a pretty snappy dresser, not like the polyester crowd we usually get. You'd think he could afford better."

"Then I guess I'll have a grilled cheese and a cola to go," Sunny said, and the waitress passed the order along. Sunny smiled, hoping she'd look just plain personally nosy, not professionally nosy. "So he used to keep coming in here even though he struck out with the staff?"

The waitress grinned and shrugged. "Started bringing his own women. Maybe he wanted to show us what we were missing. The little blonde—well, she wasn't so little, just young—she might turn up with him for breakfast, lunch, or supper. And she was just eating up anything he had to say. I don't think she paid much attention to what was on her plate. She could have eaten a dirt and dandelion omelet and wouldn't have complained."

That sounds like Dawn Featherstone, Sunny thought.

"Yeah, that one was definitely a cheap date," the waitress went on, laughing. "The older woman who had coffee with him, though—the brunette—she was definitely slumming. With those clothes and jewelry, she was a lot classier than this place."

The waitress broke off as the counterman came over with Sunny's order in a plastic clamshell and a wax cup. The waitress put them in a bag and took Sunny's money. "Oh, well. Guess it takes all kinds. I wonder what the guy did to get killed. Maybe somebody's husband did it."

Sunny thanked the woman and headed for the door and

out to her SUV, weighing the package in her hand. *Grilled cheese was probably a bad choice,* she thought regretfully. *Chances are it will congeal long before I manage to get back to the office—and I can't stretch this lunch hour and a half much longer.*

She deposited her food on the passenger's seat and got behind the wheel. *On the other hand, finding out that Martin Rigsdale apparently had at least two lady friends— and might have been two-timing them—that's priceless. It means there are at least two other people besides Jane who might have a motive to do him harm. Plus, like that waitress said, when a guy fools around with a lot of women, there might be an angry husband waiting in the underbrush with a baseball bat.*

She arrived at the office to find no more phone calls on the answering machine.

Dodged a bullet there, Sunny thought. *It would have been just like Ollie to ring up and check on me while I was AWOL.*

After sticking the grilled cheese in the office microwave to try and revive it, Sunny revved up her computer. Okay, a couple of e-mails to deal with, business as usual. She retrieved the sandwich and settled in for a working late lunch.

The grilled cheese was soggy and tasteless. Sunny didn't think she'd be adding that diner to the recommended list for tourists in the area. The soda had gone flat, too. But she chewed methodically, fueling up for the afternoon.

Just as well that she did. As soon as Sunny tossed the packaging in the trash, the phone suddenly came to life. She spent the rest of the afternoon making arrangements for three separate shopping expeditions to arrive on the coming weekend. Then, as the day drew to a close, she got a call from her dad.

"We're going to have company for dessert," he announced.

"Do I have to get out my pearls?" she asked.

"No, just the nice coffee cups," Mike replied. "Helena said she'd bring some of her coffee cake. The really good news is that she's leaving that damned puppy at home."

Sunny hurried home to find Mike had already started the sweet potatoes baking for dinner. She trimmed the excess fat off the pork chops and slipped them into the toaster oven, then got a package of frozen whipped squash out of the freezer and put it in the microwave. Flip the pork chops, give them some more time, slice one to see how done it was . . . okay, almost. She topped the chops with some applesauce and a quick sprinkling of ginger, stirred up the squash, and put it back in for a final zap.

Sunny sighed. *Dinner pretty much accomplished, even with a good-sized cat twining his way around my ankles.*

She dropped to one knee on the kitchen floor and smiled down at Shadow's gold-flecked eyes staring up at her. "And how was your day?" she asked, running her fingers down his furry sides.

"I guess we both napped," Mike said from where he was setting the kitchen table. "After Helena called, I straightened out the living room. Then I dug out the company coffee cups, gave them a wash, and dried them."

Sunny rose to her feet and smiled. "Mom had you well trained."

"Do we have anything nice to put in the cups, though?"

he asked. "We're kind of at the bottom of that coffee you picked up on sale."

"Didn't Mrs. Martinson give you a bag of fancy coffee for Christmas?" Sunny said. "I think it's in the back of the fridge."

She loaded up a couple of plates, and they had a quick supper. By the time Helena Martinson arrived, the aroma of cinnamon-flavored Christmas coffee filled the house.

The older woman gave Mike a kiss on the cheek and handed Sunny a covered dish. "I made a little cake this afternoon." She smiled at Mike. "It's fresh, and there won't be much left over for temptation."

Mike's smile wavered as he took Helena's coat. Caught between an excellent baker and the food police, there wasn't much he could say.

Shadow came into the foyer and made a wide circle around Mrs. Martinson. Then did the same in the middle of the living room and stalked off to the kitchen again.

Sunny had to hide a smile. *Either he smells dog on Mrs. M., or he remembers her mutt from last visit.*

"Why don't you sit down, and then I'll go get some coffee. What brings you over this evening?" Sunny said, hoping she already knew the answer.

"I phoned around a bit—quite a bit, actually—and I finally found out about that girl in Portsmouth," Helena Martinson said, taking a seat on the couch. Her petite figure in a cable-knit sweater and corduroys clashed with Mike's solid presence in a flannel shirt and jeans. As often happened, Sunny felt underdressed next to Helena's understated elegance. Though the older woman's blond hair may have silvered, and she sported a few more smile lines, Mrs.

Martinson was still very much like the hot mom Sunny remembered from her high school days.

Maybe I should *have put on my pearls,* she thought as she went into the kitchen, sliced the cake, added it to the tray of cups, poured the coffee, and returned.

Helena Martinson took a cup and saucer, added half a spoonful of sugar, and lightened the coffee with a quick dollop of milk from the creamer.

"I hope you don't mind skim," Mike said.

It's the same as you've been getting for the last year or so since you've been visiting Dad, Sunny thought, but she didn't say anything.

Mrs. Martinson waited until everyone had coffee and cake before she started her story. "It was nice, having a chance to chat with some people I don't usually see," she began. "The 99 Elmet Ladies have been trying to coordinate some of our programs with Portsmouth volunteer groups."

Sunny nodded. The 99 Elmet Ladies was a service group that had sprung up as times had gotten tougher around Elmet County. Ken Howell had run several admiring stories in the *Harbor Crier* about their efforts to establish a food pantry and help folks made homeless. Speaking privately with Sunny, his editorial opinion had been blunter: "There's a lot less tea and finger sandwiches and a lot more hard work than you'd expect from that crowd. Some of the more snooty groups could take a good lesson from them."

"Some of our new friends and allies from across the river live not too far from Martin Rigsdale's office." Helena looked faintly embarrassed. "I'm afraid I had to use some of the grisly details you told Mike to get the conversation going."

Yeah, gossip is often a quid pro quo proposition, Sunny thought. "What did these ladies think of Martin Rigsdale?" she asked.

"They found him very charming, of course," Mrs. Martinson replied. "He offered advice on dealing with the local stray population and spent a lot of time getting into the local social swing. His place was near a golf course, and he did some networking there with the men. And he could always be depended upon for any event where womenfolk were around."

"That sounds like Martin," Sunny said.

Mike just made a face as he sipped his coffee. "What's that old song? 'Just a Gigolo'?"

"But there was talk about him and his receptionist." Mrs. M.'s expression became disapproving. "I understand she's attractive, as one of the ladies put it, 'in a downscale sort of way.' More to the point, she's just a bit more than half his age."

"What else did you find out about Dawn Featherstone?" Sunny asked.

"For one thing, she's actually Dora Featherstone," Helena said. "She calls herself Dawn for professional reasons."

"What?" Mike burst out, spewing a little cloud of powdered sugar off his coffee cake. "She's a professional receptionist?"

"She grew up in Portsmouth, again as one of my ladies put it, 'not in one of the nicest neighborhoods.' For a while she went to Manchester for a degree in physical education.

But she dropped out of college and came back home. She worked as an aerobics instructor—"

"That would explain calling herself Dawn," Sunny said. "How many aerobics instructors have you met named Dora?"

"As I was saying, she worked in several health clubs," Mrs. Martinson went on. "Apparently, however, you need some sort of certification, and she wasn't able to get it. So she just did temp work until she wound up working for Dr. Rigsdale, who hired her full-time."

"In more ways than one," Mike muttered, but he quickly subsided when both Sunny and Helena gave him looks.

"So, has she suddenly developed a deep interest in veterinary medicine?" Sunny asked.

Helena shook her head. "From what I hear, her dream is to open her own health club." She paused, smiling. "For humans."

Sunny frowned thoughtfully as she took in that information. *Considering the front Martin Rigsdale put up, he might've looked like a good source to bankroll Dawn's dream. Maybe this isn't a case of a starry-eyed kid bowled over by the old Rigsdale charm. Maybe Dawn had her own agenda.* Sunny's frown got deeper. *And if she found out that she was wasting her time—that Martin was broke, or if he had another woman—well, Dawn is definitely well toned. She could bop somebody on the head and make sure they stayed down. And she probably knew how to administer a shot . . .*

"I hope that expression isn't a reaction to my cake," Mrs. Martinson said.

"Sorry," Sunny apologized. "I'm afraid my thoughts took me away for a moment."

"Thinking about a not very nice man," the older woman said. "And maybe a girl to match?" She shook her head. "The problem is, the women I talked to all liked Dr. Rigsdale. He fit in with them socially. When it came to Dawn, though, they talked about her 'trying to get her claws into him.'"

Sunny laughed. "They didn't know him very well. He was very equal opportunity when it came to picking up women." She told her dad and Mrs. Martinson the story she'd heard from the waitress.

"Yeah, well, maybe she's right," Mike said. "I remember my days out on the road. There was something about waitresses—" He shut up when he saw the looks he was getting from both Sunny and Helena.

Mrs. Martinson perched herself on the end of her seat, her petite features alight with curiosity. "So, are you intending to solve this mystery?"

Sunny repressed a shudder. "Definitely not," she replied. That was the last thing she wanted going out on the local gossip hotline. "I'm just worried about Jane Rigsdale. It's bad enough that she found her ex-husband dead, but now the cops are asking questions—"

She bit off the end of that sentence. "I'd appreciate it if that didn't get out and around."

"There's already a lot of talk going around about Jane," Mrs. Martinson said. "The scene in the Redbrick is public knowledge by now—probably with a lot of embroidery. I suppose the Portsmouth police know all about it."

Sunny nodded. "But we don't need to spread any more stories."

Helena fluttered her hands. "You wouldn't believe some of the things I hear. Carolyn Dowdey has been complaining that Jane overstepped her bounds in running the animal foundation. She claims that Jane is discriminating against people who took their pets to Martin instead of to her."

"Dowdey?" Sunny repeated. "Sort of a big woman in fancy clothes that don't suit her—face like a cat and a stinky perfume?"

"I've been with Carolyn while she shops for perfume," Mrs. Martinson said. "Believe me, it's not the kind of stuff you'd find discounted up in outlet-land. It would probably cost you a week's salary." She named a designer fragrance that was horrifyingly exclusive, not to mention pricey.

Sunny grimaced. "Make that two weeks' salary." She gave her neighbor a quizzical look. "Does that stuff really smell so awful?"

"Only after it hits Carolyn's skin." Helena sighed. "It's some kind of unfortunate chemical reaction that turns the best perfumes rancid. This wasn't the first, I'm afraid. I've tried to be tactful about it—several of us have—but she just doesn't seem to listen."

"Yeah, I kind of noticed that about her," Sunny said. "She barged into Jane's office last night, complaining that Jane was holding up a cat adoption on her."

"Was she?" Mrs. Martinson asked.

"Sort of, but not because she was upset about Martin. Jane wants this Dowdey woman to take a class on how to take care of pets. Apparently, she's killed two cats with kindness—overfeeding them."

"Really?" Mrs. M. looked a little worried. "Maybe I should sign up for that class, too. Toby seems ready to eat anytime—"

Mike broke in, rolling his eyes. "And anything."

"I think that's pretty standard when it comes to puppies," Sunny said. "Looks as though the two of you are going through a learning curve."

But her neighbor was on to a different subject. "Carolyn has been through some big changes, and hasn't handled them well. Her husband left her well off when he passed away. She's invested heavily in altering her house and her wardrobe—neither for the better. She wants very badly to be modern."

"Young?" Sunny interjected.

Helena gave an uncomfortable nod. "I suppose so. And even though she buys the best, it's not always the best for her."

"You sound sympathetic," Sunny said.

"And you sound surprised," Helena Martinson replied.

Sunny shrugged. "Well, all I saw was her nasty side, clawing at Jane—although she did compliment Shadow."

Mike hmphed in the background.

"She just about worshiped her cats," Helena said. "I guess they were good company in a fairly lonely life." She glanced at her wristwatch. "I hate to chat and run, but I should probably get a move on in a little while. I got a pet sitter to keep an eye on Toby. You wouldn't believe what he's managed to get into when he's left alone."

Sunny saw the stab of disappointment on Mike's face. He'd sat for all this gossip that had nothing to do with him, and obviously had hoped for more of a visit with his lady friend. "I'm afraid you'll have to excuse me," she said. "I just realized I've got to get online for a work thing. Do you mind if I say good-bye now and leave you with Dad?"

Mike brightened at the thought of some alone time with Helena.

But Helena Martinson, Sunny was sure, saw right through her flimsy excuse. Mrs. M. smiled at her. "I understand," she said.

Sunny headed upstairs to her room, followed by Shadow. Which was just as well. They'd probably like their privacy in the living room without a feline audience.

"Dad did the same thing with me when I was in high school so I could sit on the couch with a boy for a while," she whispered to her cat.

Selecting an old favorite from her bookshelf, Sunny lay on her bed to read. After a couple of pages, she felt warm breath on her right ear. She turned to find Shadow perched on top of the clock radio, looking over her shoulder.

"At least you're not tapping me on the shoulder to turn the page before I'm ready," she told the cat.

They stayed in companionable silence for a while until Mike knocked at the door and stuck his head in. "Finished with your Internet stuff?"

"It went faster than I expected," Sunny cheerfully lied. "Is Mrs. Martinson gone?"

He nodded. "She said to thank you—I guess for the coffee. And you didn't even touch your piece of cake."

She grinned at him. "Look on the bright side. You can probably have it tomorrow."

They turned in early, not listening to the eleven o'clock newscast. So, when Sunny awoke in the morning, she wasn't ready for the chilly, blustery weather that had moved in.

"Welcome back, Winter," she said, looking out the kitchen window. Wherever yesterday's snow melt had accumulated, ice patches had formed. Her dad lectured her about getting too overconfident in the Wrangler. "Some people think that climbing aboard an SUV is like getting into a tank," he said. "Those are the ones who get into accidents."

In fact, she did see someone in a big macho-wagon spin out. But she had a very careful drive into town and got to the MAX office uneventfully, before settling in for an uneventful day.

Sunny got about two hours of that until the phone rang. It was Jane.

"Well, the medical examiner's preliminary report is in," she reported. "Trumbull just called me about it."

She sounded pretty upset, which surprised Sunny. This was a murder investigation, after all. In spite of what Jane and Will might wish, Trumbull was going to keep turning up. "I thought they already figured out the cause of death," she said cautiously. "Was that so bad?"

"They found a broken needle in Martin's arm." Jane's voice was tight. "Trumbull was all over me about it. You see, I've got a case like that in my record."

9

Sunny frowned, shifting in her seat. "It's not a . . ." She fumbled a moment, trying to find a word, and then gave up. "It's not a criminal record, is it?" she asked into the phone.

"No, it's just a stupid . . ." Jane paused to take a deep breath. "Sunny, are you doing anything for lunch? I'd prefer to discuss this face-to-face rather than over the phone."

"I think I need to stay close to my desk," Sunny told her, remembering yesterday's extended field trip. It had turned up some interesting stuff, but she didn't want to try stretching her luck by being out of the office again.

"Look, I've got a gap in my appointments in about forty-five minutes. What do you say we grab some sandwiches and talk in your office? My treat," Jane offered.

"Who am I to turn down a free lunch?" Sunny replied

with a grin. They made the date and then hung up. It seemed as if Sunny had barely gotten back to her computer screen when she heard a knock at the door. Jane couldn't have gotten downtown that fast.

She looked up to see a stocky figure in navy blue opening the door. Constable Ben Semple was a member of the tiny Kittery Harbor police force. Short and heavyset, with a wide, open face and a snub nose, he didn't exactly look like a crimebuster. In fact, he probably paid his own salary and a good part of Will Price's by nailing traffic violators along the five-mile stretch of road by the outlet malls. But Sunny had seen him take charge of a crime scene. Ben knew how to do his job.

Now he hesitated in the doorway, looking uneasy.

You'll never get to work undercover if you let your feelings show so easily, Ben, Sunny thought. She smiled at him and joked, "Hey, I thought you guys only rattled the doors after we closed up for the night."

Ben's answering smile was strained. "I can only stay for a second or two." He glanced through the window at his patrol car double-parked outside. "I just wanted you to know that the Portsmouth department has gone official, asking a lot of questions about Jane Rigsdale—and Will."

Not good, Sunny thought.

"I'd have imagined Sheriff Nesbit would be tickled pink that Martin Rigsdale moved out of town before he got himself killed." Sunny couldn't keep the sarcasm from her voice. Whenever the election cycle came around, Frank Nesbit plastered the area with posters about his great job of "Keeping Elmet County Safe." The problem was, many people suspected the sheriff of enhancing that safety record by playing with the crime statistics. That was why a political faction in Kittery Harbor wanted Will Price in charge. With his background as a state trooper and then as a Portsmouth cop, Will had credible police experience.

"Yeah, the sheriff's glad about Rigsdale," Semple said, "but he's giving Will grief about his relationship with Jane." He quickly switched conversational gears when he caught the look on Sunny's face. "I mean, these days Will and Jane are friends, but years back they were pretty serious. It doesn't look good for a cop to be close to someone involved in a murder investigation." Sunny was sure her expression didn't improve when she heard that. If there was one thing that trumped professionalism, it was politics. And Frank Nesbit was a master politician. That was how he'd won and so far kept the job as sheriff.

"If the sheriff had his way, he wouldn't even let Will talk to Jane," Ben said.

So I guess the news isn't all bad, that irreverent side of Sunny's brain spoke up.

"It's going to be tough for her," he went on, "since she really doesn't have many friends here in town."

There it was—the Kittery Harbor Code, "Do right by your neighbors." Unfortunately, the flip side of that translated into a kind of clannish mind-set: "To hell with outsiders."

By moving out of Kittery Harbor, Sunny, Jane, and Will had all turned themselves into outsiders. Sunny might not like to think about it, but for a lot of folks in town, the jury was still out on the returnees. Yet Sunny also knew that she was a product of Kittery Harbor. "Do right." "Never go back on your word." Those were things that she she'd grown up believing—and still believed.

She sighed as Ben said good-bye and headed out. *Like it or not, if Jane really gets in trouble, I'll have to help her, even if nobody else does—or can.* She pressed her lips together very tightly, as if she were holding back a bad taste. *Especially if nobody can.* That was just the way of things. It was literally where she came from.

Oh, won't Jane and I have some things to talk about over lunch.

*

Not long after Ben Semple went back on patrol, Jane arrived at the MAX office door. "I thought we could go down the block to Judson's and pick up some sandwiches there," she suggested. "My treat."

Sunny nodded. "Sounds good to me."

The deli counter was pretty busy—a lot of folks in the area had had the same idea for lunch. Sunny got Black Forest ham and Swiss cheese on rye with honey mustard. Jane got fresh turkey breast, coleslaw, and tomato on a roll.

"You're brave," Sunny told her. "If I ordered that, I'd end up with coleslaw on my chin."

But Jane would probably make it look good, her snarky alter ego added.

They both got lemonades, and Jane snagged a bag of chocolate-covered pretzels. They both headed back down the block to the MAX office. Sunny checked the answering machine and the e-mail. "Okay, no messages, no disasters—let's eat!"

In moments they'd settled in around Sunny's desk and unwrapped their sandwiches. "Now what's this problem with the Portsmouth cops?" Sunny asked.

"It started with a call from that guy Fitch," Jane said. "He was asking how often it happened that a medical professional broke a hypodermic needle in a patient. I said, quite honestly, I didn't know. That certainly wasn't something I'd try to answer off the top of my head. Then he asked if it had ever happened to me."

Jane took a bite of her sandwich and chewed for a moment. "From the way he asked, I knew that he already had the answer."

"Which was 'yes,'" Sunny said.

"It was years ago, when I was just starting out, working with Martin." Jane looked hard at her sandwich, as if debating which part she'd bite next. "We were treating a big dog, a Shepherd mix. Sometime after his visit, we got a call. The dog wouldn't eat, was drooling froth, and obviously in some sort of distress."

Sunny waited till Jane raised her eyes. "That doesn't sound good."

Jane responded with a professional's shrug. "There's no nice way to say it. Dogs are kind of dopey. They'll eat stupid things. Cats do it, too, but with them it usually comes right up." She gave Sunny a rueful smile. "Wait till the weather gets warmer—you'll see."

"I can hardly wait," Sunny said.

"With dogs, especially big ones, the stupid things they eat can cause an obstruction farther along in the digestive system," Jane went on. "The thing is, in a case like that, you'd expect the dog to be vomiting."

Sunny put her sandwich down. "This is one hell of a lunchtime conversation."

"Sorry, that kind of happens when vets talk shop," Jane

apologized. "Look, I'll try to make it brief. There was obviously something wrong with the dog, and the owners went for another opinion. That vet took an X-ray to see if the problem might be in his mouth or throat. Instead, he found a piece of metal lodged in the muscles of the dog's neck, near the shoulders."

"The tip of the needle." Sunny paused for a second. "But you sound as if this came as a surprise to you."

"It did," Jane replied. "And a damned unwelcome one. You see, I'm not the one who gave the shot. Frankly, that's not an area where a vet should have even *made* an injection. A broken needle could have migrated through the muscle fibers and in between the vertebrae, causing some real problems."

"Sounds bad. But you say you didn't give the shot, so why is it on your record?"

"Martin. He was the one who gave the shot. But he convinced me to take a hit for the team."

"Because you could get away with a rookie mistake?" Sunny deduced.

"Yeah, just call me young and dumb. And the black mark went against my insurance, not his."

Definitely young and dumb, Sunny thought. *And probably already halfway in love with Martin the Charming Louse.*

Jane shook her head. "And now, all these years later, it comes back to haunt me. Even after I divorced Martin— hell, even after he's dead—I can't get rid of him!"

"Well, looking on the bright side, you don't sound like someone who killed him," Sunny said.

That shocked a laugh out of Jane. "Maybe I should

have said that to Trumbull and Fitch, the Portsmouth Manhunters."

"Or is that Womanhunters?" Sunny joked, but then got more serious. "Somehow, I don't think that would persuade them." She paused for a second, trying to choose her next words carefully. "Ben Semple stopped by today."

"That's one of the guys who works with Will, right?"

Sunny nodded. "I suppose you know that Trumbull has been asking Will some questions."

"He mentioned it." Jane made a face.

"Up to now, it was unofficial. But now he's gone to Sheriff Nesbit." Taking a deep breath, Sunny explained the political ramifications. By the time she'd finished, it was clear that Jane had heard only one thing.

"You're saying Will won't be able to talk to me anymore?" Jane's surprise made her look all the more forlorn.

Sunny was afraid that if she answered yes, Jane might just burst into tears. Instead, Jane grabbed her by the arm, talking rapidly. "He's one of the only people around here who went out in the world and came back to town. Who else can I talk to?" She stumbled over her words for a moment. "I mean, besides you. Folks are polite and everything, but I always feel as if they're measuring me, seeing if I can really fit in again."

Tell me about it, Sunny thought.

"Sometimes I can even see it in Rita's eyes when we're in the office together." Jane looked a little embarrassed, but straightened her shoulders and went on. "When times are quiet, I go back to the patient cages. It's not just to check out the animals staying with us. It's because, even if they can't speak, I know that most of them like me."

"What?" Sunny said in surprise. "Everyone likes you." The words sort of burst out of her, words she'd thought for most of her life. *Everybody likes Jane Leister.*

"Once upon a time I might have thought so." If anything, Jane looked even sadder. "But nowadays they think, 'There's that Leister girl who tried to go off, but had to come back home, and still couldn't hold on to her husband. And we had such high hopes for her.'"

Her eyes were bright with unshed tears. "And now I bet lots of them think I actually killed him!"

Sunny wasn't quite sure how to handle this kind of confession. Then, summoning up her inner Mary Poppins, she briskly dismissed Jane's worries. "It's not just the patients who like you. Anyone who's brought an animal to you knows what a good vet you are. That you care for their pets and their feelings. I know that, because I've seen you with Shadow. And then there's the work you're taking on with the foundation. You've done a lot for this town, and people know that. And they do like you."

Sunny picked up her sandwich. "Now let's stop the shop talk and eat our lunch. I want to get at those chocolate-covered pretzels."

Jane laughed, but she still wavered on the edge of crying.

Sunny leaned over and patted her on the hand. "You've got friends you don't realize—Ben Semple, for instance. And like it or not, you've got me. Will may face all kinds of problems if he talks to you, but that doesn't stop him from talking to me, and then I can talk to you. I don't work for Frank Nesbit."

Jane really started laughing when she heard that. "And

I bet he thanks God every Sunday afternoon for that." She looked down at her food. "Okay. Sandwiches, then pretzels."

Sunny gave her a bracing smile. Bur underneath it, she thought, *I hope I haven't just made a promise that I'm going to regret.*

*

The rest of lunch passed in chewing and small talk—not at the same time. They did have manners, after all. When they finished, Jane took Sunny's arm again. "Thanks. We should do this again." She sighed, but then grinned, her confidence apparently back in place. "Maybe with less police involvement."

Sunny saw her to the door and then went back to work. She had a couple of new listings to add to the local attractions database. It was a calming sort of job. Wrangling with computer code seemed so much more straightforward than dealing with people.

The phone rang, and Sunny found herself back in the human equation. Will was on the other end of the line. "Would you mind grabbing a quick coffee with me when you finish work?"

Normally, she would've accepted with pleasure. Now, though . . .

"Does this have anything to do with the conversation I had with Ben Semple earlier today?" Sunny asked.

"Could be," Will replied cautiously.

Sunny threw up her hands in surrender. What was she going to do? "Okay," she said. "How about that new little café that opened near the harbor?"

When Sunny closed up the office, she walked the short distance downtown. The cobblestone street at harborside was as quaint as ever, but almost deserted thanks to the icy wind blowing in off the water. As the only customer at Spill the Beans, Sunny got a warm welcome and her choice of tables. She chose the one in the corner under the heater and settled in to defrost. Moments later, Will came in, tall and rangy in a dark blue parka. His chiseled features looked more like ice sculpture, the tips of his ears and nose red from the cold. He unzipped his coat, showing that he was still in civilian clothes, and sat across the small table from her, blowing on his fingers.

"You can order one of those New York cappy-frappy things if you like," he said. "I just want a nice, big cup of American coffee to wrap my hands around."

"Or maybe you could wear gloves," Sunny suggested.

"They're with my uniform coat," he told her. "So they're waiting for me when I start my shift."

Before Will could say anything more, the waitress arrived and took their orders—American coffee for both of them. When she left, Will leaned across the table. "Sheriff Nesbit had me come in early today for a 'fatherly chat.'"

Since Will's late father had been sheriff before Frank Nesbit got elected to the office, there were several layers of meaning for Sunny to unpack from that sentence. Will blamed Nesbit not only for driving his dad from office, but for the older Price's death in an auto accident soon afterward.

Will sat silently for a moment as their coffees arrived. Sunny took a sip. "It's pretty good, even if it doesn't have a shot of hazelnut buffalo milk."

Will just made a noncommittal sound, stirring his spoon in his cup.

"So what do you need to get off your chest?" Sunny prompted. "What did you and Nesbit chat about? Trumbull? Jane?"

"Both," Will said. "I guess it got pretty loud. Ben must have overheard some of it." He shot her an anxious glance. "What did he tell you?"

"Well, he mentioned that there might be a problem for a cop who was—'close' was the way he put it—with a murder suspect." She frowned. "Does Nesbit think Jane did it?"

"He doesn't care." From the look on Will's face as he sipped from his cup, he might as well have been drinking pond scum. "But he gave me a great lecture on avoiding even the appearance of impropriety." He set the cup down a little too sharply. Coffee slopped onto the acrylic cover that protected the reclaimed wood of the table. "The big hypocrite."

"So what's the bottom line?" Sunny asked.

"Complete cooperation with the Portsmouth investigation," Will said. "Nesbit ordered me to answer every question Trumbull might care to ask." He frowned angrily at the memory. But then he deflated, adding in a low voice, "And no communication with Jane."

Will dabbed at the puddle of coffee with the totally inadequate napkin that had accompanied his cup, and then looked up at Sunny. "She may not show it, but this whole situation has Jane pretty freaked out."

"We talked a little about it this afternoon." Sunny decided not to tell Will about Jane's mini-meltdown. "If you have any advice you need to pass on to her, you can always do it through me."

For the first time since he'd come in, Will brightened a bit. "You're the best, Sunny. I think that's the only decent thing I've heard all day."

But his smile quickly flickered out. "I think we're past the point of giving advice," he said. "What Jane needs now is a lawyer."

"Peter Lewin has worked with her at the foundation," Sunny began, naming a local attorney, but Will shook his head.

"I'm talking about a criminal, not a civil, lawyer," he interrupted. "Someone who can practice across the river in Portsmouth."

He dug a crumpled business card from his shirt pocket. "This is a guy who knows his business." Will gave her a wry smile. "Back when I was on the Portland force, he dragged me over the coals a couple of times when I had to testify in cases. He's the youngest partner in the firm."

"Crandall, Sherwood, and Phillips," Sunny read the top line of the card aloud. "Well, at least it's not Dewey, Cheatem, and Howe."

"Tell her to get in touch with this Phillips guy." Will shook his head unhappily. "Otherwise, it looks as if my hands are tied."

He called the waitress over for more napkins and the bill. "I'm sorry, but I can't drink this stuff. Not the way I'm feeling now. It'll go right through me. And that's not a good thing when you're going on patrol."

Sunny didn't know whether to laugh or scowl as Will quickly headed out the door. *So much for the myth of the tough cop,* she thought. "Waste not, want not" was another Kittery Harbor mantra. Sunny reached over and poured the rest of Will's coffee into her own mug, and ordered a whoopie pie. With her first bite, the cream filling squelched out to either side of her mouth.

The evening's still young, she thought sarcastically. *I wonder who'll call to invite me out to supper.*

When she got home, though, all she found was a note in the kitchen from Mike:

> *Got the machine in your office and no answer on your cell phone. Have to go to a meeting. Will eat out. I promise not to eat anything with fat, salt, or flavor.*
>
> *Dad*

No answer? Sunny dug out her cell phone. "Great," she muttered. "Dead battery."

Then she smiled down at Shadow, who was still twining his way around her shins. "Looks like it's just me and you tonight. I just hope there are some sandwich makings in the fridge that aren't ham and cheese."

In the end, she wound up making a smashed fried egg sandwich, taking her plate into the living room and sitting on the floor with the cat.

*

Shadow paid no attention to the picture box, busily trying to push the plate out of Sunny's lap so he could climb in there. He usually didn't hang on her so much, but it wasn't often that they had the house to themselves.

After the Old One left, Shadow hadn't been able to settle back into his nap. Instead, he'd patrolled the empty rooms, feeling . . . lonely.

He tried to burn the feeling off the same way he would excess energy, playing the running game where he started in the kitchen, raced down the hall, caromed off the archway into the living room, and landed by the couch. The only problem was, it wasn't the same when he wasn't landing on Sunny. So he'd been especially glad to see her, even though she came home late.

When he went after her plate the fourth time, she tore off a piece of what was between the bread—huh, it turned out to be egg, which he ate even though he really wasn't interested. He just wanted to be nice to Sunny.

As she finished the sandwich, he finally got a paw on the plate and shoved it across her thigh. Then, when she went to pick it up, he swarmed over her arm and into her lap.

Halfway there, he paused for an instant, distracted. Was that Gentle Hands he smelled on her arm? Why was Sunny seeing her? His paw felt fine. To prove it, he reached out and gave Sunny's leg a good smack. No pain at all.

He swirled around in her lap and arranged himself comfortably. He certainly hadn't expected to find traces of Gentle Hands tonight. That was the interesting thing about two-legs. You never knew what they got up to once they left the house.

10

Sunny finally got loose from a surprisingly clingy Shadow to get hold of Jane Rigsdale on the phone. When she passed along Will's advice about a lawyer, Jane almost instinctively resisted. "Doesn't getting a lawyer make me look guilty?"

"Has not having a lawyer made you look more innocent to Trumbull and Fitch?" Sunny asked.

Jane didn't have an answer for that.

"Look, Jane, you're a smart person," Sunny told her. "But you haven't been at your best dealing with the police. You need someone who understands the system, and that means a lawyer. Don't take my word for it. Will is an experienced cop. He's been around for people being questioned, and if he thinks you should have a lawyer with you, you probably should."

"I—I'll think about it," Jane finally said. "You say Will gave you a card?"

Sunny read off the name and information on the card while Jane wrote it down. Then they wished each other a good night.

Hanging up the phone, Sunny looked down at Shadow, who had sat at her feet during the conversation. "Well, that's the best I could do," she told the cat. "The rest is up to Jane. If she's as smart as I think she is, she'll call that guy soon."

They went back to the living room to watch some television. Around nine o'clock, a car pulled up in the driveway and then drove off. Seconds later, Mike opened the door.

"Before you ask," he said, "Zack Judson gave me a lift, and I had soup and half a sandwich for supper."

"That all sounds pretty good,' " Sunny replied. "But what I was going to ask was why you had to go flying off on such short notice."

Mike looked at her in surprise. "I figured you would know—or at least be able to read between the lines. The sheriff has been using this Rigsdale case to bash at Will. We had to firm up his support when some folks began wavering."

"Politics," Sunny said in disgust. "I should have known it."

"That crowd up in Levett has pretty much had it their own way for years." Mike went into his standard rant about the lousy state of local government.

"Well, Levett is the county seat," Sunny pointed out. "Do you really think your Kittery Harbor crowd would do a better job if you got to run things?"

"Be hard to do worse," he grumped. "Besides, some-body had to stand up to those guys."

"But Will is the one being bashed."

Mike made a helpless gesture. "You know I like Will."

"Yeah," Sunny said. "So do I."

"Maybe not in the same way." Her dad tried out a smile, but it fell flat. "Will went into this with his eyes open. He has his own reasons to dislike Frank Nesbit."

"That's true," Sunny had to admit.

"And it's this stupid case in Portsmouth that's hurting him," Mike said. "Once that's cleaned up—"

"Just don't expect me to whip out my trusty magnifying glass and solve everything," Sunny warned.

Right, that mocking voice from the back of her head chimed in. *Just because you dug up a couple of clues doesn't mean you're investigating anything. Yup. Sure.*

From the look on Mike's face, she wondered if he had a little voice in his head saying something similar. But he only shrugged. "If there's one thing I think you've learned in life, it's not to bite off more than you can chew."

Sunny felt a little better as he turned back to put his coat away in the hall closet. Then she heard him add under his breath, "At least I hope so."

*

After a Thursday with all sorts of visitors bringing all sorts of news, Friday was kind of a letdown. Sunny tried not to think of it that way. "Maybe what I need is just a normal business day," she told herself. She had a bit more activity, helping out with weekend plans for eager shoppers and even more eager romantic couples. At least no snow-storms threatened.

Around three o'clock, when things seemed to be quiet-ing down, Ollie Barnstable called. "Nothing urgent going on in the office, is there?" he asked. "I'm thinking of spending the weekend down here in New York. Guy I know thinks he can score some orchestra seats for—"

Sunny really didn't want to hear what smash hit he was going to see, probably at bargain prices. She was saved when the other line rang.

"Can you hold for a second?" she asked. "It might be one of the shopping packages."

She switched over to hear Jane talking a bit too fast. "I did it."

"Did what?" Sunny said, hoping this wasn't going to turn into a dramatic confession.

"I called that guy—the lawyer, Phillips. He's been fol-lowing the case and agreed to meet with me tomorrow. The thing is, he's working on another big case and wants to see me around six o'clock." Jane finally paused for a second. "I hate to ask—would you mind coming with me?"

"That didn't work out so well the last time," Sunny reminded her.

"But that's part of it. You're a witness . . . and you'd be backup. I think I kind of need that," Jane admitted.

Sunny sighed. "Okay. We'll make some kind of a plan. But I've got to get off now. I left my boss on the other line."

She got back to Ollie, who apparently was engaged in conversation with somebody else. "Oh, Sunny. Yeah. Look, I may stretch this trip even longer. Don't expect me back until Tuesday, maybe Wednesday. Call me if anything comes up." He cut the connection almost before he finished the sentence.

Lucky you, thought Sunny. The rest of the day was the same old, same old. Sunny locked the door right on schedule and headed home. She even had time to take care of Shadow's oil massage before tackling the job of cooking supper.

"I'm going to miss this," she told the cat as she kneaded the oil around the pads on his paw. It had turned into a nice little ritual. Whenever she got out the bottle of oil, he'd come right over and present his paw. *Just like the way he'd do it with Jane,* she thought, looking into the cat's odd, gold-flecked eyes. *Maybe he's starting to trust me.*

"Are we having supper soon, or is the whole night going to go toward pet physical therapy?" Mike asked, coming into the kitchen. "Because there are human beings around here who are sort of hungry."

"I'll be starting in a minute, Dad," Sunny told him. "And, yes," she went on as he opened his mouth, "I'll wash my hands first."

They watched a couple of Mike's favorite programs on the TV, but Sunny didn't pay much attention, playing with Shadow. As soon as the news came on, she stood up, yawning. "I'll hear about the weather tomorrow," she said, heading up to her bedroom. "I want to get up a little early."

It was just as well she turned in a bit ahead of time, because the area was covered with fog when she got up. Sunny hurried through the morning routine and crawled into work with lousy visibility. She could hear foghorns from the harbor as she unlocked the office door.

The fog didn't lift until noontime. Sunny barely noticed. She hurried through the day, trying to accomplish any bit of work that might slow up her escape. She'd even brought a sandwich from home so she could work through her lunch hour.

When quitting time rolled around, she already had her computer off and her parka on. For once the phone didn't ring with some last-minute disaster. Sunny killed the lights and locked the door. She saw a pair of headlights make the turn onto the street and then glide to a stop. It took a moment for her to make out Jane's gray BMW in the darkness. Sunny walked to the curb and climbed aboard.

Jane made nervous small talk all the way across the bridge and into Portsmouth. "I know you probably think I'm silly," she said, "but I'm going to end up talking about some pretty serious stuff with a complete stranger. It will be good to have a friendly face in the room."

They managed to find street parking not far from the address on the business card. It turned out to be a renovated six-story brick building. According to the board in the lobby, Crandall, Sherwood, and Phillips was on the fifth floor. Luckily, part of the renovations had included installing an elevator.

The door opened onto a reception area paneled in dark mahogany instead of the blond wood in Martin Rigsdale's office. That wasn't the only difference. This receptionist actually smiled at them, and the place was obviously jumping, even at six o'clock. The young woman's desk was covered with piles of paper, and behind her Sunny could see people scurrying around with still more papers in their hands.

It took a couple of minutes to get hold of Mr. Phillips, and the receptionist apologized. Finally, a tall guy came down the hall in his shirtsleeves, a conservatively patterned silk tie pulled loose at his collar, and a cup of coffee in his hand. "Please forgive me for the delay." He gestured with the cup. "I had to refuel."

When he got to within ten feet of them, though, Mr. Phillips stopped and stared. "Jane Leister," he said in disbelief, "and Sunny Coolidge!"

Sunny stood looking into a semifamiliar face. Knock off a few inches of height, make the hair longer and messier, wind back the clock so the boyish face was actually a boy's . . .

"Toby Philpotts?" She and Jane blurted out the name almost in unison. Sunny hadn't thought of Toby Philpotts in years—well, not until she'd suggested naming Mrs. Martinson's incontinent pup after her grammar-school classmate with the weak bladder. And here he was, all grown up.

The man in front of them didn't quite grimace—he'd had a lawyer's training in controlling his expressions. "It's Phillips these days," he said quietly. "And I prefer Tobe."

He led them through a maze of cubicles to his office. It was a pretty modest space, although the bookcases were the same mahogany as the paneling outside. So was the desk. And he did have a door that shut and a window with a view toward the harbor. Toby Philpotts, a.k.a. Tobe Phillips, glanced at the empty desk outside his door. "My assistant is busy jockeying around the copying machine," he explained. "We've got to get a filing ready by the opening of court on Monday."

He set his cup down on the side of a fairly messy desk

and gestured toward the pair of comfortable seats facing him. "I've been following the case on TV and in the papers, but obviously I didn't get all the information."

"I still can't believe it!" Jane said. "I haven't seen you—since when? Middle school?"

Tobe nodded. "My dad got a job on this side of the river when I was a freshman. I wound up in a new school, made new friends, found new interests."

Got a new name, Sunny added silently. "That's right," she said aloud. "I remember you wanted to go into science."

"Law ended up paying better," Tobe said with a wry smile. "That's one of the reasons I changed my name. I kept hearing comments about pots of cash." His voice got drier. "Or pots of bovine scatology, as what's-his-name used to put it."

He cast an admiring glance Jane's way. "But then, you're a vet. You may encounter the real stuff out in the field."

She shook her head. "I don't do that much with large animals, Tobe," she said, almost as if she were tasting the name. "Most of the BS I put up with is figurative."

Tobe grinned at her. "And what do you do these days, Sunny?" he asked.

"I was a reporter down in New York," she began the same old story. "Had to come back home to take care of my dad, got laid off, though, so right now I'm in the tourism business."

"Ah," he said, obviously filing that under "Questions to Be Asked Later." He turned back to Jane. "So, tell me a bit about Martin Rigsdale. Did you meet him professionally?"

She nodded. "I worked with him, married him, and ended up divorcing him." She went on to give a pretty concise explanation of the reasons for each stage in that relationship and didn't fly off the handle when describing Martin's shortcomings.

While Tobe Phillips quietly took all that in, Sunny spent the time checking him out, hoping she wasn't being too obvious about it. The studious boy she remembered had grown into an attractive man. His sandy hair had been cut in a style that suited his face, rather than the too-long mess she remembered. And the years had pared away some of the youthful softness from that face. Tobe didn't have the drop-dead gorgeousness of a Martin Rigsdale, or even the chiseled features of a Will Price. But he was a good-looking guy, thoughtful, and judging from his reactions to Jane's story, kind.

Sunny glanced around the desk and shelves. No pictures of a wife and kids.

He asked a couple of questions to clarify some details, then said, "So you had a marriage that didn't work out and a divorce that wasn't too contentious." He raised a hand—no ring, Sunny noticed—to cut off any comments from Jane. "Believe me, I've seen worse. So why do you think you need me?"

"Because I get the feeling that the cops think I killed Martin," Jane replied a little more loudly than she'd intended. She sat back in her seat, looking embarrassed.

"We have a mutual friend, a former Portsmouth police-man who's now a town constable in Kittery Harbor," Sunny said. "When the detectives started questioning him as well as Jane, he suggested we talk to you. His name is Will Price. Apparently he encountered you in court."

Tobe sat back, thinking for a moment—and smiling. "I

remember him," he said. "A pretty savvy cop. If he thinks you may have trouble, I'd take it seriously. So back to the real question: Why do you think the police suspect you?"

"Well, we found Martin—the body." Jane faltered a little over those words. "His receptionist immediately started accusing me."

"Detectives Trumbull and Fitch took our statements," Sunny said. "When we were finished, Will came to pick us up at the station, and Trumbull saw him."

"Mmmm-hmmm." Phillips turned to Jane. "Were you in the habit of seeing your ex-husband?"

Jane shook her head. "It was almost a year and a half since we'd even talked. Then he asked me out to dinner—but that was only so he could ask for money." She explained about the foundation she was running and its generous funding. "He wanted a six-figure consulting fee, and he wanted it up front! Is it any wonder I threw that drink in his face?"

That was something Jane hadn't mentioned before, but Sunny didn't have a chance to ask any questions. Jane went on, "Then I heard from Sunny that Martin had been to see her, and I called him. He said to come over during his evening hours."

Tobe turned to Sunny. "What did he say to you?"

"He wanted my help in persuading Jane to give him money," Sunny told him. "And he suggested we might spend some of it together." Sunny rolled her eyes. "I don't know if you've seen pictures of Martin, but he was a very attractive man, and he didn't mind spreading the charm around."

"Way too much," Jane agreed grimly.

"Maybe even more than you know." Sunny related her conversation with the diner waitress. "It sounds to me as if the receptionist, Dawn Featherstone, was involved with Martin. That would explain her reaction when we showed up—jealousy. And apparently he had at least one other lady friend."

"So you're suggesting at least two other possible suspects."

Sunny opened her mouth, on the verge of also mentioning the Russian cigarettes, but then decided against it. All she had was a foreign cigarette filter suggesting that someone had been watching Martin. Given Martin's habits, that watcher could have been a detective getting the goods for a suspicious spouse. A detective with weird smoking habits, but still . . .

Tobe looked at her. "Did you want to add something?"

"Only that Jane also mentioned to me that Martin had a habit of approaching some better-off clients for money."

Tobe frowned thoughtfully. "Do you think he was spreading his charm there, too?"

Jane's cheeks went pink. "Probably."

The lawyer stood. "If you haven't guessed it by now, I'm taking this case." He outlined some of the practicalities and gave Jane some papers to sign. "If Fitch or Trumbull comes at you again, refer them to me," he said. "I know it's not easy, having your life stirred around like this. But you will come through it."

"Thanks," Jane said, taking his hand. "For the first time in a week, I feel as if I can really breathe."

Two quick raps sounded on the door, and an anxious-looking young woman poked her head in, waving some papers.

"Now I've got to get back to the present emergency," Tobe Phillips apologized. "Can you find your way out?"

They made their way to the reception area. As they did, an elevator opened and a guy came out, carrying a bulging briefcase—more papers apparently. Sunny dashed up and stopped the doors from closing. They stepped aboard.

In the elevator, Sunny said, "Well, that was a surprise."

Jane nodded. "A nice one, for once."

They got downstairs, outside, and into Jane's car. Sunny pulled out her cell phone. "I just want to check the office machine. Make sure there are no last-minute calls."

She dialed the number for the MAX office, got the answering machine, and punched in the code for messages.

"Damn," she muttered. "One message."

"This is, ah, Larry," an unfamiliar voice said, obviously flustered at dealing with a machine. "From, ah, Portsmouth Tobacconists. That gentleman you asked about? He's coming in tonight."

"Damn, damn, damn," Sunny groaned. *Looks as if I'll have to talk about those Russian cigarettes after all.*

"There's somewhere we have to get—and quickly," she told Jane, giving her directions to the shop. "I'll explain while we drive."

In between telling Jane about the exotic cigarette and where she'd found it, Sunny punched in the number for Portsmouth Tobacconists. "Hello, Larry, this is the lady with the twenty. Thanks for calling me. Has the gentleman shown up?"

"Ah, no," Larry said, sounding nervous.

"I'll be there in a couple of minutes. If he comes before then, stall him."

She hung up on Larry asking how he could do that.

They arrived at the tobacco store, and Jane looked for parking while Sunny went in, checking that the place was empty. Larry jittered behind the counter, a lot less chatty this evening.

"Has he been here yet?" Sunny asked.

Larry shook his head.

"You have nothing to worry about. I'll be outside. When the guy comes in, you can—"

"I thought you knew him," Larry interrupted.

"It's just that it's sort of dark outside," Sunny improvised. "I'd hate to miss him."

"At his size, I think he'd be hard to miss," Larry said.

Sunny hurried back outside, where Jane had gotten a space across the street from the store. Not long after, it was clear that the man in question had arrived, and Sunny could see what Larry meant about him being hard to miss: This character added a football linebacker's width to a basketball forward's height. His head and shoulders almost brushed the top of the door frame, and a gray herringbone overcoat like a big wool tent flapped around him.

"Yow!" Jane said.

Sunny had to agree. "So much for the theory about smoking stunting your growth." She peered through the windshield. "Okay, he was in the blue SUV that passed us and parked down the block. That means he may pull a U-turn to go back the way he came."

"Have you done this before?" Jane asked. "Because if you have, you can drive."

For a second, Sunny debated spinning a tale to make Jane feel better, but then decided on the truth. "This is my first time, too," she said. "But if he makes the U-turn, give him some space before you try it. And don't ride on his rear bumper."

Jane stared at her. "I guess they teach you some weird things in journalism school."

Sunny laughed. "J-school, hell. That's from watching cop shows."

The guy came out, a carton of smokes tucked under one massive arm. He walked down the block to the SUV and got in, making the big vehicle rock for a moment. A second later, the truck's rear lights lit up, and it pulled out into the street, heading to the corner and making a right.

"Okay, start," Sunny said. "He can't see us now, but we'd better get back in sight of him."

Jane brought the BMW to life and quickly took the corner. Their quarry was nowhere to be seen.

"Okay, take a right at the next corner," Sunny directed. "Maybe he's doing that instead of making the U-turn."

They made two turns and spotted the SUV with a three-block lead on them, which Jane closed to one block. The driver ahead didn't seem to be in much of a hurry, dawdling his way around downtown Portsmouth, seemingly taking turns at random. Jane sat white-knuckled at the wheel out of sheer frustration. She muttered curse words as cars cut her off or beeped at her to hurry up. "What the hell is this guy doing?"

"Maybe he's got a meeting somewhere and is just killing time," Sunny suggested.

They followed the SUV into a more industrial neighborhood. The few stores that fronted on the street had closed. "Well, this is a good place for a meeting—if you like spy movies," Jane said.

The big guy's SUV made a sudden turn into a narrow alleyway.

"Cut off your lights and turn in," Sunny said. "If he keeps going, we can follow him. If we don't see his lights, we'll pretend we're making a K-turn—"

"And get out of here?" Jane suggested.

"I guess so," Sunny said. She'd hoped the guy they were following might lead her to some hangout where they'd be able to watch him discreetly, maybe even eavesdrop. As the thrill of the chase died down, Sunny's more cautious side weighed in. This guy was a possible killer, after all. Maybe it wouldn't be such a great idea to get too close to him. Still, if they got an idea where he stopped in this dark alley, they could come back in the daytime and get an address.

Jane made the turn, and had to jam on the brakes—the SUV was right in front of them.

And then, a second later, another SUV came pulling up behind, boxing them in.

Sunny and Jane looked at each other. *Well, Dad, looks as if you were right,* Sunny thought. *I've definitely bitten off more than I can chew.*

11

A **figure in** a heavy overcoat got out of the truck behind them and stepped over to Jane's window, his hand in one pocket. At the same time, the big guy had appeared beside Sunny's door, blocking her in, too. And he also had his hand in a pocket of his big, floppy coat.

The guy by Jane rapped on the window with his free hand. She lowered it a little.

"We have to talk," the man said in a pleasant tenor voice. Sunny caught a slight accent. "Please to come out."

With his big friend keeping watch over both Sunny and Jane, the smaller guy went into the alley and opened a door. Sunny exchanged a look with Jane. They really didn't have a choice in the matter. So they got out of the BMW and went inside.

They found themselves in a sort of foyer, a plain,

concrete-floored box with a heavy metal door facing the entranceway. Sunny was pretty sure if she tried the handle, she'd find it locked. As for the way back out, the big guy planted himself in front of that, more effective than any lock.

The fellow who'd spoken before put out his hand. "Identification, please."

Sunny and Jane wordlessly handed over their wallets. While he looked through them, Sunny noticed that, despite his heavy overcoat, he was actually a slim guy. The big man would probably make about three of him.

Mr. Slim held up Jane's driver's license, his sharp features relaxing a little. "Mrs. Doctor Rigsdale," he said. "Please accept my excuses. And you, too, Miss Coolidge. When Olek here calls me, says someone is following him, and asks for instructions, you might understand why we worry."

"But now that you know who we are, you're not worried?" Jane asked.

"Yes," the man said simply. "I am Dani, by the way. And while I don't know you, I do know—did know—Mr. Doctor Rigsdale."

He breathed hard through his nose. "He owes me money."

Hmmm, Sunny thought. *He uses past tense for Martin, but present tense on the owing part.*

"I tell you a story," Dani said, handing back their wallets. "It goes back to the time I live in Kiev—Ukraine. My father, he has a business . . . let us call it moving things."

"That can be a useful business," Sunny said. "Like when people need to get their furniture to a new house."

Dani shrugged. "That's not exactly what we'd do."

"Or when you need to get food from the country into a city," Jane suggested, but Dani shook his head.

"There are things that people might want," Sunny said slowly, remembering her friend Vanya's comments on Ukrainian smuggling rings, "That other people—like a government—wouldn't like to move."

Dani nodded and smiled. "Exactly right. Sometimes it could be cigarettes, or vodka—or even money."

"Sounds like a good business," Sunny said.

"Thank you." Dani gave her a courtly bow. "But then my father dies, and since I am a younger son, I must go from Kiev, or there will be trouble. So I go to Montreal, where some of my countrymen are, to start my own business there. Olek comes with me, because, well, because he takes care of me since I was a small boy."

He shrugged. "But instead of business, I get trouble again. So Olek and I leave Montreal and come to this city. Everything looks good so far. But I have to ask—do you want to make trouble, too?"

Jane was pale, but she didn't lack for nerve. "I just want to find out who killed my husband. It's bad enough that I'm being blamed for it. But nobody should get away with murder."

Dani nodded. "Oh, yes, that makes trouble for me, too—on top of the trouble your husband makes. But first a question. How is it that you follow Olek?"

Sunny explained about finding the cigarette and tracking down a source. Dani shot his bodyguard a reproachful look. Olek ducked his head, like a big dog who realized he's done wrong.

"How many times do I tell you, 'Don't smoke those things, Olek!'" Dani scolded. "If you want to burn your tongue, there are American cigarettes like the Camels! They're cheaper and they're bigger!"

Looking downcast, Olek mumbled an apology. His voice was so low and rumbly, Sunny couldn't tell whether he spoke in English or Ukrainian.

Dani reached up to clap his bodyguard on the shoulder. "I can understand, Olek. You want a taste of home, even if it tastes terrible. But see what you do here? These lovely ladies are thinking we killed the Dr. Rigsdale."

"We'd be just as happy if you could show us we're wrong," Sunny suggested.

"I can tell you you're wrong, and I can prove it," Dani said. "It is a thing of business. The Dr. Rigsdale is better for us alive than dead." He gestured as if he were carrying a large imaginary package in his hands. "We have much money coming in from people who owe us. The doctor, he has a bank account. We put our money though his bank—"

Sunny stared. "You were using Martin's practice to launder money?"

Dani nodded vigorously. "He helps us make nice, clean money."

"Let me guess," Sunny said. "You gave Martin the money to try and fix up that house—at least to build that impressive-looking office."

"Looks good, doesn't it?" Dani said. "He had all kinds of plans to set up things just the way he likes it. But it all costs more money than he expects."

Sunny nodded. "And what happened when he couldn't pay it back?"

"Then he had to do favors for us. It's only fair." Dani adopted a virtuous look that morphed into a crafty smile. "Besides, it's a good kind of business. Many people pay in cash. That makes it easy to bring in money from other places."

"And that's what you do," Jane said, "move around money?"

Dani beamed. "Exactly. So we have a good thing with your husband. To keep it going, we needed him alive."

"But you said he made trouble," Sunny pointed out.

That dimmed Dani's smile a bit. "He was a very charming man. Very handsome and charming. He got a bank officer—a very foolish woman—to tell him when an important transaction would clear. And then he took the cash."

"Well, that sounds just like Martin," Jane snorted. "Handsome, charming, and untrustworthy as hell."

"It also sounds like the kind of thing that could get a person hurt," Sunny said. "Or even killed."

"No, no, no. I am still starting out here and would rather not have trouble," Dani replied. "But I find out about this quicker than Dr. Rigsdale expects, and I tell him he is not as smart as he thinks he is. He promises it was all a misunderstanding, that he just needed it to impress an investor. It will go back. To make sure, I have Olek keep an eye on him."

That explains the observation post and the cigarettes, Sunny thought. "Did Olek see anyone come to the office the night that Martin died?" she asked.

Dani shot off a question in quick Ukrainian. Olek rumbled an answer, shaking his head negatively.

Claire Donally

"He saw no one," Dani reported.

When he saw the look on Sunny's face, the mobster burst out, "If I wanted him dead, you don't think Olek could do that? He could—" Dani slammed his hands together as if he were squishing a snowball. "We don't need to fill him with poison."

"That might be another way to avoid trouble," Sunny said, "making it look as if other people did it."

"I tell you again, it bad business to kill the Dr. Rigsdale," Dani insisted.

"Maybe you decided to make an example of him," Jane suggested, "because he made trouble for you."

"Listen." As Dani's tone got less friendly, his English got worse. "You don't kill nobody if they aren't telling you where the money is first."

"How much money was it?" Sunny asked.

Dani named a six-figure sum. Jane gasped. It was the same amount that Martin had been trying to get from her—the amount that had earned him a glass of wine in the face.

"Oh, Martin," she muttered.

"It's a lot of money," Dani somberly agreed. "And it isn't only mine. Sooner or later, the people in Montreal, they start to ask questions. I need to find that money. You want to find who kills your Dr. Rigsdale. Maybe we help each other, eh?"

"Maybe." Sunny was willing to go along with Dani if it meant getting out of there. But other than discovering this Ukrainian connection, she hadn't found out anything useful yet.

"Because I think whoever kills the doctor, that person stole my money," Dani said. "And I got to get it back."

He looked intently at Jane.

Oh, God, he knows about the foundation, Sunny thought.

"Your husband that used to be, he talked about you," Dani said. "How when he finished with you, then all of a sudden you have money."

"It's not my money," Jane tried to explain.

"But would you use it to save a life?"

Jane looked stricken.

Would it have made a difference if Martin had explained about getting in over his head with the Ukrainians instead of trying to charm the money out of her? Sunny wondered. And then, *Wait a minute. Why would he need that much from Jane? He still had the money he stole from them.*

Or did he?

Dani shrugged and spread his hands. "Because if we don't find our money, we got to get it from somewhere."

He gestured to Olek. "So now we let you go. But we be in touch, eh?"

Olek opened the door to the alley, politely holding it as Sunny and Jane made their way out. As they got into Jane's BMW, Dani stepped past them into his SUV. He pulled it away so it no longer blocked their path. Then he got out and made a sweeping gesture with his arm.

Jane took the hint. She started her car, backed it onto the street, and drove off. When they were about ten blocks and two turns away, she pulled to the side of the street. "I've got to stop for a minute," she said. "My hands are shaking too much to drive."

Sunny knew what she meant. She was shivering, and it had nothing to do with the cold outside.

Jane slowly sank forward until her forehead rested on the wheel. "Oh, Martin," she moaned, "what have you gotten me into?"

"The first question is, do we tell anybody?" Sunny said. "Our new friend Dani was trying to be nice, but he's obviously a mobster."

"And that Olek . . ." Jane just shuddered. "Following him was not one of your better ideas, Sunny."

"My enthusiasm got the better of my common sense," Sunny confessed. "It's the kind of mistake a real rookie reporter would have made." She shrugged uncomfortably. "Maybe being such rank amateurs is what saved us. I don't think they'd have been so pleasant and forgiving if Will had been along."

On the other hand, she thought, *Will would have stopped us.* But she didn't actually say that.

"Maybe." Jane sounded doubtful, not to mention worried. "But they're expecting us to help them—or give them a big chunk of money."

"Well, we definitely have to find out more about them," Sunny said. "I can ask Ken Howell at the *Crier* to see if his buddies on the other local newspapers have heard anything about new loan sharks in town. And maybe, if I'm careful, I can ask Will—"

"You can't!" Jane sat bolt upright, staring at her in panic. Then, a little more quietly, "I don't think they'd like you passing along what they said."

"I can talk about finding cigarettes, and give the names

as something I overheard." Sunny tried to calm her down. "Then we'll see what Will can find out."

She raised a hand to stave off any more protests from Jane. "When Sheriff Nesbit ordered Will to cooperate, he gave him a direct order. Will has to answer any question that Trumbull wants to ask him. As far as I know, Trumbull hasn't asked anything about Ukrainian gangsters. We're just trying to find out about Martin's finances."

Jane gave her a long, odd look. "The longer I hang around with you, the more I'm willing to bet that you have a very perverted view of the truth," she finally said.

Sunny could only shrug. "You probably wouldn't lose money that way. Sadly, there's one thing that always comes with a reporter's job: you get to hear a lot of lies."

When they got back across the bridge into Kittery Harbor, Sunny got on the phone. "Hey, Dad? Sorry I'm running a little later than I expected. Have you eaten yet?"

"Kind of hard, when the cupboard is just about bare," Mike replied. "I've been looking at one of those little cans you feed your friend, wondering if I put in a little chopped onion and mustard, maybe it would taste like tuna salad."

Sunny laughed. "Trust me, Dad, it would take a lot more than a few condiments to make cat food taste like tuna salad." She dug out her wallet. "What do you say to a pizza? Maybe half mushroom and half broccoli."

"You know," Mike said, "when I was younger, there used to be this stuff called pepperoni . . ."

"Yeah, and I used to have a dad who had a healthy heart," Sunny shot back. "Be happy I didn't suggest pineapple chunks."

She looked in her wallet and scowled. Then she glanced over at Jane. "Would you mind some company? A pie is a little much for two people. Jane, would you like to join us?"

"What?" Mike said into the phone.

"Are you sure—" Jane began.

"Fine, it's all set up. See you in about half an hour, Dad." Sunny ended the call and gave Jane a big smile. "There's just one thing. You'll have to pay the freight on the pizza. I don't have enough money with me." Jane laughed, and readily agreed.

About twenty minutes later, Jane turned onto Wild Goose Drive. Sunny sat in the passenger's seat, the cardboard pizza box in her lap, feeling the heat of the pie on her thighs, smelling the sauce, the cheese, and yes, the pepperoni on a couple of slices. She had to swallow deeply, or she'd have started to drool. How long ago was that sandwich she'd eaten at her desk?

Jane parked, and Sunny got out, carefully balancing the pie so that the cheese didn't shift, and walked to the door. Since she was only carrying a sack with their free liter bottle of soda, Jane got there ahead of her and rang the bell.

"Figured it would save you doing contortions to get the key," she said.

Mike's voice sounded on the other side of the door. "Coming, coming." He swung the door open and smiled at Jane. "Welcome, dear." Then he turned to Sunny. "Let's get the guest of honor into the kitchen."

"And by that he means the pizza," Sunny explained.

Shadow came up, drawn by all the commotion in the doorway. His eyes went wide and his ears perked up when he saw Jane. He came trotting over immediately. But about a foot from their shins, he stopped, wrinkling his nose. Then he stalked away ahead of them.

Must be the smell of Ukrainian mobster on us, Sunny thought. *Well, the good news is that if any of them comes ringing the bell, I'll have Shadow sniff under the door and warn me.*

The three of them ate in the kitchen, Mike doing his best to play the genial host while shooting sidewise glances at Jane and then at Sunny.

He's been rooting for me to kick her butt when it comes to Will, she realized, *and he can't understand why I've invited her home.* But in between her dad's nervous glances, Sunny was shooting him "knock it off" looks. *The three of us must look like a nervous tic convention.* The wry thought made Sunny chuckle, earning her another laser-glare of death from her dad.

"This must be a very *serious* time for you," Mike said to Jane, emphasizing the word "serious" with an exasperated look at Sunny. "Is there going to be a funeral?"

"That's an interesting question," Jane said, sipping at her glass of diet soda as if she wished it were something much stronger. "The chief medical examiner hasn't yet released Martin's body. And when I got in touch with them, I found out that someone else had already been making inquiries."

"Who?" Sunny and Mike said together.

"Dawn Featherstone." Jane shook her head. "It seems she wanted to save him from my clutches. As if I would want Martin back."

"Well, this sounds kind of awkward," Sunny said.

"No, we found a way to resolve it," Jane told her. "Martin always wanted to be cremated."

Might give him a taste of what he's in for, the irreverent voice in Sunny's head suggested.

"So when all that is taken care of, Dawn will organize a memorial service, and I'll pay for it."

Mike looked scandalized. Cremation was definitely not the Kittery Harbor way. "No funeral? No family?"

"Martin's parents both passed away before I even knew him," Jane explained. "My dad is no longer with us either, and my mother is in Arizona. She says the heat makes up for all the Maine winters she lived through. Also, although she's never said it . . . she never liked Martin. Guess Mom is a better judge of character than I am. And neither of us have any siblings. So I figured I'd let Dawn make whatever arrangements she wants in Portsmouth. That was where Martin went off to have his new life. Let him stay there."

"Uh-huh," Mike said, looking a bit thoughtful—and relieved.

So it won't be Kittery Harbor business after all, Sunny thought. *Well, Martin was a stranger in town. It shouldn't be that big a deal.*

After that, the conversation settled down a bit. Mike and Jane talked a little politics. Before the Leisters moved away, Jane's father had been an alderman. No mention was made of the police investigation . . . or of Will Price.

"Well, that really hit the spot," Jane said as she dug into the last of the broccoli wedges. "I don't like the reheated taste of pizza by the slice. And getting a whole pie for one person, that's just wasteful."

Mike nodded with approval. That was good Kittery Harbor thinking.

"You could always freeze it," Sunny offered. Back in her New York days, the freezer section of her refrigerator often held relics of several pizza binges.

Mike and Jane both shook their heads. "It never tastes the same."

When they were done, Jane helped with the dishes and thanked Mike for a pleasant evening. Beaming contentedly, he headed off to the living room to catch up with his shows.

Jane took Sunny by the arm. "Oh my goodness," she said. "Your car is still downtown. I think it's only fair that I give you a lift to pick it up."

They said good night to Mike, pulled on their coats, and went out into the chilly night to Jane's BMW. As she drove, she said, "Thanks, Sunny. That was worth the price of the pizza. After our little adventure, I needed to be around normal people."

"And here I stuck you with my dad," Sunny joked.

Jane laughed. "Oh, it took him a little while to settle down, but then he was a lot of fun." She glanced over at Sunny. "You're lucky to have him around."

"He's lucky to be around." Sunny took a deep breath. "At least when he got the chest pains, he had the good sense to call for help immediately instead of trying to tough it out." She shook her head. "Even so, he was awfully sick—awfully weak."

"I think you did the right thing, coming up to take care of him." Jane was silent for a moment as she negotiated a hill. "Oh, I know it screwed up your job. But it's good that the two of you are together. My dad was gone too quickly. I barely got to Arizona in time to say good-bye."

"I didn't know that," Sunny said.

"Well, who would I tell?" Jane burst out. "That's why I say it's good to have your dad underfoot. Someone you can shoot the breeze with, someone with roots around here. Look, I know you and I have had kind of a rocky start. But the two of us—and Will—we have a different perspective from the folks who've spent their lives here and only know how the world looks from Kittery Harbor. Like it or not, we're sort of outsiders in our own hometown. I appreciate that you looked out for me tonight."

"Well, I had to, after those guys just about kidnapped us," Sunny said modestly.

"Yeah, I just about ruined a good pair of pants when you all but accused Dani of murder." Jane laughed, but her voice was a bit shaky again. "I know how to handle animals so they won't bite me. But that—you've got guts, Sunny."

"More like reporter's instincts," Sunny said. *And a whole lot of luck,* she added silently.

By then, they had reached the silent strip of New Store shop fronts, all of them dark by this time of night. Jane pulled up behind Sunny's Wrangler and waited until she was in the driver's seat, then waved good-bye and took off. Alone.

Sunny drove back toward home, her ornery dad, and even ornerier cat.

Which reminds me, she thought. *Got to remember to take a shower tonight. I want to wash off whatever is repulsing Shadow.*

Cat Nap

*

It was nice to enjoy a lazy Saturday morning. Sunny was able to sleep late—well, late-ish. She awoke to find Shadow with his forefeet on her pillow, standing nose to nose with her.

"All right, all right, I'll take care of the food situation," she muttered, wrestling her way out of the covers. "Sheesh."

With nothing pressing, Sunny was able to enjoy a leisurely breakfast, listen to some oddball radio shows, chat with her dad, and make a list for an afternoon food-shopping expedition.

She planned to call Will, but waited till after one o'clock. Will's tour on the swing shift ended this morning, and she wanted to give him some time to sleep before pestering him. She timed it right. He was yawning as he spoke to her on the phone, but conscious.

"Have you had breakfast yet?" she asked. "What do you say to swinging by the waffle house?"

The restaurant was a sort of tourist trap aimed at the outlet-land shoppers, but they made waffles all day, and the maple syrup was real.

"Sounds good," Will said. "Shall I swing by to pick you up, or do you want to meet me there?"

"Meet, I think," she replied. "I've got to go shopping afterward."

They set a time that would allow them both to wash up and get dressed. Sunny whistled as she drove until she was about halfway to the restaurant. Then she began to plot what she was going to tell Will.

*

He sat staring at her, a plate piled with waffles sitting disregarded in front of him. "A cigarette?" he said. "Really?"

"It's what I found," she told him.

"I guess I haven't read your monograph on the subject, Sherlock." He gave her a skeptical look as he finally tucked into his meal.

"I didn't need to fool with cigarette ashes, there was a name on the side—in foreign letters," she told him. "But I recognized the type. It's called a *papirosa*. I saw people smoking them in a café in Brooklyn that a friend took me to—Russian mafia types."

Will choked so badly, maple syrup practically came out his nose. Sunny gave him her napkin to help clean up. "You're saying Martin Rigsdale was involved with Russian gangsters?"

She shook her head, remembering her promise to Jane about soft-pedaling the Ukrainian connection. "I'm saying that I found a store in Portsmouth that sells the same brand, and I found a guy who buys them by the carton." The next part was going to be the tricky one. "I overheard the guy talking on his cell phone. It seems his name is Olek, and he was talking to someone called Dani."

"You just happened to be eavesdropping on a guy in the Russian mob?" Will sighed and then gave her a stern look. "I don't suppose you thought for a moment that might possibly be dangerous?"

Well, I did, just a little too late, Sunny had to admit. But she kept those words to herself. Instead, she asked, "Have you heard about any guys like that in Portsmouth?"

"Not while I was on the force there, no," Will replied. "When I was way up north with the troopers, though, we dealt with some biker gangs with organized crime connections."

"Can you ask any of your friends about those guys?"

He frowned. "It's not going to be easy. They were willing to pass on a little information to help out when the crime was on this side of the river. But this is a murder in their melon patch. People have to know that Trumbull is questioning me. It's like I'm radioactive—contact with me may be fatal to their careers."

Will sat silent for a moment, thinking. "But if they're in Portsmouth, these guys may be active on this side of the river, too. Maybe if I put it that way . . ." He looked down at his rapidly cooling stack of waffles. "Boy, Sunny, you really know how to ruin a guy's breakfast."

12

"Hey, I'm sorry," Sunny said to Will. "Does this mean you're going to talk to Trumbull?"

"How can I?" Will stabbed his fork into the pile of waffles on his plate. "It's a pretty thin connection to begin with, and you've fooled around with the evidence. Trumbull might even think you planted that cigarette to distract attention from Jane."

"I wouldn't do that!" Sunny protested.

"I'm trying to see this from Trumbull's viewpoint," Will replied. "He's already asked me if, based on my experience, you were likely to interfere in his investigation."

"My dad asked me the same question," Sunny admitted.

"I wonder why." Will took a sip of coffee.

"I'll tell you what I told him," Sunny growled. "The

Portsmouth cops have their best detective on the job. Why should I get involved?"

"Why do I think I hear a 'but' coming up here?" Will said wearily.

Sunny nodded. "It seems to me that Trumbull is concentrating all his attention on Jane. You've talked with the guy. Can you tell me that I'm wrong?"

Will frowned, toying with his fork. "When a detective questions anyone—a witness, a source, a suspect—he purposely doesn't give them the full picture."

"Yeah, but as a cop yourself, you can sort of fill in the blanks between the questions and catch the drift of the investigation. Is Trumbull going anywhere other than after Jane?"

He hesitated for a long moment. "No. I don't think so. That's why I thought Jane should see a lawyer."

"Well, she did," Sunny told him. "And it was a pretty funny meeting. Turns out that Tobe Phillips is a grammar school classmate of ours under a different name—Toby Philpotts." She decided not to mention the young Toby's bladder problem—or how nice-looking he'd grown up to become.

"That's one piece of good news." Will sighed, not buying Sunny's attempt to change the subject. "I wish you hadn't messed with that evidence."

"It's not as if I meant to." Sunny tried to defend herself. "I stumbled onto the observation post, trying to get out of the snow. So my footprints were there before I even knew there was something to find."

Will shook his head. "But when you did find something, you took it away with you. That's tampering at best. At worst, it means the cops can't use it in their case." He pushed his plate away. "It also means they can't use it as leverage to get any information. We don't know when that smoker—Olek or whatever—was standing there. But if he saw anything going on at that office near the time that Rigsdale died, we won't be finding out about it."

Sunny wanted to reassure him that Olek hadn't seen anything, but of course she couldn't. Mentioning that fact would open the door to a lot of questions she just couldn't answer.

"Look," she said, "I really am sorry about messing up your breakfast. Why don't I pick up the bill for it?" She had a few extra bucks in her wallet—household money, meant to pay for the food shopping.

Guess I'll have to find a few places to economize, that's all, she thought.

They finished their coffees, Sunny paid, and then Will said good-bye. "I think I'm gonna get some more sleep." He stifled a yawn and climbed into his pickup, heading back into town while Sunny aimed her Wrangler deeper into outlet-land. There were a couple of supermarkets out there as well, and Sunny was working on a diminished budget.

She was pretty lucky, managing to get everything on her list or slightly less pricey alternates. The only problem, weirdly enough, was the low-sodium turkey she needed to get for her dad.

"Sorry." The guy behind the deli counter apologized. "The low-sodium turkey was on sale, and we just had a run on it. There's none left, not until Tuesday." He turned around to the racks of deli meats and ran a big chunk of turkey through the meat slicer. "I've got this. A lot of folks like it."

He handed Sunny a single slice on a piece of waxed paper. She chewed, swallowed, and shook her head. "Way too salty."

"Sorry," he said again.

"No problem," Sunny told him, and then pushed her shopping cart to the checkout line.

But it was a problem. She had gone for all the bargains, starting at the farthest store and working her way back toward town. This should have been her last stop. She didn't want to turn back now with a carload of all the other food she'd gotten.

Well, she thought, *I could stop off at home, unload the car, and then go down to Judson's for the turkey. It might be a bit pricier than I'd hoped, but I can swing it.*

Sunny came quietly into the house. Mike was sprawled asleep on the couch with some sort of NASCAR race going on the television. From the middle of the sunny spot near the window, Shadow drowsily raised his head, slit his eyes at her for a moment, then rested back on his paws again.

"You'd think that he at least would be a little more enthusiastic, knowing I was coming home with food," Sunny muttered as she unloaded her grocery sacks into the refrigerator.

Then she went back out. Perversely, parking downtown was much worse on the weekends than on weekdays. Even on a wintry Saturday, Sunny found herself walking for blocks to get to the strip of shops known as the New Stores.

Judson's Market took up the equivalent of two storefronts. This was the second location for the grocery, Mike often told her. The original Judson's had opened four generations ago in the redbrick part of town. Her dad's friend Zack Judson had moved the market to the New Stores in search of more space and more customers. Over the years, to compete with the supermarkets springing up farther out of town, Zack had taken his operation considerably upscale. You could get exotic coffees, fancy cuts of meat, fine chocolates, and foreign cheeses. Even his cold cuts were expensive. But they were also very, very good.

Sunny walked in the front door to find the aisles jammed as if Zack were giving the stock away. Well, Saturdays were always busy at Judson's. The rich folks over in Piney Brook called in their orders for delivery. The not-so-rich folks in their McMansions drove in to do their weekend shopping. And local residents still came in to get their milk and bread.

The meat and deli departments were in the rear of the store. Sunny had to wend her way through the shoppers to get back there, and then join a long line waiting for service.

This is a hell of a thing to go through for a pound of turkey, she thought, but nevertheless she stood and waited, until finally there were only three people ahead of her. And then she heard a loud, complaining voice over by the meat counter.

"I hope you have an explanation for this, Mr. Judson."

That woman sounds familiar. Sunny turned to see Zack Judson making placating gestures to an older woman who looked like a cranky Persian cat—Carolyn Dowdey. Mrs. Dowdey was waving something in Zack's face, a brown paper parcel—the old-fashioned packaging that Zack's butchers used. In this case, though, the original packaging was wrapped in a clear plastic bag, and with good reason. Even ten feet away, Sunny could see that half of the brown butcher paper was soaked with blood.

"You can imagine my shock and surprise when your deliveryman arrived with *this*." Mrs. Dowdey held up the offending package again. "I was under the impression that your staff knew the proper ways to prepare cuts of beef for cooking—and didn't just hack bloody hunks of flesh off half-cooled carcasses. When I call in my weekend order, I expect the best—not body parts that will bleed all over the other items I had asked for."

"Mrs. Dowdey," an increasingly desperate Zack said, his eyes just about spinning as he took in all the customers eavesdropping on this conversation. "Please accept my apologies, and let me take that from you." He practically snatched the bloody parcel from her hands. "Of course," he went on, "we'll reconstitute your order and deliver it—gratis. And I'll personally supervise the preparation of a replacement cut of meat."

Still carrying the bloody package, he went behind the butcher counter.

With that look on his face, it might not be a good idea to go walking into a room where there's a whole lot of cutlery lying around loose, Sunny thought.

Carolyn Dowdey stood her ground, waiting for Zack to return, a look of triumph on her face.

Yeah, yeah, Mrs. D., that irreverent part of Sunny's brain thought. *You struck a real blow for the consumer today—for the little guy.*

Sunny's lips twitched as she hid a smile. Carolyn

Dowdey would probably pop a blood vessel if anyone were to suggest that she was one of the little guys.

Then their eyes met.

"Young woman," Mrs. Dowdey said, "don't I know you?" She frowned, squinching her facial features into an even smaller area, and then smiled as she recalled where she'd seen Sunny.

"You had the beautiful cat with the gray coat and the tiger stripes," Carolyn Dowdey recalled. "At the vet's office."

Her condescending smile stiffened a bit as she likely also remembered her performance during that particular visit. "I'm not sure that young woman is the best person to be treating your cat, I'm afraid." Mrs. Dowdey sniffed.

Sure, Sunny thought, *make a fool of yourself and then throw a little mud on the person you picked a fight with.*

"I've only had Shadow for a few months, but Dr. Rigsdale has taken excellent care of him."

Carolyn Dowdey actually unbent a little. "Shadow— that's a good name for him." But then she got back on her high horse. "Perhaps you were lucky enough that he didn't have a serious illness. I had two cats go through treatment at the Kittery Harbor Animal Hospital. They had kidney ailments." The extra flesh on her face quivered a little. "It's the same problem that took my late husband."

Sunny had to bite the tip of her tongue to keep from saying something stupid like "maybe it's something in the water."

Carolyn Dowdey didn't notice, having built up a good head of steam by now. "It's almost like extortion. 'We want to do the best for your cat, but if you feel it's too expensive . . .' "

I could just imagine good old Martin saying that, with a wonderfully concerned look on his face, Sunny thought.

"My last cat, Mrs. Purrley, went through a string of intravenous treatments, and then surgery." Mrs. Dowdey's face stiffened. "And all of it for nothing. I had to have her put to sleep by Dr. Rigsdale—the other one, who was in Portland."

"The whole vet thing is a racket," the guy in front of Sunny on the deli line burst out. "My wife took our dog all the way across the bridge to that quack in Portsmouth. Why? Because he's so *nice.*" He drew out the word in disgust. "The guy was a pretty boy who played up to all the women so they'd bring him their pets and pay him a fortune. Damn vets and their phony 'treatments.' I told her, 'Madge, this guy is robbing us. It's not like we've got some prize-winning purebred. Chester is a mutt, and if he gets really sick, maybe we should let him die.' "

Carolyn Dowdey drew herself up, and for a second Sunny thought she was going to slug the guy with her purse. But then the deli man distracted the dog owner by asking him what he wanted, and Zack Judson appeared, carrying a nonbloody parcel. He led Mrs. Dowdey off to get the rest of her order, and peace if not quiet was restored.

Sunny ordered her turkey and waited while the deli man sliced it. As she headed with her packet to the ten-items-or-less line at the front of the store, she was deep in thought, remembering how she'd told Jane that everyone liked her.

Maybe I was a little hasty, saying that, she thought, *because it looks as if a lot of people don't like veterinarians.*

*

Sunny arrived home to find the living room empty. "Hey, Dad!" she called. "You here?"

"In the kitchen," Mike called back.

Boy, I hope he's not looking for the turkey, she thought as she headed for the back of the house.

If Mike was searching for turkey, he was definitely looking in the wrong places. He stood at the top of their step stool, his head in one of the top kitchen cabinets, moving cans down onto the counter.

"What's up?" Sunny asked, quickly stashing her package in the fridge.

Mike extracted his head from the cabinet and came down to floor level. "Got a call from Helena Martinson," he explained. "She's trying to stir up some donations for the food pantry. They're getting more business than they can handle. I figure there's stuff up top and in the back that's probably been lurking since before I got sick."

He sighed, thinking back to those wonderful days when he could eat anything he pleased. "Some of that stuff can probably go—like these."

Standing front and center on the counter were a couple of small canned hams. "They were on sale right before I got sick. I remember picking them up, figuring I could slice them up and nuke myself a dinner, maybe make sandwiches. Or chop one up and make hash." Mike shrugged.

"Now I figure there's too much fat and salt in 'em for me to eat—but they might help a family make dinner."

Sunny nodded. "And there's probably soup and canned veggies with more salt than you need. How about I climb and you sort?" She glanced around. "Where's Shadow?"

Mike pointed. "His usual perch—on top of the refrigerator."

As she climbed up the steps, Sunny found herself level with Shadow, who watched these unusual proceedings with a suspicious eye.

"Take it easy," she assured him, "we're not going after your food."

Sunny bent to get into the cabinet and began passing cans down to Mike. "Yikes!" she exclaimed as she found one that was so swollen, it wobbled as her hand brushed it.

Carefully picking up the container, she looked at the label. "When did you ever buy canned apricots? And why?"

Mike shrugged. "Can't say." Then he held up a finger, frowning. "Wait a minute. There was a recipe in the magazine that comes with the Sunday paper. It was for homemade barbecue sauce. You started out running canned apricots through a blender."

"And when was this?" She nervously eyed the deformed can. Its top and bottom made little domes.

"Barbecue season," her dad replied. "Summertime." He squinted into the air, trying to call up the memory. "Can't have been last summer. I was still pretty much out of it. Didn't go shopping on my own. Maybe it was the summer before? Or the year before that?"

"Whenever it was, we're lucky this thing didn't explode

and leave us cleaning apricots and sticky apricot juice from all these shelves," Sonny said. "Why don't you get a bag, and we'll put this away separately."

She carefully combed each shelf, but luckily the can of apricots was the only time bomb she discovered. The contents of each shelf got divided—what could go, what should stay—and the keepers were returned to the cabinet. By the time they were done, they'd accumulated a good-sized collection of stuff that Mike shouldn't be eating anymore—canned hash, sloppy Joe mix, Vienna sausage, jars of meat sauce, and a lot of salty canned vegetables.

"Canned potatoes?" Sunny said in disbelief, hefting a can. "You couldn't just cook a potato?"

"They're cut up in little chunks." Mike defended his choice. "Good for making potato salad."

They also contributed some dry food to the collection. For some reason, Mike was heavily overstocked on corn muffin mix. And he also added most of their boxes of flavored gelatin. "I had more than enough of that stuff in the hospital," he said. "And when I came home here, flat on my back, I ate it to please you. No more. If I get really sick again, let's stick with applesauce."

Mike went into the garage and returned with a cardboard carton marked "Books."

"One of the ones you already emptied," he quickly explained when he saw the look of dismay on Sunny's face. "I figured if it could stand up to your library, it should be able to hold this stuff."

Sunny agreed and, after they got everything stowed away, asked, "Do you want to drive over now?"

"It's getting kind of late." Mike glanced out the window.

The light was already fading. "We'll both go tomorrow. That's when Helena will be there," he added in as offhand a tone as possible.

"Okay," Sunny said, reaching up to the top of the fridge to pet Shadow while he nuzzled against her hands. That let her hide her grin from Mike. *If he wants to impress his lady friend, it's not my business.*

"Besides," Mike went on, "I've got some buddies to call. After I tell them what we found in our cabinets, maybe they'll decide to clear theirs out and donate, too."

*

Sunday morning was bright but chilly, although it warmed up in the afternoon. Mike finished his three miles of hiking around the outlets, then they loaded their donations into his car.

"Where is this food pantry?" Sunny asked as they drove off. "Is it downtown?"

Mike shook his head. "Real estate there is too expensive. They're in a store on Stone Road—what used to be a store. Place went bust, and the landlord can't get a new tenant, so he's letting the Elmet Ladies use it."

Sunny nodded. Even in a long-settled development like the New Stores, there was always one hard-luck shop. Sunny had seen three tenants, for example, in the space next door to the MAX office. As a landlord, though, it was probably against Ollie Barnstable's principles to let the place out for free.

As they neared their destination, Sunny recognized the place. It was a stand-alone store with a good-sized parking lot. First it had been a showroom for high-end car stereos and alarms, and then a guy had tried to operate a computer repair shop. Its last incarnation had been as a ninety-nine-cent store, and even that had failed.

"They couldn't get people out here even to buy cheap crap," Mike said, nodding at the number 99 that still showed in the plastic sign over the door. "They left it up because it's the 99 Elmet Ladies."

A hand-painted poster saying FOOD PANTRY had been taped to the inside of the window.

Sunny got out their box of food. Mike held the door for her as she entered the store. It was a very bare-bones arrangement. A makeshift counter stretched across the interior space, cutting off the back corner of the former store. It had obviously been knocked together out of plywood, although an attempt had been made to create a homier atmosphere by stapling gingham-style plastic tablecloths over the bare wood. Behind the counter, industrial-style metal bookcases stood at right angles against the walls. Helena Martinson and several other women stood stocking or rearranging the contents. While the shelves weren't quite bare, they weren't overflowing either.

Mrs. Martinson spotted them and went to the counter. "Oh, thank you, Mike! And Sunny," she added.

"Not many customers," Sunny said, glancing around. Except for herself, Mike, and the Elmet Ladies, the store was empty.

"Officially, we're closed on Sundays," Mrs. Martinson explained, "except for real emergencies—and to restock." She began unloading the carton they'd brought, arranging the contents into different piles.

"Ah," she said in satisfaction when she came across the

hams. "We try to come up with three meals a day for each customer, but it's hard to offer anything balanced when we're depending on donations. Zack Judson tries to help, giving us some of his overstock, and we're trying to shame the big supermarkets into helping, too."

She noticed the hand-lettered label on the side of the box. "If you've got any books you'd like to get rid of, Sunny, we'll be holding a sale next month." Her cheeks got a little pink with embarrassment, but she continued her pitch. "We've got to raise funds any way we can."

"I'll see what I can do about that," Sunny promised, remembering the hectic job of getting her stuff out of her old apartment. "Thinning the herd might be a good idea. It will give us a bit more space in the garage, although Shadow will miss the piles of boxes. He likes to play at mountain climbing."

"Toby likes to climb, too." Helena bobbed her head a little, grimacing. "At least he tries. Most of the time he tumbles and takes something down with him."

"Youthful energy," Sunny said hopefully. "Sooner or later, he'll settle down."

"It's a lot more responsibility than I realized, taking on a pet." Mrs. Martinson finished her sorting and called over a couple of the other ladies. "Maybe I should have listened to Carolyn Dowdey—"

"Carolyn Dowdey!" One of the other women made the name sound like a bad word. "When we set up the 99 Elmet Ladies and made plans, she was right in the middle of everything, voicing her opinions on how to do everything. But when it comes to volunteering to help out—I haven't seen her in almost a year."

"Her cat was very sick, and Carolyn had to spend a lot of time taking care of her," Mrs. Martinson offered weakly.

But now she has the time to go and squawk at Zack Judson, Sunny thought.

"Towards the end, she had to give the poor animal some sort of shots," Helena Martinson went on.

The other volunteer loaded up her arms with one of Helena's piles. "You see it in here," she said, "like this one family. They were doing fine until the husband lost his job at the shipyard. The wife sold Avon or something, but even with that and unemployment, they had a hard time feeding themselves and a kid, much less a pet. And when their dog got sick, what could they do? A vet's bill comes to about a month's rent."

Sunny nodded, but she was still chewing over Helena Martinson's last comment.

If Shadow got sick, would I have the heart to stick him with needles?

She wasn't sure.

13

Sunny let her father chat with Mrs. Martinson for a while, and then she and Mike returned home. As they opened the door, Shadow came out of the living room and strolled over to give them a sniff. Apparently, they didn't bring home any interesting scents. The cat just turned around and searched out a new patch of sunlight to nap in.

"That looks like a pretty good plan," Mike said, looking down at Shadow. "But maybe we could have some lunch first."

They sat at the kitchen table, making some inroads into the sliced turkey that Sunny had bought.

"Pretty interesting, what the 99 Elmet Ladies are trying to do with that food pantry," Mike said in between bites of his sandwich.

Sunny nodded. "It looks like practical help that a lot of

people around here need." She found herself thinking about the story Mrs. M.'s friend had told about the family torn between getting treatment for the dog or paying the rent. What had Carolyn Dowdey talked about? Intravenous treatments and surgery? With the salary Sunny made at MAX, how would she afford something like that if Shadow got sick? He'd been lucky enough to bounce back quickly from his misadventures so far, and it helped that Jane seemed to feel she owed Sunny favors. But if Shadow really got knocked down by some illness, how could she watch Shadow suffer?

"Earth to Sunny." Mike waved a hand in front of her eyes. "You've been sitting there for a couple of minutes, looking at that sandwich as if you wanted to strangle it."

"Sorry." She looked over at him. "I was thinking about that family with the sick dog. Could Jane do something with the animal fund to help out people like that?"

"It's not easy, getting people around here to accept charity," Mike said slowly. "I bet it must kill some of those folks, just going to the food bank, and Helena and the other ladies try to keep it as nonofficial as possible. What you're talking about, there'd have to be hoops to jump through— *administration*." He made that sound like a bad word. "Plus, you're poking your nose into how Jane makes a living. That can get kinda . . . personal."

Sunny thought about that for a minute. "I can see what you mean," she said finally. "But then, people get awfully personal about vets. That's something else I should talk to Jane about."

She got on the phone to see if Jane was busy and got an invitation to come over and visit the pet hospital. Jane let her in and led Sunny to what she called "the observation wing." It was just a room equipped with cages for patients who had to stay overnight. Jane did some housekeeping chores and gave quick checkups to the three dogs and two cats who were in residence.

"I have a suggestion for you and Tobe to consider," Sunny said as Jane worked. "Could Martin have been killed by a dissatisfied customer?"

Jane sighed. "There are certainly enough of them." She put on a pair of heavy gauntlets to deal with a hissing cat that kept making clawing gestures at her. "And not this kind either."

She succeeded in calming the cat down and checking her vital signs. When Sunny complimented her, Jane replied, "That was easy compared to dealing with the humans. They come in half hysterical because their pet is sick. And if you make the animal better, well, that's your job, isn't it? But if, God forbid, poor little Bobo doesn't get better, well, then you're a worthless quack. Worse, you're a money-grubbing quack."

She shook her head. "Look at you and Shadow. I suggested a treatment that you could take care of by yourself. In a lot of cases like that, people will come back to me with a pet that's still limping. They 'couldn't find the time' to take care of the animal. I guess I really shouldn't be surprised. Most people can't find the time to take care of themselves. So many of the illnesses among people today could be treated with diet and exercise. Heck, a lot of them could've been avoided in the first place with diet and exercise."

Sunny nodded, thinking of her father.

"Instead, though, people wind up going to the doctor

to ask for a pill." Jane looked disgusted. "I try to see if the animal's human partner can be depended on to help in treatment. Martin, who had a lot more experience, automatically wrote the humans off. He'd do procedures that hurt the animals a lot more than home treatment would."

"Because of money?" Sunny asked.

"Maybe—in later days," Jane admitted. "But he also had stories of patients coming in much worse because their owners couldn't follow a simple course of treatment. Martin argued that he was merely protecting his professional reputation. He put a lot of money, training, and time into his practice. He said he didn't want to depend on some civilian who might screw up even simple instructions."

She wrote a couple of notes on patients' charts. "For my part, if I think a pet's human is trustworthy—like you—I'll suggest a home treatment option where it's feasible. Otherwise, it's my professional responsibility to see that the animal gets the necessary care. And if that means a paying visit, so be it."

Sunny remembered Mike's comment about poking her nose into how people make their living. But Jane had a point.

And the vet was on a roll now. She continued, "It's not an easy job, Sunny. I treat the pet, but I've got to deal with the human side of the partnership. Sometimes that's difficult. It can take people a while to come to grips with the fact that their pet is extremely ill—or worse, that their pet can't really be cured. While that process goes on for the human, I have to make sure that the pet isn't suffering."

Jane turned to survey her patients in their cages. Some of them were pacing around. Most just lay in a corner, looking unhappy. Sunny couldn't tell whether their unhappiness came from boredom or illness.

"Sometimes I have to extend treatment longer than I'd like to—beyond what I think is humane," Jane admitted. "But that's because the human can't bring himself—or herself—to make a decision about ending the pet's suffering, not because it's adding a bit more profit to my bottom line."

Sunny nodded somberly. "The other day, I heard about someone who had to give her cat injections, and I was wondering how much harder would it be, deciding to end things for him, if he were so sick—"

"I think you would make the right choice," Jane said quietly. "Sometimes, it's worth doing everything you can. But sometimes you realize that it's selfish, keeping a pet with you when the animal is in terrible pain."

"I hope you're right." Sunny shivered a little, even though the room was warm. "But it must be a terrible decision to make. And it's easy to see how some people could end up blaming the doctor."

"Even the nicest folks can get pretty nasty," Jane agreed. "You have to let them vent their feelings, and if you can, help them get through it. You might not believe me, Sunny, but I think grief counseling comes into this. It's like losing a member of your family. You're still pretty new to the experience of having a pet. You have to go through this kind of loss yourself to understand what I'm saying. The problem is, dealing with that kind of grief is a case for a human psychologist, not a vet. We try to do what we can. Whenever we had a euthanasia case, we'd give the person a DVD to watch."

She gave Sunny an embarrassed smile. "Maybe it

doesn't sound like much, but a lot of people have told me it helped."

Her expression darkened a little. "Martin and I had a long-running argument over those damned discs. He used to give them to people, and then tack a charge onto their bill—at a big markup."

I can't tell if it's grief or anger, Sunny thought. *But Jane is still thinking a lot about Martin.*

"It took a long time, but I finally convinced him that giving the disc as a gift was the decent thing to do. It's weird, what you count as a success in a marriage. Fact is, he left not long after that."

Jane knelt by one of the cages, petting the dog inside. "I wonder sometimes what Martin did when he set up his own practice. Did I really change his mind, or did he go back to charging folks for that little bit of comfort?"

"I can't answer that," Sunny said, determined to change the subject. "But I think you have a lot to talk about with Tobe Phillips."

Jane glanced up at her. "What do you mean?"

"From what you say about vets in general, there are probably a lot of people who were seriously annoyed with Martin in particular."

"I suppose that's true," Jane said.

"So you should mention that to Tobe," Sunny explained, "and he should mention it to Detective Trumbull."

"If my own practice is anything to go by, the detective would find himself with a lot of possible suspects," Jane admitted. "But lots of people grouse about the treatments, or the costs. I don't ever remember a dissatisfied client putting a vet to sleep," Jane joked. "Sorry, gallows humor."

She smiled, then frowned. "Checking out all those people, though—that's going to be a major distraction. He'll end up wasting time that should be used to find the real killer."

Sunny took a deep breath. How to put this delicately? "Finding the killer isn't your concern, or Tobe's. It's Trumbull's job. You're just trying to make sure you don't get accused of something that you didn't do."

Let's face it, Sunny added silently. *Martin Rigsdale was not a nice guy. He cheated on you, he was probably cheating on his new girlfriends, no doubt he cheated his patients—he cheated the Ukrainian mob, for heaven's sake. You can be sad that things didn't turn out as you might have hoped, even mad at the guy. But that's about as much as you should invest in Martin. If Trumbull finds whoever murdered him, fine. But if it remains an unsolved mystery forever, it's not gonna break my heart.*

Jane might not be sure about distracting Mark Trumbull, but she was apparently willing to be distracted herself. "I still can't get over seeing Toby—Tobe—after all these years," she exclaimed. "He looks good."

"And since he's in court all day, I guess he's either overcome or outgrown his old problem."

Jane's mouth dropped open. "Yikes! I'd forgotten all about that."

Sunny looked at her in disbelief. "You forgot that we nicknamed him Toby P. Philpotts, because he always had pee in his middle?"

"Stop it!" Jane begged, trying to stifle giggles. Then she got thoughtful. "Is that a problem you can outgrow?"

"I bet they have pills for it now," Sunny told her. "'Ask your doctor if Pee-no-more is right for you.'"

"Or maybe there's something to do with tubing," Jane suggested. "Like a stadium buddy."

"Don't even start going there," Sunny warned her. "My dad drove over half of the Northeast, delivering salt. When I asked him about bathroom breaks, he told me about the trucker's very personal assistant. All the fun of a catheter, but with a—ah—external connection, if you catch my drift."

Jane made a face. "Gross!"

"Says the lady who tells stories about vomiting dogs while we're trying to eat lunch," Sunny said. "I guess the device probably exists. What I don't know is if my dad actually used it, or if he just used the story to keep me out of his dresser drawers."

"I'd say that would work—either way," Jane replied with a grin. Her tone changed as she went on. "Let's hope that Tobe's problem is history. From what we saw, he grew up to be a really nice guy—as well as a nice-looking one."

Oh, wonderful. That critical voice from the back of Sunny's head joined the conversation. *Now we're back in high school talking about what's gross and who's cute?*

Sunny squelched the complaints. She'd rather hear Jane talking like this instead of rehashing old fights with Martin or stressing over Trumbull. "Yeah," she agreed, "Tobe does seem nice."

"I wonder if he's available," Jane idly asked.

"Oh, come on," Sunny said. "You didn't check his finger or do the office once-over? How out of practice are you?"

"And I suppose you got the full story, Ms. Ace Reporter?" Jane shot back.

"I noticed that he wasn't wearing a wedding ring, and

that there were no pictures of a wife or kids on his desk or bookcase."

"So—what?" Jane asked. "He's single?"

"Maybe, though from what I understand, single guys don't usually become law partners," Sunny objected. "If a person is going to be that involved in a firm, the other partners want to make sure he's settled." She shrugged. "Or he may be just very, very good at what he does, and they wanted to keep him. You mentioned your marriage and your divorce, which gave him an opening. He did say that he'd seen worse divorces than yours, but he didn't add anything personal there."

"So what's the bottom line on his availability?" Jane pressed.

Sunny shrugged her shoulders and threw out her hands. "Insufficient information." She grinned at Jane. "But probably worth more research."

Jane laughed, but shook her head. "If you're anything to go by, I'd have to say that reporters are very, very strange."

But we have needs, too, Sunny thought. *If you're chasing Will Price, can't I go after Tobe?*

That was something she couldn't say out loud. Sunny picked her words carefully. "Speaking of distractions, you'd better remember that Tobe is your lawyer. He's got to keep his eyes open and his mind clear for the duration."

"Oh, come on." Jane's cheeks got a little pink. "That's something that even these guys in the cages know about. Don't poop where you eat."

"I don't think pooping is the activity I'd worry about," Sunny told her.

Jane's face got pinker. "Okay, point taken. Sheesh."

Jane was a little teed off now, ready to leave the topic of Tobe Phillips. But under that, Sunny caught a flash of loneliness in the pretty vet's eyes as she turned back to her patients.

*

They chatted a little longer while Jane finished up at the pet hospital. As they stepped outside, Sunny glanced at the sky above. Clouds were gathering, but she still considered suggesting that they stop off for a cup of coffee. Maybe they could even stop at Spill the Beans and have a whoopie pie. But her finances argued against that course. After bribing a tobacconist and shelling out for a breakfast that Will didn't even eat, Sunny couldn't take on any more unaccustomed expenses this week. And no way was she about to let Jane treat her again.

I guess that's another Kittery Harbor commandment— "Thou shalt not mooch." Instead, Sunny put on a cheerful face and said good-bye.

As Jane's BMW pulled out of the parking lot, Sunny sat behind her wheel for a moment, thinking. Then, instead of heading home, she steered for downtown Kittery Harbor and the offices of the *Harbor Crier.* As she hoped, Ken Howell was hanging around in there, threatening weather or not.

The long, narrow room housed the newspaper operation and Ken's printing business. Sunny was never sure which supported which. An ancient rolltop desk housed a fairly modern computer, which Ken used for writing and composing. Scattered around the room were generations of different printing presses. That wasn't surprising. Howells had been printing and publishing in here since before the Civil War.

Ken had a house somewhere. Her dad had even told Sunny he'd visited there. But the newsroom was Ken's home. If he wasn't out distributing papers or gathering news, Sunny usually saw him in the office. Today he had a practical reason. One of the presses was clattering away, spitting out some sort of newsletter. In order to make ends meet, Ken not only printed the paper, but also took on all sorts of other printing jobs.

When he spotted her coming in, Ken gave Sunny a companionable nod and pointed at the chair beside his desk. For him, that was a warm welcome. He'd been almost hostile a year ago when Sunny had approached him about a reporter's job. But that ice had been broken. They'd worked together on a couple of stories and developed a healthy respect for each other's abilities. The sad fact of the matter was that a local weekly couldn't afford to take on Sunny, or anyone else, full-time.

After a few minutes, the clattering stopped and Ken came over, wiping his hands on a rag. "What brings you down here on a Sunday?" he asked, white eyebrows rising on his long, spare-fleshed face.

"Moneylending," Sunny replied.

Ken looked at his shoes. "I wish I could help," he began.

"I mean professional moneylenders. Or rather, loan sharks." Sunny quickly jumped in.

He jerked his head up, his eyes sharp. "My advice—don't get involved there. If the Elmet Bank won't help you, try a credit union. I think your dad—"

"It's not for me," she promised. "I'm just trying to get an idea of where people would turn. Are there operations that could take over whole businesses?"

"I've heard about that," Ken said slowly. "But bear in mind, this is pretty much a blue-collar town. The loans are small, comparatively speaking, and so are the sharks. The big business these days involves mortgages, screwing people out of their homes, or quasi-legal deals like payday loans. Which seem to me like going after people in a bad position and trying to make things worse."

His eyes took on a speculative gleam. "Maybe there's something to write about there. We've got a lot of people around town hurting in this economy, and they'll do really foolish things to try and stay afloat."

He looked a little self-conscious. "To tell the truth, I nearly did it myself a couple of years ago when the bottom first fell out. I looked around for a loan to keep the paper going. Banks were no help—they were afraid to lend money. One of my horse-player friends set me up with a guy in Portsmouth. He looked straight out of *The Godfather*—he's passed away since.

"When I looked at what the deal would finally cost me, I realized I'd never get out from under. That was probably the idea. Most payments we get are in cash, so they could play with the books."

"Money laundering," Sunny said.

Ken gave her a brief nod. "And then Ollie Barnstable came along, offering to buy in. He was bad enough. I didn't need anyone else trying to make me an offer I couldn't refuse."

He straightened his storklike form to its full height. "But I really considered the idea for a while, crazy as it was. That's the problem. You'll do crazy stuff for something you love."

The picture box made noise—confused noise, many voices shouting while two-legs ran up and down on grass. They seemed to be fighting or running to catch something. Shadow had seen it before—many times now. Sometimes, the Old One would sit up on his couch, wave his arms, and shout, too. Shadow didn't really understand why. It was just one of those weird human things.

Today, though, the Old One had fallen asleep. Not for the first time, Shadow wished he knew how to make the picture box shut up. From what he could see, it involved pointing a smaller box at the larger one, but every time he tried to investigate, the smaller box was moved away from him.

He tried moving to a patch on the rug behind the couch. It was a little cramped and could have been warmer, but at least the bulk of the piece of furniture blocked a lot of the noise. He was just beginning to doze when he heard a key in the lock.

Darting out from behind the couch, he ran for the door just in time to catch Sunny coming in. As he came close, he caught a confusing collection of scents. One he recognized—he definitely smelled Gentle Hands.

Why did Sunny keep going to see her without me? He paced around Sunny, sniffing more deeply. There were traces of several more animals on her—both cats and Biscuit Eaters. Shadow wrinkled his muzzle and squinted his eyes. He didn't like that.

This could be worse than the Old One's female friend bringing the young dog here. Shadow had lived in places where the humans brought younger animals to stay. And then, all of a sudden, Shadow didn't have a home.

But Sunny wouldn't do that to him.

Would she?

Sunny bent over, reaching her hand out to him. It smelled of Gentle Hands, but no other animals. That was good. Shadow rubbed his face against her fingers, to mark a little bit of his own scent there. Okay. If Sunny tried to pick him up, he'd let her.

Instead, the doorbell rang. Sunny went to answer it, letting in a blast of cold air and snowflakes and a shriek of wind that Shadow had only heard as a faint whisper before.

The female Old One stood in the doorway, with the Biscuit Eater pup straining at the leash in her hand.

Shadow hurriedly backed into the living room. What was going on here?

*

Helena Martinson looked apologetic as she struggled to hold the golden retriever pup in check. "Forgive us for turning up like this," she said. "We were out for a walk, and the weather turned so nasty all of a sudden."

"Come right in," Sunny told the older woman. If she held the door open much longer, they'd have to start shoveling the front hall.

Mrs. Martinson came in, clumps of snow dropping from her dark gray parka—not just the same cut as the one Sunny had picked up, but the same color, too. "We shouldn't have a problem with Toby," Mrs. M. promised. "He did his business early on our walk." She used a piece of tissue to wipe at the puppy's paws.

Toby stretched to his full height, his paws resting on Helena's right thigh above her knee. He rattled the ID tags on his collar as Mrs. Martinson undid his leash. Then he dropped his paws back to the floor and gave himself a good shaking.

"I've been trying to get him to do that before he goes any farther into the house," Helena explained, reaching down to pet Toby's head. "Good boy."

Toby gave a happy yip and wagged his tail. Then he turned and headed for the living room.

Sunny glanced around. Where had Shadow gone?

"Hey, Dad," she called. "We have company."

They came in to find Mike Coolidge blinking awake on the couch. "Helena!" he said in surprise and pleasure. Then he spotted the dog, and his pleasure dimmed a little. "And Toby. What a surprise."

Sunny spotted Shadow standing off to the side of the arched entranceway. Toby saw him too, and started bumbling his way toward the cat. Either he'd forgotten the unfriendly welcome he'd gotten on his last visit, or he was willing to let bygones be bygones. As Mrs. Martinson joined Mike on the couch and Sunny took a chair, Toby kept coming after Shadow, who in turn kept retreating. Shadow obviously didn't want to be driven out of his territory, but Toby's dogged pursuit kept him on the run.

In a desperate leap, Shadow bounced into Sunny's lap. But even there he wasn't safe. Toby tried to climb up after him—not very successfully, his antics making Sunny, her dad, and Mrs. Martinson all laugh. Finally, Shadow swarmed to the top of Sunny's chair and launched himself in a leap to the remaining chair in the room. He set himself on the chair back like a sailor clinging to a refuge while Toby circled mournfully around, unable to reach him. From the way Shadow's tail lashed about, he didn't find the situation funny at all.

Helena declined coffee or a snack and just sat chatting. The snow squall blew itself out in about forty-five minutes. But in that time it had deposited a fresh coating of a couple of inches on the dirty remains of the previous snowfall. The sunlight was definitely fading by now, and Mike offered Helena a lift home.

"Nonsense," she replied. "It's just a short walk, and Toby will enjoy a chance to play in the snow." She put on her parka, attached Toby's leash, and started down the drive. Mike stood in the doorway waving good-bye. Sunny stayed in the living room, approaching the chair that

Shadow had appropriated, but when she went to pet him, he disappeared from under her hands.

A little skittish today, aren't we? She turned around to find him. *Maybe he's smelling dog on me from my visit with Jane.*

Suddenly Mike yelled and dashed out the door. Sunny followed, shivering in the frosty air. She saw Mike slipping and sliding along the snowy pavement to a dark form lying on the ground. Toby circled around, whining.

Sunny reached her dad as he helped Helena Martinson onto her knees. "Are you okay?" His voice was loud, agitated, making Toby spin around and huff at him. "Did that damn pup pull you off balance?"

"I'm all right," Helena said in a breathless voice. "That tumble just knocked the air out of me for a second." Then, more in her normal tones, she went on, "And no, Mike, it wasn't Toby's fault. I just hit a slippery patch, and my feet went out from under me."

"Just take it easy and make sure everything's okay," Sunny said. She didn't want to aggravate any possible injury by hauling the older woman to her feet. On the other hand, Sunny could feel herself shivering. She was pretty sure that standing around in a whipping wind with just a sweater on wasn't the best thing for a heart patient either, but Mike insisted on helping Helena to her feet. Sunny retrieved Toby, holding him in her arms, and together they headed back to the open door.

Mike kept an arm around Helena as they went up the step to the doorway. "You're limping," he said in concern.

"It's nothing to worry about." Mrs. Martinson sounded

a bit testy now. "This isn't the first time I've slipped on the ice, you know."

They stood in the hallway for a moment, Helena brushing snow off herself, Sunny and her dad warming up.

"You're sure you're okay?" Sunny asked as she returned her neighbor's dog. She'd taken some falls, too—it was kind of hard to avoid ice, given the local weather—but Mrs. M. had a good thirty years on her.

"I'm perfectly all right," Mrs. Martinson assured her, cuddling Toby. "I guess I landed on someone's lawn, since the ground wasn't too hard. And the snow broke my fall— so I didn't break anything." She shook her head. "We weren't walking all that fast. Tody was a making a new path through fresh snow. I guess I didn't watch where I was going. All of a sudden my feet were off the ground— and then the rest of me was hitting it."

"You scared the hell out of me, going down like that," Mike told her. "I was afraid you'd cracked your head."

"But I'm fine now," Mrs. Martinson insisted. "Let's not make a big deal out of it."

"Okay," Sunny said. "But you are getting a lift home." She made sure she had her car keys and pulled on her parka.

Mike wanted to come, too, but Sunny told him to stay home and warm up. His exposure to the cold had left him looking pale instead of pink.

"I'll be back in a few minutes," Sunny said. Then she, Helena, and Toby headed out to the Wrangler parked in the driveway.

As they pulled onto Wild Goose Drive, Sunny said, "You're sure you're all right?"

"Just a little shaky," Mrs. Martinson admitted. "I didn't want to say so in front of Mike. You know how he'd worry." She rubbed her right knee. "And I guess I took a good knock here when I hit the ground. I'll probably have a bruise to show for it tomorrow."

She smiled down at Toby, who sat in her lap and worriedly licked her fingers. "I'll be fine with my little friend here."

"Just don't expect him to dial 911 for you if you end up feeling worse than you think," Sunny warned. "You can call us—we're not that far away."

That was true. A couple of turns, a few blocks, and they were pulling up in front of Mrs. Martinson's house. Sunny insisted the older woman hold her arm as they came up the walk. She tried to lighten things up. "After getting you through all of this, I don't want you to skid and fall at your own doorstep."

Sunny got Helena inside, out of her coat, and installed in her favorite chair. Toby resumed his place in her lap. After brewing some tea and making sure Mrs. Martinson was settled in, Sunny was ready to head home. Before she left, though, she had one question. "Did you have the hood on your parka up when you went out before?"

Mrs. M. nodded. "The snow might have stopped, but the wind was pretty bad." She looked up at Sunny. "Why do you ask?"

"I just think it's a problem with these parkas," Sunny said. "You wind up with a kind of tunnel vision when you pull the hood up."

"I'll try to be more careful," Mrs. Martinson promised. They said good night, and Sunny went out to her car. She frowned as she got behind the wheel. The snow may have stopped now, but the wind had picked up, sending showers of newly fallen flakes whipping around. It felt as if the temperature had dropped, too. Sunny had to concentrate on getting home along much more slippery roads.

When she arrived, she found that Mike had made a simple supper—soup and grilled cheese. He growled about the need for more salt—not on his food, but on the roads and sidewalks around town. After skidding her way home, even in the Wrangler, Sunny wasn't about to argue with him.

They finished and did the dishes. Mike headed for the living room and the television. "There's a good game on tonight."

Sunny begged off. "I want to do a little research," she said, going up the stairs. Once in her room, she fired up her laptop and got on the Internet.

I asked Mrs. M. to get some personal information on Dawn Featherstone, Sunny thought. *Maybe I should have gotten some public info first.*

All through dinner, she kept remembering Ken Howell's comment. "You do crazy stuff for something you love." But Sunny also knew that people did crazy things for people they loved.

She'd had a theory that Dawn tried to pin the blame on Jane for a simple reason: Dawn had committed the crime and was looking for a patsy. But what if Dawn was afraid that someone else had objected to her relationship with Martin Rigsdale and had taken him out? A father, a brother, an old boyfriend? Dawn might have been trying to cast suspicion on Jane—and even Sunny—to protect somebody close to her.

Using tricks she'd learned in her first weeks as a reporter, Sunny dug up the basics on Dawn—make that Dora—Featherstone. Here was a birth certificate from the right time frame. Not too many babies named Dora these days. That gave Sunny the names for both parents. She also learned that Dawn was an only child.

Looking for the Featherstone name in local newspapers brought sad news. Both of Dawn's parents had perished in a house fire while Dawn was away at college.

Some things you'd rather not know, Sunny thought, leaning back from the keyboard. *Well, that's a perfectly good hypothesis shot to hell. Dawn doesn't have a family to protect her.*

She closed out her search window but then paused for a moment. *There could be a boyfriend, though.*

Unfortunately, she was unlikely to find anything like that online, unless things had gotten as far as an official engagement. So Sunny got her phone instead and punched in Helena Martinson's number.

"I just wanted to check in and hear how you were doing," Sunny said.

Mrs. Martinson laughed. "You should coordinate better with your father," she said. "I just got off the phone with him a couple of minutes ago."

"I was upstairs doing some work," Sunny explained. "I haven't gotten a report from him. So, how are you?"

"I'm fine," Helena told her. "I rested a bit in my chair, had something to eat, and will probably go to bed a little early tonight. Tomorrow I may be a little stiff, and my knee will be a bit sore. As I told Mike, nothing life-threatening."

Busily concentrating on the question she wanted to ask, Sunny stumbled a bit. "I'm glad." She grimaced. "I mean, I'm glad that you're fine, not that you're going to be sore."

"It could have been worse," Mrs. Martinson agreed. "So what's on your mind, Sunny? You usually don't flub things up."

"It's just a question that came up, and you might have heard the answer already. When you were asking about Dawn Featherstone, did anyone mention her having a boyfriend?"

On the other end of the line, Mrs. Martinson paused for a moment. "Most of the people I spoke with were in Martin's social circle, not Dawn's," she said slowly. "But there was mention of a serious boyfriend who went into the military—the Army, if I remember correctly. They sent him off to Iraq or Afghanistan, and he hasn't been back since. Someone mentioned that he'd gotten married and either settled down south somewhere, or he's on a base down south somewhere."

Another possibility scratched off, Sunny thought. "Well, thanks, Helena," she said. "It's just a question that popped up."

"Yes." Mrs. M.'s voice was dry. "I wondered if there might be someone who'd object to Dawn carrying on with Martin Rigsdale. This fellow, Joey Something-or-other, was the closest possibility, but since he was out of the picture, I didn't mention it."

"But there you were with the answer," Sunny said. "Thanks. Look, if you need anything—"

"Your father already volunteered, at least for the daylight hours," Mrs. Martinson told her with a laugh. "And he said that you'd be on call if I need anything after dark."

Sunny shrugged. "Well, he's right to put my name up. Just bear us in mind if you do need anything." They wished each other a pleasant rest of the evening and then hung up.

Rising from her chair, Sunny stretched and looked around. Usually when she was upstairs this long, Shadow came padding in to check on her. She went downstairs to find Mike watching his football game.

"Hey, Dad," she asked, "has Shadow been with you?"

Mike's shaggy eyebrows rose in surprise. "I thought he was upstairs with you."

15

Sunny flew around the house, calling Shadow's name and checking usual places where he liked to get out of the way. Top of the refrigerator: empty. Under Sunny's bed: no cat. She peered under the dining room table—sometimes Shadow perched himself on one of the chairs there—and even got on her stomach to get a look under the couch. That was usually Shadow's hiding place of last resort.

"Where is he?" she asked, beginning to get worried now.

"Well, he was pretty mad at being chased around by that pup," Mike said.

Sunny remembered Shadow standing at bay on the living room chair, his tail sweeping back and forth like a metronome. "Maybe he took off to the garage."

But while the garage was full of a lot of things—like

all of the stuff Sunny had saved from her New York apartment—it was definitely devoid of cat.

"That was the last time I saw him," she said, "up on the chair."

"A lot of stuff happened after that," Mike pointed out. "We had that nasty spill for Helena, we rushed over to help her—"

"We left the door open," Sunny said through a suddenly tight throat.

Mike blinked. "You think he wandered off while we were getting Helena back on her feet? Why would he do that? It had just snowed, for heaven's sake. And between the wind and the cold, well, I was glad to get back indoors."

"Maybe he came out to see what was going on, and we didn't notice him." Sunny sped back into the house, to the front door.

"We'd have noticed him, all right," Mike said, coming after her. "That hairball is a regular Pavarotti when it comes to yowling and meowing. I'd have definitely heard him. Hell, *you'd* have heard him, even upstairs."

Sunny threw the door open to expose a carpet of white. There were tire ruts and sections of Wild Goose Drive where the snow had been scraped away. But the wind had pretty much erased her footprints coming back from the Wrangler. As for any other marks in the snow from earlier, they were just gone.

A blast of wind froze Sunny's face and sent a spray of loose snow onto the hall floor. But however frigid it was outside, that was nothing compared to the cold that Sunny suddenly felt around her heart.

Mike gently touched her shoulder. "You thought he might be sitting there, waiting?"

"I guess it was a silly idea, but yes," Sunny admitted. "It's freezing cold out there. Where would he go? *Why* would he go?" That question almost came out as a wail.

"We don't know that he went anywhere," Mike told her. "We know he was upset at having his place invaded, and that he can hold a grudge—and sulk—for a while. Maybe he's found a new hiding place and is using it to punish us. Maybe tomorrow he'll wake up in a better mood and we'll find him in the kitchen. I'd leave a little food in his bowl. If anything is likely to bring him out, it's that."

"That's probably good advice," Sunny said. But she couldn't keep the quiver from her voice as she spoke.

She did as Mike suggested, even splurging on the canned stuff that Shadow particularly liked. But she spent the rest of the night patrolling the house, looking for any signs of her cat. Then she put on her coat and searched outside, too.

Sunny awoke the next morning bleary-eyed. She hadn't slept well, worrying about Shadow, and she certainly didn't feel any better when she came down to the kitchen and found his food and water untouched. Mike was already down, starting on breakfast. He looked at Sunny and just shrugged.

Bracing herself, Sunny opened the kitchen door to test the weather. It was cold and calm—no wind at all. Sunny held tight to the doorknob until her hand hurt. The newest layer of snow on the lawn had been disturbed. She saw footprints, and they were too big to be a squirrel's.

No, those were cat prints, and they led down to the newly plowed road and disappeared.

*

Maybe I'm being hasty, Shadow thought as he trotted along the side of the road. He hadn't seen the usual things that happened before he got kicked out of a house. No arguments, no cutting back on food, no kicks or shouting. They'd just made such a big deal out of that stupid Biscuit Eater.

Letting it chase me around my house! The memory still burned. If the beast had been older, a little bigger, he might have let the claws come out. But doing that to a little one, that was a sure way to get tossed out of the house. So he'd been forced to the top of the chair, like a stray chased up a tree, not by a real Biscuit Eater, but a toy one. And all the two-legs had made happy noises!

He hadn't seen much to be happy about. Oh, Sunny had come to him after the pup had left, but Shadow had had no intention of being second best. He had avoided her hands.

And then Sunny had just left him! She'd run out and hadn't even bothered to close the door. When he saw it standing open in front of him, Shadow had taken the hint. He'd left, too.

Not the best planning. If he'd been smart, he'd have eaten something first. It would have been too much to hope that he could bring his pleasant bed or the furry thing that gave him comfort. He'd found shelter under the deck, a place he'd used before. There were still leaves to curl up under, and most of the wind hadn't been able to get in at him.

So, now . . . from his wandering days, he knew a couple of houses where the two-legs inside left out food for traveling cats. It would be cold, and he'd have to keep an eye out for competition, but he didn't think he'd starve. He'd need to find a warmer place to sleep. The deck was all right for an emergency, but it wasn't a long-term proposition.

Besides, it was too close. When he'd wrapped his tail around his paws and settled himself as comfortably as possible, he'd spotted a light dancing in the darkness outside. And he'd heard Sunny calling his name. For a wild moment, he'd considered bursting out of his hiding place and running to her.

Instead, he'd kept silent and lain quietly. He'd had disagreements with humans before, and they'd made up and been happy . . . for a while. Sooner or later, though, Shadow had ended up looking for a new home.

He just couldn't stand to do that with Sunny, to hope that things would be better and then have them not be better . . . No. He had gotten by without her before, and could do it again.

A truck came by, sending a thin spray of slush that Shadow dodged.

He just wished it had happened in spring, not in the middle of winter.

*

Sunny went in to work, but luckily, winter Mondays were pretty light, because not much MAX business got accomplished that morning. She ran through the incoming e-mails with half an eye and made a few notes for later. Then she used the office resources for her own project.

Before she left the house, Sunny had transferred several photos of Shadow from her laptop to a flash drive. Now she moved the pictures to her work computer and started composing a poster. LOST CAT, the headline read in nearly two-inch-tall type. Then she inserted Shadow's picture, one where the stripes showed through on his gray fur. Then, GRAY TIGER-STRIPED CAT. ANSWERS TO THE NAME SHADOW. IF YOU FIND HIM OR HAVE ANY INFORMATION, CALL 207-555-4841.

And after considerable thought, she centered a final word at the bottom of the page: REWARD.

How much that would be, she couldn't be sure. It would depend on whatever information she got, what condition the cat turned up in.

God, she thought, *I hope he turns up all right.*

She'd raided some of the boxes from her old apartment. The one holding stationery had the remains of a ream of fluorescent orange paper that she'd used for party invitations. If nothing else, it would catch people's eye. Sunny printed out the finished poster, proofread it one last time, and then ran off copies on the office copier until she'd exhausted her paper supply.

The pile of posters went on one corner of her desk with her stapler on top. She'd start putting them up around town during lunch hour. Now it was time to tap into the Kittery Harbor Gossip Hotline. Sunny had already asked her dad to spread the word, although she hadn't mentioned the idea of a reward to him. Mike might find that just a bit too much.

Sunny managed to time her call to Helena Martinson just right. Her neighbor was home and awake, but hadn't gotten the news about Shadow yet.

What Sunny hadn't planned on was how upset Mrs. M. became when she heard. "He ran away? I know he got a little annoyed when Toby tried to play with him, but I didn't think he'd run off."

"We're not sure what happened," Sunny said. "Things were pretty confused."

"You and Mike came out to help when I fell down." Helena's voice only got more distressed. "And you left the door open. Is that when he got out?"

Maybe this was a bad idea, Sunny thought as she tried to calm her neighbor down. "We really don't know," she said. "Speaking of that fall, how are you doing?"

"I'm a little stiff," Helena replied. "But that won't affect my dialing finger! I'll get the news out." She paused for a second. "Are you putting up posters?"

"Just made a bunch of them," Sunny said.

"Don't waste time trying to put them all up yourself," Mrs. Martinson advised. "Have your dad pick up some— he can post them around the neighborhood. I'll take a few as well, to get them up in some other areas."

If she wants to turn into Cat-Finding Central, okay. Sunny's hard-bitten reporter alter ego sounded a little rueful today. *It's better than having her blame herself.*

When Sunny estimated her father had finished with his three miles of hiking off in outlet-land, she called him at home. "I've got some posters to put up," she told him. "And Mrs. Martinson asks that you bring her some."

"Always glad to see Helena," he said. "I just hope that puppy of hers doesn't try to chew on them." He promised to be in shortly. Sunny set aside half of her pile for him.

Even as she waited, Mrs. Martinson's telephone tree began to bear fruit. First came a call from Ken Howell. "I hear your cat has gone missing," he said.

"I don't think that's front-page news," Sunny told him.

"No, but I think we could run a notice in the community bulletin board on the back page," Ken replied. "Do you have a picture?"

"Yes, but—"

"It's not an ad," Ken told her. "It's just professional courtesy."

"It's darned nice," Sunny corrected. "I'll e-mail you a picture right away."

"Got an office cat, you know," Ken said. "In an old building like this, you sort of need one."

Sunny blinked in surprise. "Really? I've never seen him."

"He hides whenever people come in," Ken explained. "And there are a lot of places around here for a cat to vanish himself."

"That's true," Sunny had to admit.

"I call him Harvey, because people think he's my imaginary friend." Ken paused for a second. "I'd sure hate it, though, if he started hiding from me."

No sooner did Sunny hang up the phone than Zack Judson appeared at her door. "I heard about Shadow," he said. "You know, before he went to live with you, he'd stop by the store sometimes."

Sunny sat straight in her chair with surprise. "Really?"

Zack nodded. "If he turns up, I'll try to keep him there—and at least let you know." He looked down at her pile of posters. "And I'll put one of these up in our front window. If you can spare a few, I'll give 'em to my delivery guys to post farther out of town, get those Piney Brook people looking for him, too."

Sunny peeled off a sheaf of posters for him. "I really appreciate—"

Zack shrugged off her thanks. "Your dad and I go way back. Happy to help."

He left, and Sunny sank back in her seat. *Maybe I'm not as much of an outsider as I imagined,* she thought.

Just as she was considering closing up the office to plaster the downtown area with posters, Will Price knocked on the office door.

"If you're coming to tell me that the sheriff's department is joining in the hunt, that'll just be too much."

"What hunt?" Will asked in bafflement.

Sunny handed him a poster. "Oh," Will said. Then he looked at her more closely. "Oh, I'm so sorry to hear this." Even though he was in uniform, Will dropped his usual cop persona. "I'm back on the day shift now, so I'll try to keep an eye out for Shadow." He smiled at her, trying to cheer her up. "I don't know if I can convince Sheriff Nesbit to join in the hunt, but you have a couple of friends among the constables. I'll get the word out there."

"Thanks," she told him. "Every bit helps." She took a deep breath, thinking of how quickly Shadow had adopted her. "Even if he's landed with another family, I just want to know he's all right."

"I know," Will said gently.

"So, if my cat didn't bring you in, what brought you by?"

That snapped Will back to police mode. "I spent the weekend carefully reaching out to some buddies on the Portsmouth force," he said. "They tell me there are some newcomers in town, lending money."

"Oh-ho," Sunny said. "From foreign parts?"

Will nodded. "Turns out they're Ukrainian, not Russian. Guy named Danilo Shostak seems to be the brains of the operation, with someone called Olek Linko acting as the muscle."

Sunny nodded. *The names matched what she knew, and what she'd told Will.*

"It seems the Ukrainians made a specialty of smuggling, which includes moving money around," Will went on. "Nobody is sure how big a deal this is, but it sounds like the major players in Providence gave the okay, and a Ukrainian operation in Montreal sent Shostak down. So far he's kept a real low profile."

"Avoiding trouble," Sunny murmured.

"That's one way to put it," Will agreed. "So if Jane's ex was involved with him, he can't be very happy with Rigsdale getting killed. Sooner or later, Trumbull is going to start shining some light where this guy won't want it shone. I mean, he's got to be going over Rigsdale's books."

And when that happens, Dani will have to go on vacation, Sunny thought. *He'll either have to find the money Martin stole to give his bosses, or he'll squeeze it out of Jane.*

Will misread her expression. "I'm sorry to come in and mention this stuff while you're worrying over Shadow."

"No, I think it helps to take my mind off that," she told him.

Because now I can worry about Jane, and the money, and who might have it. Sunny tried not to let her feelings show on her face. *Because I haven't got a clue.*

16

Sunny went through the motions, gobbling a quick sandwich she'd brought from home and then putting up posters in the hopes of finding Shadow. Store owners offered space in their windows or by their cash registers. Some people she knew and many she didn't stopped to read the notices and offer their good wishes. A few seemed to know about Shadow's disappearance already. Sunny looked at the picture on her poster. *You're getting famous around these parts, little guy.*

Unfortunately, none of these folks had any information to offer. They promised to keep an eye open, though.

Through all that time, Sunny's brain kept spinning its wheels on the question of where Martin Rigsdale had hidden his ill-gotten gains. Stealing from the Ukrainians in the first place suggested that Martin had intended to get out of Dodge. She was sure that Dani—not to mention Olek—would take a dim view of him making off with the money, especially since it wasn't even really theirs.

Equally obviously, something had gone wrong. Dani mentioned finding out about the bank withdrawal before Martin had expected him to. He also mentioned a very foolish bank officer—another victim of Martin's charm. Apparently, though, Dani didn't consider the banker to be a coconspirator of Martin's, which suggested that she had been squeezed dry of information already. Sunny could only hope she hadn't been squeezed in other ways. She remembered Dani's graphic demonstration of what Olek could do if he had to.

If Olek wanted some information out of me, I'd just tell him. Sunny might follow the guy, but she knew her limits.

Knowing Martin's preference for feminine companionship, Sunny was pretty sure that he'd planned to run away with someone. But if Dani and Olek had pretty well dismissed the bank officer, it had to be someone else.

Dawn Featherstone seemed the strong contender—young, impressionable, and looking at her from Martin's viewpoint, easy to control. Of course, Martin might have been wrong about her. She could be the one who'd killed him. But whether or not she was his girl of choice or his murderer, she should have her hands on more than a hundred grand. She could go someplace far from Maine and open her dream fitness club. Why was she hanging around?

On the other hand, maybe she didn't have her hands on the money and was looking for it. In that case, the only way that Sunny would know that Dawn had succeeded was if she suddenly disappeared. That might help Jane with the suspicion of murder thing, but it wouldn't help her with the Ukrainians.

Wait a minute. There was another woman in Martin's life, the dark-haired classy one. Unfortunately, Sunny had no idea whatsoever who that might be.

Sunny returned to the MAX office feeling tired and drained. And she still hadn't started any of the day's business. Stifling yawns, she went to work answering e-mails. The phone rang, and she snatched it up eagerly. Thankfully, she remembered to answer it, "Maine Adventure X-perience," and not "Any news?" because the voice on the other end was Ollie the Barnacle's. "Anything exciting turn up today?"

Sunny decided he didn't need to hear about Shadow running away. "Nothing that requires an executive decision," she told him.

"Okay, it looks as if I'll be getting back in sometime late tomorrow," he said. "I'll probably be in on Wednesday."

Sunny was surprised. Ollie usually didn't give her advance notice on when he was stopping by the office. *Maybe he wants to make sure I get rid of all the pizza boxes and beer bottles before he comes in,* she thought.

"Okay," she said. "If you need anything, you know where to find me." At least he hadn't called while she was out putting up posters. At least she didn't think so. Sunny paused for a second. "Do you know anything about loan sharks?"

"What?" Ollie's voice got a bit belligerent. "Is somebody saying I'm a loan shark—or that I need one?"

"Nothing like that," Sunny assured him. "I've, uh, got a friend who was thinking of borrowing some money. I thought with you being more business savvy, you could help me explain things—"

"Don't get involved with a shark," Ollie interrupted. "You start off borrowing to buy buttons and end up losing your shirt. The way they compute the interest, you never get to pay off the principal that you borrowed in the first place." He chuckled sourly. "It's as bad as credit cards—except they don't have people who come to your house and threaten to beat you up."

"Do they really do that?" Sunny asked.

"Yes." Ollie tried to sound patient. "That's the big difference between them and your neighborhood bank."

"Do they kill people?" Sunny pressed.

That got a moment of silence out of Ollie. "Jeez, Sunny, how much are you figuring to borrow?"

"It's not for me—really," Sunny insisted. "I just thought you must know more about this kind of financial stuff than anyone else I know."

"If you think I hang out with loan sharks, that's not much of a compliment," Ollie complained. "I know some guys who got in bed with the sharks. Almost all of them ended up regretting it. These were guys who owned businesses, but because of what they owed, the sharks became their partners—and often, their bosses." He harrumphed into the phone. "That said, it's bad business to kill the golden goose. The problem is, not all the guys who go into the loan-sharking line are businessmen. Some of them—I guess you'd call them sadists. But they're more likely to kidnap someone to get a little leverage when they put the squeeze on someone."

"And . . . killing?" Sunny pressed.

"I guess it's been known to happen," Ollie said. "Usually when they really don't expect to get their money back, and an example has to be made."

"Thanks, Ollie. That's what I thought."

"Yeah. Make sure your 'friend' hears that. Oh, and I'm definitely counting the petty cash when I come in." Ollie cut the connection, and Sunny went back to work, such as it was.

The phone rang yet again. This time it was an excited-sounding Jane Rigsdale.

"Two things," she said. "First, I'm really sorry to hear about Shadow. Several of the people who came in mentioned that he'd taken off on you."

"What can I say?" Sunny replied. "I'm sorry, too."

"You know he's a bit of a wanderer," Jane pointed out. "He didn't stay all the time with Ada Spruance."

"Yeah," Sunny recalled. "That's the first thing she told me about him."

"I was going to warn you when springtime came a little closer that he might develop a case of wanderlust," Jane said. "I just didn't think it was likely to happen when the weather was this cold."

"He was kind of angry with us—with me," Sunny confessed. "A neighbor had brought over a puppy, and he didn't like it."

Jane made a sort of noncommittal noise. "Maybe he felt threatened."

"Jane, it was a puppy. He wasn't in fear for his life. If it had caught up with him, it would have probably licked him."

"I don't think Shadow would have allowed that," Jane

said wryly. "But I wasn't talking about a physical threat. Judging from the way he gets along with people, I'd say Shadow has had a lot of homes in his life. Some, like Ada's, he might have left on his own, but others, it's more likely that he was kicked out. He might have seen the puppy as taking over his place."

For a moment, Sunny couldn't talk because of the lump in her throat. "Now I feel horrible. Mrs. M.—Helena Martinson—was only bringing the puppy around because she'd just adopted him. I never thought that Shadow might see it that way."

Jane tried to offer some hope. "He might turn back up after a couple of nights in the cold. Also, it's mighty slim pickings out there, eating-wise. Shadow is a practical little critter. If you see him, you can convince him it was all a mistake." She got a little more professional. "And if need be, I can help with some suggestions on helping the two animals get along. Pet psychology isn't my specialty, but I've done a little bit of it."

"If he appears on my doorstep, you'll be the first to know," Sunny assured her. "What's the second thing you had to tell me?"

"I think I may have found out who Martin's dark lady is." Jane's voice was back to full excitement now. "Martin has a sub in right now at his practice—like most medical practices, we arrange with other vets to substitute for us when we're not available."

"I see," Sunny said. "Martin is definitely unavailable these days."

"And in some cases, his substitute has ended up over-booked," Jane picked up the story. "So he asked if I would take one of Martin's cases. I should have gotten suspicious when the lady in question tried to cancel. I had to shame her into bringing her dog in, and when she did, I found myself examining a perfectly healthy animal who was booked for monthly appointments. And when I took a look at Martin's notes, I found a whole lot of fancy language that boiled down to observation and administering the occasional supplement—dog vitamins. This is a nice animal—a purebred—but he's not a show dog. There's no need to be so obsessive about the dog's health."

"So either Martin was cheating this woman . . ." Sunny began.

"Or cheating *with* her," Jane finished in a stage whisper. "This would cause a stink if it got out. The woman is Christine Venables."

"Why does that name sound familiar?" Sunny asked.

"Because you have a dad who's interested in local politics," Jane told her. "State Representative Ralph Venables? This is his wife."

"Oh, wonderful," Sunny said. "It's not messy enough, we have to add a political scandal."

"Also, Tobe managed to track down the waitress you bumped into, and they've talked some more."

"Tell him to skip the grilled cheese," Sunny advised.

"He's going to try and get a picture of Christine Venables and run it past this woman." Jane sounded a lot less eager now. "I'd rather not use it—I know what it's like to have a marriage blow up in my face. But it's sort of an insurance policy if Trumbull really comes after me."

"I'm glad it's not a decision I'd have to make," Sunny

honestly said. "So, if you've been chatting with Tobe, any more news on his availability?"

"Unmarried," Jane reported briefly. "He made partner because they wanted his skills."

"Just be careful," Sunny joked. "Lawyers are trained in persuasion."

*

Sunny finished the day's work and sat for a long moment in front of her computer, thinking. Then she called Helena Martinson. "Are you all set for milk and stuff?"

"You really shouldn't bother," Mrs. Martinson replied.

"I'm three stores away from a market," Sunny pointed out. "How much of a bother is that?"

"Well, I suppose I could do with a quart of the one percent milk," Mrs. M. said.

"Fine," Sunny told her. "I'll see you in a bit."

She turned off her computer, got her parka, locked up the office, and headed over to Judson's.

When she arrived at her neighbor's house, Mrs. Martinson had coffee perking away. "I thought we might find a use for some of that milk," she said with a smile. But when she took the sack, Sunny could see that she limped her way into the kitchen. And she had trouble negotiating the baby gate she had set up in the doorway, beyond which Toby the pup yipped in excitement to see a visitor in the house.

"Let me help with that." Sunny hurried after her hostess.

"It's not as bad as it looks," Mrs. Martinson insisted.

"I've got a bruise on my knee, and it slows me down walking."

"Well, you should take it easy while it heals properly," Sunny told her, taking the tray with the cups, saucers, milk pitcher, and sugar bowl. "Let's sit down and enjoy this properly."

They settled in the living room with Toby whining after them.

"So what would you like to talk about, dear?" Mrs. M. asked with a guileless smile.

"Oh, you're good," Sunny said, laughing. She took a sip of coffee. "What can you tell me about the Venables family?"

"Well, obviously, Ralph Venables is a state representative. He's married to Christine, and they have a daughter, Kristi, who's a year or two out of college. She'd been working in Boston, but lost her job and is home now." Helena frowned, trying to bring up details. "They're fairly well off. Ralph came from money and was involved in a real estate business, but got out before the bottom fell out of that. As far as I know, he hasn't invested in anything foolish. Ralph got reelected last November and is starting his second two-year term. Christine's people came from farther north, respectable but not rich. She actually helped to set up the 99 Elmet Ladies and would have liked to be more involved. But it might look too much like politics."

"And that's what anybody who searched the newspapers would find," Sunny said with a smile. "But what's the dirt?"

"We-e-ell," Mrs. Martinson drew out the word, "they have a beautiful house over in Piney Brook, but I hear Ralph has been spending most of his time up in Augusta."

Sunny nodded. "You think that's more than the press of government business?"

"He wasn't so diligent in his first term." Mrs. M. took a sip of her coffee. "He may be trying to earn some brownie points—what do the politicians call it? Carrying the can?" She pursed her lips. "But he hasn't really been home in months. And when he does come down, he rarely stays overnight."

"I bow to your years of experience," Sunny told the older woman. "What does that say to you?"

"A possible separation, but they're trying to keep it quiet," was Helena Martinson's verdict. "They may have held it together for the election, but now they're easing into a divorce. There have been some rumors. I've heard them, but so far it's been all talk."

She aimed bright eyes at Sunny. "But maybe not anymore, I suspect."

" 'Suspect' is a good word," Sunny replied. "This, as they used to say when I was working, is definitely not for publication." She briefly told the story of Martin Rigsdale's two ladies. "The blonde is pretty obviously Dawn Featherstone, but the dark lady could be Christine Venables."

"Very Shakespearean," Mrs. Martinson said. "I just hope it doesn't turn out to be one of those revenge tragedies."

"If they're heading for a divorce anyway, is there any reason to get all dramatic about it?" Sunny asked.

"One word: 'politics.' Two people might dissolve a marriage with a minimum of fuss and bother. But the threat of political scandal could complicate things considerably. It could hurt Ralph's electability for the office he holds or keep him from getting any higher up the ladder."

"Possible motive," Sunny admitted. "But enough to kill for?"

"It does seem a little cold-blooded," Mrs. Martinson agreed. "But consider this. It's one thing to decide that a marriage is over, to come to that rational conclusion. Even so, it's something else to discover that your wife is sleeping with another man. That could lead to a hasty reaction."

"And a bigger scandal to keep quiet," Sunny finished. "And, of course, if there's a divorce settlement to be made, any kind of scandal hurts Christine."

Mrs. Martinson nodded. "As you say, motive. Strong enough to kill over? I can't tell. But I can say this—Martin Rigsdale had a lot to answer for."

Sunny fell uncharacteristically quiet for a few moments. She'd been involved with a guy who'd been getting divorced, living apart, just waiting for the final papers.

And then Randall hadn't gotten divorced at all.

Maybe this is just hitting a little too close to home for me, Sunny decided. *I'm seeing too many sides to this one.*

"As you said when we started, this story is definitely not for publication." Mrs. Martinson sat very straight in her armchair, her cooling cup of coffee held between both hands. "But I wonder if there are more pieces to put together. Let me see what I can find."

*

Shadow regarded the sandwich suspiciously. In his experience, food did not usually appear in the middle of a road, especially a sandwich that didn't even have a bite in it. He tried to remember anything like this. Sometimes humans threw papers from their go-fast things, and sometimes there was food in there. But that was usually in warmer times. This time of year the two-legs didn't leave windows open. He remembered once seeing a car with a sack of food left on the roof. The car had moved, the sack had fallen, and Shadow had investigated. But there was nothing in there that a self-respecting cat would eat. Here, though . . .

He could smell the rare roast beef even before he came around the curve in the road. Shadow looked around. A car sat still on the side of the road not too far away. But nothing moved in the failing light. He peered at the sandwich again, and his stomach rumbled.

Shadow had walked very far since he left the space under the deck. He hadn't had as much luck as he'd hoped in finding food. In fact, he'd had none. He was tired, and cold, and very empty. Soon he'd have to find a safe place where he could sleep. It would be good to do that with a full belly.

He looked both ways along the empty road again and, crouched low, approached the sandwich. One of the pieces of bread had fallen away, leaving the meat out in the open.

I was lucky to find this before some other animal did, he finally thought, tearing a morsel free with his teeth. Oh, it was good to have food.

And then, all of a sudden, things were very, very bad. Something swooped down on him, and he suddenly found himself trapped in folds of fur. What kind of creature was this? It apparently could fly, but it had fur. And it stank! Shadow had seen Biscuit Eaters who liked to roll in dead things. But whatever this animal had rolled in was worse than dead. It made Shadow a little light-headed to breathe this reek.

Still, he tried to fight, kicking, unsheathing his claws. But he couldn't land a good blow or draw blood in the stifling folds.

And then it got worse. He felt himself pulled from the ground, as if some gigantic bird was taking him away. Shadow couldn't help himself. He yowled in terror.

And then he found himself falling, landing with a thud partially softened by the fur around him. Then came a sharp slamming sound. Shadow continued to fight against the furry folds enveloping him, finally getting free. This was no animal! Or rather, it might have been once, but now it was a dead thing. He had the horrible suspicion that it was now a human coat. And now that he was out of its folds, he could sense that he was in a fairly small space crowded with other things. He felt metal, and what seemed like a rug. Very faintly, he saw an outline of light. But no matter how hard he clawed at it, he couldn't make the outline bigger.

Then the whole space began to move, and Shadow knew where he was. It was the back part of a go-fast thing—the part for holding things!

He'd investigated a few of them in his travels, but he'd always been careful not to get caught inside. There had been interesting smells and odd things that could be played with, but he'd always stayed outside.

Just my luck, to be trapped in a place that smells so bad. In the close confines of the trunk, the stink from the furry coat drowned out almost everything else.

This was very bad, indeed. He had to get out! Shadow scratched, and cried, and hurled himself at the metal walls around him until he lay panting on the floor, sick and hurting. His claws went for that faint outline of light, growing fainter now. They scraped uselessly at metal.

He tried to get to his feet, but his legs wouldn't cooperate. Shadow flopped down, his head spinning, that dreadful scent clogging his nostrils. He gagged, and what little he had eaten came back up again. Twisting around, he managed not to choke. But the darkness inside this space seemed to grow darker yet.

So dark, he couldn't even think . . .

When Sunny got home, she found her father sitting at the kitchen table, having nuked himself a bowl of frozen soup. "Sorry to be getting home a little late," she said. "I picked up a quart of milk for Mrs. Martinson, and we got to talking."

She got herself out another pouch of soup and began heating it up. "How was your day?"

"It feels a little odd around here without Shadow, I have to admit," he said. "The only thing odder was some of the phone calls I got. I wish you hadn't mentioned a reward, Sunny. A bunch of the calls I got were people checking to see whether the information they had was worth enough to leave. And most of the information that people gave for free—well, that's about what it's worth. We've got about ten thousand people living in this town, and from the sound of it, there are about five thousand gray or striped cats around here. I tried to mark where people saw these cats on a map, and it was all over the place, from the Piscataqua River to Piney Brook, up to Sturgeon Springs and Saxon."

He smiled at her, trying to sound positive. "I guess the good news is that the word has certainly gone out far and wide. People are being very generous with their information. I just hope we'll be able to figure out what's useful. One nut actually claimed she saw a cat being stolen off the street. I figure by tomorrow, we'll be hearing about the saucer people either dropping cats off or taking them away."

"Poor Dad." Sunny reached across the table and took his hand. "This must be such a waste of your time."

He shrugged. "In between, I got out of the house. Went to some of the stores up in outlet-land where I take walks and persuaded them to put up posters there." Mike gave her a lopsided kind of grin. "If we don't ask, we don't find out anything, do we?"

"I guess not," Sunny said. "And thanks, Dad." She got up to make some sandwiches to go with the soup. They still had lots of turkey in the fridge.

When they'd finished supper, they went to the living room. Sunny found it a bit odd to be sitting in an armchair again instead of on the floor, playing with Shadow. She also found that paying full attention to a lot of the shows did not improve them.

The phone rang, and Sunny picked it up, bracing herself for either a demand for a reward or some new crazy theory about Shadow's disappearance.

Instead, it was Mrs. Martinson. "Did you know that

there's a memorial for Martin Rigsdale tomorrow evening? One of my friends from Portsmouth called with the news."

"I knew there was going to be a memorial," Sunny said. "It was supposed to depend on when the chief medical examiner released the body."

She could almost feel her neighbor's shudder over the phone. "Not that I'm going," Mrs. M. hastily put in. "But don't you feel it's odd that Jane Rigsdale is doing this on the other side of the river?"

"Jane isn't," Sunny explained. "She's paying for it, but letting Dawn Featherstone make the arrangements. As she always kept reminding me, Martin was her ex-husband. He went off to Portsmouth to start a new chapter in his life."

"A final chapter, as it turns out," Helena Martinson added disapprovingly.

"Well, it's a chapter he didn't share with Jane, and I guess she doesn't feel the need to take part in any farewell."

"It still seems strange," Mrs. M. repeated.

When she ended the call, Sunny punched in Jane's number and asked about the memorial.

"That's right," Jane confirmed. "The ME released Martin's remains late today, cremation tomorrow, and the memorial starting at seven o'clock."

"That seems a bit rushed," Sunny said.

"Yeah, well, look at it from Dawn's point of view." Jane's tone became considerably more sour. "Tuesdays are when I have evening hours, so she can be sure I won't turn up like an unwelcome guest. Not that I have any intention of showing my face."

"Okay," Sunny said. "Just wanted to make sure."

"Any luck on the Shadow front?" Jane asked.

"No news," Sunny reported. "A lot of tips that point in all directions, but nothing solid."

"Keep your chin up," Jane said. "Shadow is a survivor. I'm betting he'll find his way home."

"I hope so," Sunny sighed. She hung up and turned to Mike. "Mrs. Martinson called to tell us that the memorial for Martin Rigsdale is tomorrow."

"I guess that means an early supper," Mike said.

"What?"

"We have to pay our respects," her father said.

"Martin Rigsdale was not what you'd call a respectable person," Sunny argued. "And he certainly didn't give me much respect. The one time we met, he hit on me."

Mike looked uncomfortable, but determined. Obviously, this was the Kittery Harbor Way. But he did unbend enough to say, "Your mother always had a good explanation about going to wakes and memorials. She used to say it's not for the guest of honor—wherever they are, they could probably care less. It's for the living people. That's why we're paying respects."

*

Shadow woke up to find himself in a strange room. It was pretty much empty, except for things that a cat might like—or use. He found an enclosed bed, like a cave, but with comfortable padding. Just outside the opening for that stood a scratching post. Toys were scattered across the carpeting. Against the wall he found bowls for food and water, but nothing in them.

The only human furniture in the room was a single

chair. One wall had shelves built in from the floor to the ceiling, like the setup in Sunny's room where she kept her books. But here, the shelves were bare.

All in all it had the makings of a Good Place, except that Shadow couldn't get out the door. And then there was the smell. It wasn't as overpowering as when Shadow had been trapped in the trunk, just about wrapped in a coat saturated with the powerfully unpleasant scent.

Here, in a bigger room, the smell was more diffuse. But it clung in the nose like a nagging undertone. Now he recognized it—not dog and dead things, but the scent of that weird Old One who came to screech at Gentle Hands.

The One Who Reeks has been in here, Shadow thought. *She's sat in that chair often enough to mark it with her scent.*

He prowled around the rest of the room, trying to see what else his nose might tell him. Nothing much.

In the area around the bowls, he detected traces of another cat—a female—and the scent of sickness.

But he didn't smell the she in the sumptuous bed. In fact, that had store smells, like the bed that Sunny had brought home for him.

Shadow stood very still for a moment, not wanting to mewl. He missed Sunny. He missed having his bed next to hers. He missed being able to climb into bed with her. Why did she let that Biscuit Eater come into the house? Why couldn't she be happy with him?

He pushed the miserable feelings away with anger, leaping onto the chair that stank of the One Who Reeks. Give him a scratching post, would she? He'd show her what claws were for!

Shadow didn't ignore the smell that tore at his nose. Instead, he used it to fuel his fury, clawing at the upholstery until the stuffing showed. He dropped to the floor, panting from the exertion.

He didn't know how much later the door opened. For a moment, the One Who Reeks stood frozen in the doorway with bowls of food and water in her hands, staring. Then she began screeching.

Shadow leaped for freedom, but the door slammed shut. He hissed in disgust.

And she took the food with her.

*

Sunny made an effort to get into work a little early on Tuesday. After all, she intended to leave right on the dot that evening. She tended her computer and took care of all the usual jobs. It had been a while since she'd reconciled the petty cash, but she did that right before lunch. Ollie might have been twitting her about needing the services of a loan shark, but she wanted to make sure the office finances were in good order—just in case he really did check.

She was in luck—income, outgo, and cash in hand all balanced out perfectly.

One less thing to worry about, she thought.

As quitting time came around, she stepped into the bathroom and checked her reflection. Sunny had abandoned her usual business casual dress code for the day. She'd gotten out a dark gray suit—something she used to save for serious interviews back in her reporting days. With a muted silver blouse, it looked good without being too flashy. In fact, *she* looked good. The only problem was that her hair was getting a bit out of control again. Sunny did what she could, closed up the office, and headed home.

She found Mike in the living room, watching the news in what he called his "wedding and funeral suit."

"Looking good, Dad," she complimented him.

With a crisp white shirt and a sober tie, Mike could have been a model in a shopping circular. He hooked a thumb in the waistband of his trousers. "It does fit better," he admitted. "Last time I wore this outfit, I felt a bit squeezed in. Figured when it was my turn to be front and center in the casket, they'd have to slit the suit up the back to make it look like it fit me."

"Dad!" Sunny stared at him. She didn't know what got into her father when he had to deal with funerals.

"It's true," Mike insisted. "I had a friend who used to work at Saxon Funerals. That was one of the tricks they used if the guest of honor turned out to be a little too fat for his good suit."

He shrugged. "It's not as if people are going to see."

They had a simple supper and set off for Portsmouth. The funeral chapel was pretty close to Martin's office, a white brick structure with a large parking lot.

"Looks like a good-sized crowd," Mike said, glancing around. "I guess Martin was fairly well liked."

Sunny parked her Wrangler toward the edge of the lot. She'd put on a black wool coat that had seemed warm enough in New York but failed to deal with the chilly wind whipping among the cars. Mike jammed his hands in the pockets of his heavy trench coat, muttering, "I'll be glad to get inside."

Martin's memorial took up the whole ground floor. Instead of the traditional casket, easels featured a collage of pictures—Martin playing golf, Martin looking convivial at parties, Martin accepting awards, even a few shots of Martin with some four-legged patients.

A few of the pictures included Dawn Featherstone. None of them included Jane.

While Sunny perused the photo montage, Mike unabashedly studied the crowd. "I know a few folks here," he murmured.

Sunny felt a presence at her elbow and turned to see Dawn Featherstone glaring at her.

"What are you doing here?" the young woman asked, her usually soft features taut with stress. She looked as if she'd lost some weight over the past week. Dawn was dressed all in black. On a closer look, though, the pants she was wearing didn't quite match the shade of her jacket. Her blouse was buttoned all the way up to the neck. Two strong spots of color showed on her cheeks.

"I'm not here looking for trouble," Sunny told Dawn quietly. "I only knew Martin briefly, but my dad felt we should pay our respects."

Dawn gracelessly shook hands with Mike, her expression suspicious.

"Dad mentioned seeing several acquaintances in the crowd," Sunny went on. "I'll just stand in the back while he says hello. And then we'll be gone."

True to her word, Sunny found a quiet corner and stood looking on while Mike worked the room like a seasoned politician, shaking hands and speaking with people, being introduced and chatting some more.

I bet Martin would be pleased with the turnout, Sunny thought, watching the visitors. *Pretty well-dressed crowd, too.*

A lot of the men had designer suits. The women had winter tans and real jewelry. For a moment, Sunny felt a little sorry for Dawn. She was trying to be a good hostess, greeting people, talking about the photos. Most of the people were treating her like the maître d' at a restaurant. No, they'd be more considerate of a maître d'—he had the power to stick them at a bad table. Dawn, with her mismatched suit and strained manners, was going to a lot of trouble . . . for damned little in the way of appreciation.

As Mike worked his way toward her, Sunny amused herself by searching for brunettes in the crowd. Had Christine Venables shown up for this sad occasion?

Mike finally rejoined Sunny. She leaned toward his ear. "If you've had enough, I'm ready to go. No need to overstay a pretty brittle welcome."

"Okay," he said. They turned to look for Dawn—and found her shaking hands with a woman who had a few glints of silver in her glossy dark hair. The woman was very serious and polite, compared to the perfunctory way a lot of the guests treated Dawn. But the girl's face had gone dead white, and her polite smile had become more of a grimace.

"Let's wait a minute," Mike said. "Let her finish talking with Christine Venables."

Sunny nearly burst out at her dad's innocent identification. She hadn't shared with him what Mrs. Martinson had told her. As they approached, Sunny could see Dawn nodding jerkily to something Christine said. The older woman nodded back and then moved off. Sunny stepped up. "We'll be going now. Thanks for your consideration."

Dawn was still obviously changing mental gears. She stared at Sunny blankly for a moment, then remembered who she was. For a second aggression flickered through her eyes, but then Sunny's words sank in. "You're welcome," Dawn finally said. "Excuse me—there are some more people—"

Mike offered his condolences, and then they escaped to reclaim their coats.

"Okay," Sunny said. "We rushed to get here, got crushed in with a lot of snooty people, caught some attitude from Dawn, and now we're outside freezing in our good clothes. Was it worth it?"

"You were decent to that girl when a lot of other people weren't," Mike replied. "That's paying respect."

They'd just gotten to Sunny's Wrangler when her cell phone began bleeping. With a practiced movement, Sunny answered it and put it to her ear to hear Will's voice. He sounded worse than anyone at the funeral had.

"I tried you at home and wound up getting the machine," he said. "Look—I got a call from one of my old Portsmouth friends. Trumbull and Fitch got Jane out of her office and brought her down to the station again." His voice got more strained. "I can't go down there. It's a lot to ask, but could you—"

"Actually, we're pretty close by," Sunny told him. "Tonight was the memorial for Martin Rigsdale, and Dad felt we should go." She glanced over at Mike. "Would you mind a trip to the police station?"

"As long as I'm not in custody, okay," Mike replied, a twinkle in his eyes.

"Okay. We're heading there now," Sunny said to Will.

They got in the Wrangler and headed for the municipal complex.

"I don't know how long this may take," she warned Mike.

"It's not as though I have anything pressing tomorrow morning," he said. "You'll have to worry about getting to work."

As it turned out, neither of them needed to worry.

Sunny brought her Jeep up to the porch outside the station entrance just in time to see Tobe Phillips and Jane emerge from the building, laughing and smiling.

Behind them, she could see a glowering Detective Mark Trumbull standing at the glass panel.

Sunny shook her head. *He's just not seeing things he likes through that door.*

18

Sunny opened the door of her SUV and got out. "Are you guys all right?" She honestly wondered if Jane and Tobe might not have been drinking, they were so giddy.

"We're fine." Jane got her laughter under control, but she still smiled at Sunny. "They came in towards the end of office hours, Fitch and one of the sheriff's men. Rita was kind of hysterical—" Jane glanced at Tobe. "Or was that me? Anyway, Rita knew to call Tobe, and he was here waiting for me. Damn good thing, too, because without him I'd probably have said something stupid and be sitting in a cell by now."

She lowered her voice, leaning toward Sunny. "I have to thank Will for suggesting Tobe. He was really great in there."

Then Tobe took up the story. "I think they honestly

expected to close the case tonight." He wasn't loud, but his face shone like a member of the winning team being interviewed in the locker room after the big game.

"They weren't at all prepared when I brought up the connection between Martin and Christine Venables, and I think the political side of it really knocked them for a loop. They'll have to do a bit of homework before they even start thinking of questioning Jane again. Thanks, Sunny."

Mike opened his window and leaned out. "I guess I should say congratulations," he said. "You don't usually see people coming out of a police station looking so jolly. What had you laughing like that?"

"Hi, Mr. Coolidge." Jane took a moment to introduce Tobe. "It's nothing, really. I was just so sure when they took me in here that I wouldn't be coming out. And then, as we were walking away, I began to tremble. I guess Tobe must have realized it. He took my arm and mentioned something silly from school." A giggle escaped her at the memory. "It's something I probably hadn't thought about in twenty years. Next thing I know, I'm laughing, and so is he."

"I guess that's a good thing to get your spirits up," Sunny said. "But did you realize that Detective Trumbull was on the other side of that glass door watching you?"

Hearing that sobered Jane up pretty quickly. She shot a glance at the door, but the space was empty now.

"Maybe that wasn't such a good thing," she said quietly. "I wouldn't want him to think we were laughing at him."

Tobe got a bit more serious, too. "Well, I don't think it's a good idea to go back inside and try to tell him," He sent a considering gaze over Sunny and her dad. "I'm pretty impressed that you two showed up so quickly. Did Rita call you also?"

"Oh, Kittery Harbor has the fastest gossip service on the whole East Coast," Sunny assured him, without giving her source. "That's lucky. Also it's lucky that we happened to be nearby. If we'd been a little longer hearing about Jane, you'd have gotten her out before we even arrived here."

Jane, in the meantime, had finally taken in the way they were dressed. "You were at the memorial."

"Briefly," Sunny said. "Dad thought that making an appearance was the right thing to do. We were just on the way out when we got the call."

"What memorial?" Tobe asked.

Jane explained about allowing Dawn to run a service for Martin.

"You didn't do her any favor with that," Sunny told her. "Martin's snooty clients, or associates—I don't know if you'd really call them friends—were treating her like one of the servants."

"I didn't twist her arm," Jane said. "She wanted to do it."

"Looks to me as if she was regretting that." Sunny gave Jane a sidewise look. "Especially when Christine Venables showed up. A little bit of tension in the air."

"Really?" Tobe spoke up. "Christine Venables is at this memorial?"

Jane shot him a look. "Before you ask, I don't want to go there, even if I am on this side of the river."

Tobe shook his head. "The thought never crossed my mind. I think you should go home."

"We could give you a lift," Mike offered.

At the same time, Tobe said, "I've got my car here."

Jane had the grace to look embarrassed. "I don't want to put you out."

"It's no problem, really." Tobe smiled.

"And I suppose you guys have legal things to discuss," Sunny added, thinking, *Sheesh, it's like high school all over again. All the guys want to go with Jane.*

Tobe led Jane off to his Lexus, and Sunny got back behind the wheel of her Jeep. "Okay, Dad," she said, pulling on her seat belt. "Let's get this show on the road."

"Are you going to call Will and let him know how things turned out?" Mike asked.

"Yes," she replied. "When we get home. I don't like the idea of yakking on the phone while I'm trying to drive."

Tobe and Jane pulled out of the parking lot ahead of them, and Sunny didn't see the dark blue Lexus on her way home. The drive was uneventful. They arrived in time for Mike to catch his nine o'clock shows. Both of them changed out of their good clothes. Sunny pulled on a set of old sweats and went up the stairs to her room and the phone.

When she got Will, he already knew what had happened at the station. "So Phillips did a good job of getting Jane out, but Trumbull is furious. Apparently, they were laughing their heads off at him as they left."

Who is he tapped into, Sunny wondered, *the Mrs. Martinson of the police force?*

"That's not quite true," she told Will. "Jane was wound pretty tightly after being hauled down to the station and questioned again. Tobe tried to loosen her up by reminding her of something silly that happened back in school. She sort of overreacted, and so did he."

"And so has Trumbull," Will said grimly. "He's riding everybody to eliminate this Venables woman as a suspect so he can go back to concentrating on Jane."

"Okay, not the best result, but that means he'll be concentrating on somebody besides Jane—at least for a little while."

"How was Jane?" Will's voice got a little awkward as he asked.

"After she stopped laughing, she seemed like her usual self," Sunny reported. "She declined to go to Martin's memorial service, even though she wasn't all that far away. And then she turned down my dad's offer of a lift to go home in Tobe's Lexus."

"Did she?" Will was a good cop who didn't give much away. But Sunny was willing to bet right now that he was wondering if he'd created a monster.

*

Shadow slammed into the window, bouncing off painfully and falling to the floor below. He tried to shake the pain out of his shoulder and grimly trotted to a new angle, running, leaping, slamming into the glass, and rebounding again. The problem was there was no place level with the window, no place that allowed him any chance at a running start.

He sighed and sprang to the windowsill. Even if he could run straight at the glass, he wasn't sure he could break it. Certainly, it had held up against his best efforts so far.

Shadow leaned down to lick at his shoulder. But that wouldn't make the dull ache go away. He tried to distract himself by taking in the view. Outside, a big, snow-covered lawn stretched to a line of trees far away. Shadow pressed a paw against the glass, feeling the chill from outside work its way into the pads of his foot. It must be freezing out there for that much cold to come through the window.

But being out there would still be better than staying trapped in this place, he thought.

The rattle of a key outside the door stirred him to action. He dropped to the floor and scurried to the cavelike bed against the wall.

Shadow hunkered down in the semidarkness, trusting in the color of his fur for concealment. He lay quietly as the One Who Reeks came in, quickly closing the door behind her with a heel. Again, she carried food and water in her hands. She peered around, trying to find him.

It would have been easy to leap out of hiding and frighten her. But it would be useless. As long as the door to the room remained closed, Shadow knew he had no escape.

The One Who Reeks came closer, filling the bowls against the wall. Tensed in the darkness of his artificial cave, Shadow held his breath as waves of scent poured off her. He wanted to make a noise of protest, but that would involve inhaling. He didn't want a lungful of that stink.

Having arranged the food and water, the human retreated to the chair. Even though he'd slashed at it with his claws, it was still sturdy enough to sit on.

The One Who Reeks sat quietly, glancing in various

directions. But Shadow saw that sooner or later, her eyes would flick over to the opening to this bed.

Of course, he thought, *there are no other places in here to hide.*

The female two-legs rocked almost imperceptibly in her seat, waiting for Shadow to show himself. Grimly, he kept his place, motionless, watching her. It wasn't easy. Under the stink she gave off, he could catch the whiff of food. That was torture, to have food in his nostrils and none in his belly, but he refused to follow the temptation out into the open.

Then came other torments. His stomach might be empty but other parts of him were getting full. He had to use the litter box—and soon. Otherwise, he risked fouling this pleasant nest, the one Good Thing in this awful place.

The urge became painful, but still he held his place. He didn't know how long the One Who Rocks sat there, trying to force him into the first move.

At last, though, she gave up. The human rose and went to the door. For a wild moment, Shadow considered leaping after her, running for the door as she opened it. But the long inactivity had sapped the strength of his muscles. He'd probably fall over his own paws—and worse, considering his overfull condition, mess himself.

So he forced himself to stay motionless while the One Who Reeks opened the door and closed it behind herself. Then, ever so carefully, he climbed out of the bed and went to the litter box. And then, when he was comfortable again, he went for a drink of water and some food.

In spite of his hunger, Shadow didn't eat greedily. He

checked the impulse, taking small bites. Then he went back to the bed. He still hated this place, but at least there was food.

*

Sunny shut the kitchen door. The morning sun was bright but treacherously misleading. Not only was the air cold, but chilly blasts of wind made it feel worse.

I only hope Shadow is someplace safely indoors, she thought. *He picked a really awful time to go a-wandering.*

Ice patches had reappeared in the roads, messing up traffic. But Sunny managed to get in at a reasonable hour and started work.

She'd just about cleared her desk of the day's major tasks when Ollie Barnstable came in. He was more of a mess than usual, wearing a leather trench coat that he seemed to believe gave him a secret agent–style image. Instead, it made him look more like an overstuffed piece of furniture. He couldn't get the thing buttoned across his widening middle, which meant he must be freezing in this weather. That, and the flight up from New York, made his always uncertain temper a little worse than usual.

He came in waving a fluorescent orange poster. "This is your cat, isn't it?"

Sunny gave him a smile. "Don't tell me you found him!"

Ollie glowered at her. "Don't tell me you used office equipment to make these."

She did her best to look innocent. "Well, Ollie, we don't have any paper like that around here, do we?"

"Guess not." Still looking suspicious, he loosened the belt that barely managed to keep his coat closed and dropped into the chair opposite Sunny's desk. "Sorry about your cat. You weren't out traipsing around looking for him during office hours, were you?" That was the important point for him.

For a second, Sunny thought about referring Ollie to Tobe Phillips to improve his cross-examination technique. But she decided no good could come of being snarky. Instead, she contented herself with a simple, "No. But a lot of folks were very helpful, putting up the notices around town."

He nodded absently, not really paying attention. "And nothing else interesting happened while I was gone?"

"Just business as usual," Sunny told him. "How was your trip?"

"A waste of goddamn time," Ollie growled. "This guy kept stringing me along, keeping me in New York, because his buddy was busy scaring up investors down in Miami. Supposedly, this clown had a million-dollar idea. They'd picked up this resort down in the islands—a place that went bust—and planned to renovate it for a whole new market. I wasted nearly a week trying to figure out what it would be. Gays? Rehab junkies? Religious nuts? Sex freaks? So when this guy comes to show me his plans, it turns out to be a concierge hotel for pets! What a stupid idea! Who the hell cares that much about pets?"

He glanced down at the Day-Glo flyer in his hand, and his usually pink face turned almost a radioactive red. "Uh, not to say that people don't care about their pets. I mean—"

Sunny decided to let him off the hook. "I know what you mean, Ollie."

As she spoke, the office door opened. In came a very

unhappy-looking Ben Semple, accompanied by Detective Fitch.

"The sheriff sent me over," Ben said, his words and expression showing that he didn't want Sunny thinking this was his idea. "I believe you know Detective Fitch of the Portsmouth police."

Fitch's thin face looked more like a ferret's than ever—a ferret about to make a snack out of a baby mouse. But his voice was bland and official. "Ms. Coolidge, I'm asking you to accompany me down to the station. We have some additional questions to ask you about the murder of Martin Rigsdale."

Ollie's eyes went from the uniformed cop, to the detective, to Sunny. "Oh, yeah," he muttered. "Business as usual."

19

Sunny rode in Detective Fitch's car—in the back. "Procedure," he said.

At least he's not doing the bit where he presses down on the top of my head while I get in, Sunny thought ruefully.

They drove through town, with Ben Semple accompanying in his patrol car until they got to the bridge. Then Ben peeled off. *Sure,* Sunny thought. *Now I'm in Fitch's jurisdiction.*

The Portsmouth cop didn't gloat over Sunny's situation, or threaten, or even say much of anything. She shifted her perch on the back seat. *Guess he wants me to stew in my own juices until he gets me in the interrogation room.*

They arrived at the police station, and sure enough, Fitch escorted Sunny straight over to an interrogation room. She looked around at the acoustic tiles and the mirror at one end of the room. Was anybody watching behind there?

Fitch got her seated and then said, "Detective Trumbull will be with you in a minute."

I wonder if this means I'm getting the good-cop treatment, Sunny wondered. A moment later, Mark Trumbull came in carrying a file folder. His jacket was off, and the cuffs of his shirt were rolled up. Sunny could see the holstered pistol on his belt. His usual mournful expression shifted to a slight smile. "Thank you for coming down, Ms. Coolidge."

As if I really had a choice, Sunny thought.

Aloud she said, "It's a little unfortunate. The day my boss comes in after being away for a week, and I'm pulled away from work."

"Then I'll try to make it as brief as possible." Trumbull consulted his folder, although Sunny was pretty sure he had everything in there memorized by heart. "I understand you were the person who put Mrs. Rigsdale's attorney on the trail of Christine Venables."

"I wouldn't exactly put it that way," Sunny protested.

"How would you put it?" Trumbull asked. "You found a witness and told Mr. Phillips about her."

"I was in Portsmouth on business." Sunny had already decided not to mention what kind of business. "I stopped at a diner to pick up something for lunch. Martin Rigsdale's face was on the TV, and the waitress recognized him. We talked about it. She mentioned that he frequented the place. Apparently, he tried to pick up some of the wait-staff and later brought some female company of his own." Sunny tried to make her story as direct as possible.

"And did she identify those companions?" Trumbull

had his usual sorrows-of-the-world expression, but his eyes were sharp. "Did you?"

Does he think I primed the pump with a little information of my own? Sunny tried not to frown. *Or that I planted something?*

"The waitress didn't mention names." Sunny shrugged. "In fact, I can't remember hers, if she even gave it to me. But she described the women. One pretty much matched Dawn Featherstone—young, blond, athletic, very taken with Martin. The other was brunette, older, and more sophisticated. I didn't know who that was."

"You don't know Christine Venables?" Trumbull pressed, his eyes getting sharper.

"I only know the Venables name from local politics," Sunny answered. "If I'd caught a glimpse of her, on TV or out campaigning, I don't remember it. Until my dad pointed her out last night, I don't recall ever seeing Mrs. Venables before."

Trumbull pounced. "But you saw her last night?"

Sunny nodded. "We went to Martin Rigsdale's memorial service last night. My dad is kind of—well, he felt we had an obligation to go. That it would be traditional to pay our respects. We spoke briefly with Dawn Featherstone, and my father mingled with some folks he knew. We were just about ready to leave when my dad pointed out Christine Venables."

"So your father knew her," Trumbull said in the tone of a man trying to nail something down.

"He recognized her," Sunny said, loosening the nails a little. "But then, my dad is a lot more interested in local politics than I am."

The detective nodded. "Mrs. Venables is the wife of a Maine state representative." He tilted his head a little. "And this wouldn't involve any sort of political . . . activity on your father's part?"

Sunny had to fight back a flash of anger. *I don't care what you insinuate about me, but leave Dad out of it.*

"Dirty politics, you mean? That's not the kind of politics my father is interested in," she said flatly. "He just mentioned the name in passing. In fact, he wasn't even aware of my interest in Christine Venables. Jane had mentioned her name to me."

Trumbull settled back in his seat, frowning. "Yes, she told me about that."

Then why are you rehashing it with me? But Sunny didn't ask that question. She knew that the cop wasn't just asking for her story, he was also using it to check out Jane's. *Well, that should jibe with what Jane told you,* Sunny thought.

Trumbull sighed and placed both hands palms down on the table between them. "Well, unless you have anything else to add, I guess that covers what I wanted to know."

Sunny felt muscles in her back relax—muscles that she hadn't even been aware of tightening.

"One thing, though," the detective added in an offhand manner. "What brought you over to the station last night?"

Whoa, Jane is right. This guy is great with those old Columbo zingers. She couldn't see any way of sidestepping or coming up with a palatable answer. It would have to be the truth. "I got a call from a friend," she said, "Will Price.

He thought that Jane might have been taken into custody."

For just a second, Trumbull's features tightened, the merest disarrangement of his mournful mask. Heads would roll if he found out who'd spoken to Will. Sunny didn't know who Will's source was, and what she didn't know, she couldn't tell Mark Trumbull. "He didn't mention how he got that idea. But since we were comparatively nearby, we came to the station to see if Jane needed help."

Trumbull's oversized head gave the tiniest of shakes. "No, Mrs. Rigsdale had all the help she could possibly need."

"She was certainly glad to be getting back outside," Sunny told him. "I don't have to tell you that talking to the police, even if you're innocent, can be a pretty intense business."

The hint of a smile played around the detective's lips. "You seem to handle it well enough, Ms. Coolidge."

"I was a reporter," she replied. "I have some experience. Jane doesn't. All I'm saying is that she needed to be loosened up, and Tobe Phillips did that by reminding her of something stupid from twenty years ago." Sunny glanced at Trumbull. "I guess you know we were all in school together way back when. Anyhow, I think Jane overreacted—you know, the whole laughing in church kind of thing. If you start, it's hard to stop."

Very quickly, Detective Trumbull's face went to surprised, thoughtful, and wary . . . and then shut down into that sad, basset hound look again.

He's wondering why I mentioned that. Sunny did her

best to mask her own satisfaction. *Did I see him through the door last night, and how did he look? Enjoy that, Detective. You're not the only one who can throw a zinger.*

The moment ended with a knock on the door. Fitch came in with a sheaf of papers. "We finished checking out the Venables," he said. "The husband was definitely up in Augusta during the window of opportunity. He was doing some sort of legislative committee work with several other state representatives."

Fitch looked at his papers. "And the wife was home with her daughter."

Sunny looked sharply from one detective to the other. In her old job, she was all too familiar with leaks. Some happened accidentally and some were carefully planned and orchestrated. Her overhearing this had a strong smell of accidentally on purpose.

Had Trumbull and Fitch actually gotten alibis from the Venables family members, or was this misinformation? And if it was real, why were they discussing it in front of her? Was this to serve notice that, as Will had predicted, Trumbull was bursting to eliminate Christine Venables as a suspect so he could get back to nailing Jane?

Certainly, they have to expect that Jane and Tobe will hear about this. Sunny couldn't keep the wry look off her face. *They've got to know which side I'm on.*

Whatever mind games he was trying to pull, Trumbull was decent enough to arrange for a lift to get Sunny back to Kittery Harbor. She wound up in the back of another patrol car, perched on the edge of her seat. From some of the stories that Will told, who knew what could be lurking on the seats from previous occupants.

She was very glad to escape the perp's-eye view of life by the time the car arrived at the MAX office.

Unfortunately, Ollie the Barnacle was still there, seated behind her desk. He looked at the oversized, expensive watch on his wrist. "Two hours gone. If I'm a nice guy and subtract an hour for lunch, that means you still owe me an hour."

Sunny slipped off her parka. "And were there any important developments during my absence that you need to bring me up to speed on?"

He gave her a sour look. "Don't push it," he warned. "Damned phone didn't ring at all. Sometimes I wonder what I'm paying you for."

"You know that winter is our slow season," Sunny told him. "What you're paying me for is to have a human on hand to take care of things when they need to be taken care of."

As if on cue, the phone rang. Sunny reached across the desk to pick it up. She grinned as she listened. *Thank God, another shopping expedition to outlet-land.*

"And you'll need accommodations for how many?" she asked in her most professional voice. "A full busload—twenty-six people! Will they want motel or B&B lodgings?"

Sunny came around the desk, shooing Ollie away. He vacated the chair—making money was more important to him than comfort. Sunny began calling up pages on her computer, discussing locations and rates. By the time she was done, she looked up to discover that Ollie had quietly left.

Well, now he knew what he was paying her for. It wasn't the hours; it was what she knew.

Yeah, knowledge is power, Sunny thought, flopping back in her seat. *Too bad it's not money, too.*

*

Shadow lay on the topmost shelf of the bookcase, surveying his prison. It had been a good thing to work off some of his pent-up energy in climbing. And it was always good to be able to look down on everything around him.

He stared at the door between him and freedom. However hard he wished, though, it wouldn't fall down, or break, or just swing open. But the next time the One Who Reeks opened it . . .

Shadow tried to estimate the angles. If he pushed off from here with all his strength, how high would he be when he reached the other side of the room? If he were head high, he could go for the face of the human who imprisoned him. The last two times she'd come in, she'd been carrying food, so her hands would be occupied.

He blinked that thought away, pleasant as it might be to consider. It was a long, dangerous leap from up here to down there, and most likely he would be much lower by the time he reached her. If he landed on her clothes, he wouldn't be able to do much damage. And Shadow knew he'd have to hurt her, not just surprise her, if he really hoped to escape.

Finally, there was the thought of landing on her, of having to cling to the source of that awful stench . . .

He shuddered for a second, fighting to make that thought go away. Then, laying his head on his paws, he closed his eyes, trying to relax. Speaking of scents . . .

Maybe Shadow's sense of smell had suffered, being

trapped in close quarters with a human that emitted such an offensive odor. But up here, as he put his face close to the wooden shelving, he caught a trace of a different fragrance, a trace left by one of his own kind, not a human smell.

He rose on all four paws, nosing along the wood. Yes, definitely he was sniffing another cat. It reminded him of the scent of a she that he'd encountered down on the floor by the bowls. But he'd sensed sickness down there, pain and sickness nearly to death.

Then he realized. This was the scent of the she before she became ill. Yes, it made sense. A cat that sick wouldn't be able to climb any great height. This was where she had gone before she became weak.

He followed the spoor to the other side of the shelf, noticing it get stronger as he moved. Not only did she come up here, but she spent a lot of time coming up here.

Well, if I were trapped in a room like this, with a human like the One Who Reeks, maybe I'd look for the farthest place away.

Realization made him stop in his tracks. He *was* trapped, just as the she had been. Would sickness and death be his only escape?

He reared back at the thought, sitting on his haunches. And when he did, Shadow discovered the real reason the lost she had come up here. Somehow, he caught a whiff of fresh air!

Shadow peered up at the ceiling above him. It wasn't like the walls or floor—or the ceiling in Sunny's room, which he'd explored one day from the top of her bookcase. The noise she made when she found he'd left a paw print up there! But that had been all in one piece, solid and immovable. This ceiling, though, was broken into squares, with thick borders. Looking more closely, he saw seams at the end of those borders. That's where the trace of fresh air came from.

He stretched out a paw—no, still too short. So he pushed up with his rear legs. That was dangerous; it nearly sent him toppling to the floor. Was that what had happened to the she? Had she perhaps fallen and injured herself? Maybe she was just too short to reach that tantalizing square above.

But Shadow was longer than most cats. He backed up a little on the shelf and then extended his rear legs as strongly as he could, trying for a vertical jump while pressing up with his forepaws. He struck the rough-textured square—and it moved!

Again and again he tried, leaping at full extension, sometimes having to dance back desperately to avoid plunging off. A low guttural growl came from deep in his chest as he leaped, catching his claws in the rough-textured stuff . . .

He fell back again. But he had dislodged the square so that a narrow sliver of darkness showed above him.

A way out!

*

Sunny sat at her desk, watching the clock on the wall reach quitting time. At least, it would have been quitting time, except for the hour that Ollie the Barnacle was holding over her head.

Should I just call him now and say I'm staying late to pay off my debt?

She made a face, looking down at her computer screen. The problem was, nothing was happening now. No one would be calling or getting in touch when they expected the office to be closed. It wasn't just unfair, putting in an empty hour to make up for what Ollie had described as an empty hour. It seemed stupid.

"To hell with this," Sunny muttered, closing down her computer and then the office. Standing outside, she still felt rebellious—ready to do something stupid. So she left her Wrangler parked on the street and started walking toward the harbor.

The weather was milder this evening, and the wind had died down. When Sunny reached Spill the Beans, the café had a lot more people. Sunny could care less—she didn't want a table; she just wanted a whoopie pie. All they had to do was sell her one, maybe put it in a bag so she could carry it to eat on the drive home.

Sunny looked around to ask if they did takeout—and froze. The table in the corner, the one where she and Will had sat and talked, was occupied by people she knew. Jane Rigsdale and Tobe Phillips sat with their knees touching below the tiny little tabletop, and their faces nearly touching above.

They burst into laughter. *Seems as if they do that a lot,* the tough reporter in the back of Sunny's brain commented. And she couldn't fail to notice the high color in both their cheeks. *I don't think that's from the coffee—or from the overhead heater.*

A waitress finally noticed her and came over. "How may I help you?" she asked.

Sunny shook her head. "You know, I don't think you can."

She got out of there. Better to leave the two some privacy. The whoopie pie would have to wait.

20

Before going up into the darkness overhead, Shadow
climbed down to the floor, to the food and water bowls.
Better to finish off what he had before venturing into the
unknown. With a full belly, he scaled the shelves again.
Then he positioned himself under the opening he'd created
and leaped. After a brief, undignified scrabble, he was up
in a dim world, sneezing. Well, he'd learned one thing: the
unknown was dusty.

Using his forepaw, he batted at the square he'd dislodged. Finally, he managed to get it back in place. That
made the dimness darker. But unless the One Who Reeks
could track by scent, she wouldn't know where he'd gone.

Shadow set off across this new domain, walking slowly
and carefully. Now that they were underfoot, the squares
that made up the ceiling tended to give alarmingly as he

stepped on them. By trial and error, he learned where to put his weight—and where not to.

Then he raised his head, trying to follow the crosscurrents of air up here. He also flicked his ears around. There was some sort of low, machine-made noise ahead and off to the left.

Shadow padded along gingerly, letting the sound get louder until he came to the source, a boxy metal construction that stretched off on either side into the darkness. When he extended a paw, Shadow found it was warm to the touch and let off a low, droning vibration. When he climbed on top, it felt a little bit like the refrigerator back in Sunny's house.

For a second, he felt so low, he wanted to yowl.

Oh, Sunny! Why did I leave you? Nothing has been good since. If I could come back, I wouldn't mind the Old One's friend bringing the Biscuit Eater around. You could have a house full of Biscuit Eaters, so long as I had you.

But then he roused himself. This was no time to give in to feelings. If he wanted to get back to Sunny, he had to get out of here first. This metal was much steadier underfoot than the squares. He'd follow this pathway and see where it led.

The first place it led was to a wall—a very solid wall. But a hole had been roughly cut through it to accommodate the metal path, and by pressing himself almost flat against the metal, Shadow managed to squeeze through the jagged opening. It was dirty work, and when Shadow reached the other side, he paused for a moment to try and clean himself. That tasted terrible. He quickly gave up the attempt.

Who knew what other unpleasant things he'd have to crawl through to get out of here?

Shadow closed his eyes, trying to get a sense of this new space. There must be a bigger room below. He heard music, muffled by the squares of the ceiling, and a stronger sense of the stink coming off the One Who Reeks. Either she spent a lot of time in the room under his feet, or she was there now.

Taking care to be silent, he continued along the path.

It was many more steps before he came to another wall, this one flimsier. He was able to claw himself a bigger opening to get through. But a short journey after that, he came to a dead end. The metal path he'd been following didn't go through this wall, it went into it. Tapping and scratching showed this was a formidable wall, indeed. And when Shadow crouched to examine where the metal went into the wall, he smelled clean air, sweet, fresh . . . and chilly. Beyond this wall was the outside world. The problem was, there was no way he could get through.

He shook himself philosophically. This was only one end of the path. Where did the other go?

Turning around, he retraced his steps until he reached the room where he'd been incarcerated. He heard a voice below, calling his name, getting louder and angrier. He recognized that screech. It was the One Who Reeks. He lay silent as he heard the voice again, calling to him, making kissing noises. From the sound of it, the One Who Reeks was moving among several rooms. So she realized that, somehow, he'd gotten out of the room. He heard the sound of full bowls tapping together and suffered a moment of temptation that was easily fought off. It was better to crouch up here in the dark, dusty and hungry, than to put up with that one below.

*

Sunny came home to find Mike and Mrs. Martinson sitting on the couch, a bit of space between them. But from the self-satisfied look on Mike's face, they'd probably been a lot closer before Sunny's key rattled in the lock. Mrs. M. just ran a hand through her hair, looking prim and proper.

I guess without Shadow around to cramp his style, Dad's getting a lot luckier these days. The flip comment from Sunny's reporter alter ego failed to amuse. It just reminded Sunny that Shadow was gone, and that the new normal was also lonelier. At least for her.

Still, she tried to look cheerful, engaging in a little chitchat.

"George Welling is debating putting an addition on his house," Mike announced. "Between his son who's finished college and can't afford to move out, and a mother-in-law who had to move in, he's running out of space."

Helena Martinson nodded. "A lot of people who thought they'd be facing empty nests are finding them filling up again nowadays."

Sunny didn't say anything to that, painfully aware that she was one of those birdies who'd been forced home to roost.

Maybe Mike realized that, too, because he quickly shifted the topic. "Anyhow, George was talking about Allerton Contractors—"

"More likely he was hearing about them from Carolyn

Dowdey." Mrs. Martinson pursed her lips in disapproval. "She tells everyone that Joe Allerton is a wonderful builder. I'm afraid he's more of a wonderful actor, always very deferential when Carolyn is around."

"From what I've seen of her, she'd like that a lot," Sunny said.

Helena nodded. "You think she'd have more sense, but I'm sorry to say you're right. She recommended Joe to Martin Rigsdale when he built that new office. I wonder how that turned out."

"It looked pretty good—what I could see of it." Sunny remembered some of the comments Dani Shostak had made about Martin getting into his financial hole. "I think it might have turned out more expensive than anticipated, though."

"That's usually the case with Joe Allerton," Mrs. M. said grimly. "And however nice it looks, you can bet he cut corners wherever it didn't show." She shook her head. "And the people he works with! The Dowdey place was a nice, classic Colonial house. But the architect Joe brought in added this *thing* to the side of the house where everyone has to see it. He didn't even have the decency to hide it in the backyard."

"A thing?" Mike asked, taking the words right out of Sunny's mouth.

"Makes it looks as if a house from here had a head-on collision with one of those glass and cedar places you see in California," Helena complained. "It's one thing to add a sunroom or maybe enlarge the kitchen, but it seems just vulgar to tack a whole wing onto a house—especially when it's a completely different style."

She sighed. "They put drop ceilings in to give it a more 'intimate' feeling, and added a new fireplace for the family room. Not that there's any family. Carolyn is alone in the place. But it's very modern, and she tells everyone that she loves it."

"So long as it makes her happy," Sunny offered with a shrug.

Mrs. M. looked doubtful. "I'm not sure Carolyn knows what might make her happy anymore."

She stopped, suddenly self-conscious, and looked at her watch. "I don't know where the time goes when I sit with you, Mike. I should be working on my supper."

"And so should we, I guess." Sunny said good-bye and headed back to the kitchen to start whipping up a meal, giving her dad and Helena Martinson some privacy for a warmer farewell.

Later, at dinner, Mike asked his usual half-jocular question: "Anything exciting happen today?"

"Well, I got hauled off to the Portsmouth hoosegow for a while," Sunny told him. "Detective Trumbull wanted to ask me some questions, and did it in the most disruptive way possible—damn!" She broke off.

"Finally think of something good to say to him?" Mike joked.

"No, it's something I should have said to somebody else." After dealing with Ollie and proving she had a job to do, she hadn't contacted Jane or Tobe about Trumbull's game playing.

And they were right in front of me at Spill the Beans. Sunny shook her head. *I must really be losing it.*

On the other hand, she didn't know if they'd have welcomed the interruption. It hadn't looked like a legal consultation to her.

"Would you mind dealing with the dishes tonight?" she asked Mike. "I have to go upstairs and make a phone call."

Jane picked up her home phone when Sunny punched in the number. *So I guess coffee after work didn't turn into something more elaborate—unless Tobe is sitting there beside her.*

"Sunny!" Jane said. "What's up?"

I was wondering the same about you. But Sunny quickly quashed that thought. "Trumbull had me come down to the station today."

"The guy just doesn't stop, does he?" Sunny could imagine Jane scowling on the other end of the line. Then, "Are you okay?"

"They didn't bring out the rubber hose," Sunny told her. "Fitch was his usual sunny self, but he didn't give me much attitude. Trumbull tried to pick my story apart when I told him about meeting the waitress, but all in all, he was just double-checking."

"Even so, it can't have been fun." Jane spoke with the certainty of someone who'd gone through a real interrogation. "I'm sorry you had to get hauled off. Seems to me he could have come to you, or even sent Fitch to ask his questions."

"He could have," Sunny said. "But I think he had another reason for getting me down there."

She described the byplay between Fitch and Trumbull. "They had no reason to discuss alibis in front of me," Sunny finished. "And knowing that I'm friendly with you, they had good reason not to."

"Unless they wanted me to hear about it." Jane's voice grew tight. "If he's crossed Ralph and Christine Venables off his suspect list, then he'll be coming after me again."

"If." Sunny emphasized the word. "The thing is, police can lie."

"So we've got to check up on those alibis right away," Jane said. "I've got to call Tobe." But instead of hanging up, she paused. "How would you feel about an undercover assignment?"

"Questioning Ralph or Christine? I don't think that's a good idea," Sunny said.

"Actually, I was thinking you might have a chat with their daughter, Kristi." Jane rushed on before Sunny could interrupt with objections. "I happen to know where she'll be from about noon till one tomorrow. I always bump into her at the beauty salon."

"It's a small world," Sunny said. *And a weird one,* she silently added. This Kristi kid is supposed to be unemployed. How can she afford a weekly visit to a pricey salon? It must be nice to have well-off parents. For that matter, why would someone as gorgeous as Jane need such regular beauty treatments?

"I can switch you into my appointment," Jane went on, her enthusiasm growing. "And you can do your reporter thing on her. It would be perfect. And you know you need a trim, Sunny. Come on. I'll pick up the tab."

"All right," Sunny capitulated. "On one condition. You'll have to cover for me at the office. If any important calls come in, you'll have to get me on my cell."

They made the necessary arrangements, with Sunny silently shaking her head. If Ollie Barnstable caught wind of this, she'd probably end up owing him a week's work.

*

The next morning went smoothly enough. The good news was that Ollie didn't turn up to try and make life difficult. Jane arrived at the office early, so Sunny had a chance to get her set up comfortably. Then Sunny got in her Wrangler and headed for the salon. The place was actually on the outskirts of Saxon, the next town up the coast, which in recent years had gone considerably upscale, and this beauty parlor was definitely part of that process. It wasn't just a hairdressing establishment anymore; it was a day spa—not that Sunny had a day to spend there.

She sat in a gown provided by the management, waiting for her shampoo and looking over the other clients. Kristi Venables was easy to spot. Most of the customers were somewhat older than Sunny. Kristi looked like a younger edition of her mom, her face perhaps a bit plumper, with the start of bags under her eyes.

No wonder she's in here every week, that critical voice in the back of Sunny's head whispered. *Either she's out partying all night, or she's up worrying.*

As the two youngest people waiting for treatments, it was easy enough to strike up a conversation with Kristi. "It's nice to get away from the job for a little bit, even if it's only a long lunch hour," Sunny said.

Kristi sighed. "I just wish I had a job to get away from. When I graduated college, I thought I was lucky, scoring a public relations gig in Boston. I thought the two summers I'd worked for them as an unpaid intern were paying off."

She scowled. "But then they laid off my whole department, I couldn't keep my place in Boston, and I ended up back here with my folks. Do you know how hard it is to get a PR job around these parts?"

Actually, Sunny did. When she couldn't find any journalism work, she had made the rounds for any job that might use her skills at writing copy. "You probably have a better shot than a lot of people," she said, trying to put some sympathy in her voice. "You've got some experience, but not so much that you'd price yourself out of the market here."

Kristi looked a little surprised. "I never thought of it that way. All I'd see when I went on interviews was a lot of people with better résumés than mine."

"A better résumé doesn't necessarily get you a job—not when a company figures you'll be out the door as soon as you can use that résumé to find a better salary." She'd had several interviews where she'd heard as much. "You just have to keep trying."

"That's for sure," Kristi said. "I hate depending on my mom and dad for everything. I'm even on their insurance again. I kinda need it, since I have asthma. That doesn't mean I have to like it."

She looked very young for a moment. "Most of the time, it's not like I'm even with them. Dad's away in Augusta, 'running the state,' as he likes to say. And Mom isn't home much. Sometimes I think they just don't like to see me hanging around."

"Maybe we just majored in the wrong stuff in college," Sunny suggested with a smile. "We should have gone out for something more practical, like being a vet."

Kristi laughed. "I don't think my allergies would let me do that. And maybe it's more dangerous than you think. A vet got killed in Portsmouth last week! My mom used to bring our dog to him, and do you know what? The cops came yesterday, asking questions. I guess they must be getting desperate if they thought my mom could tell them anything."

Sunny kept her voice light. "What was it like? Were they all, 'Where were you on the night of the twenty-third?'"

She did her best cop voice, and Kristi laughed again. "You know, you're pretty close. They did ask where Mom had been, but as it turns out, she was home with me all evening. She was supposed to go out, but then she didn't."

The girl looked a little embarrassed. "It's the first time I ever saw it happen. Mom opened a bottle of wine—and finished it. I had to put her to bed. She was out like a light"

21

Sunny returned to the office feeling a little bit lighter and definitely more stylish. Her stylishness factor declined considerably when she saw Jane sitting behind her desk. The office furniture might be on the beaten-up side and the computer was definitely last generation, but Jane looked high-fashion and perfectly groomed in spite of missing out on her weekly beauty fix.

"I'm back," Sunny announced as she opened the door. "Please tell me that Ollie didn't stop by."

"*Nobody* stopped by," Jane told her. "The phone didn't ring. This was the quietest hour and change I've spent in I don't know how long."

"I'm surprised," Sunny said with a grin. "With you in the window, I'd have expected our foot traffic to go up a couple of hundred percent."

Jane gave her a skeptical look. "When you start spreading it that thick, I know you're setting me up for bad news."

Sunny shrugged. "It looks as if Trumbull isn't playing head games. The police did talk with the Venables family, and Kristi did indeed give her mom an alibi."

Jane slumped in the desk chair, her hands clasped together way too tight. "That means he'll be coming after me again. I guess the only thing that's slowing him down is that he can't put me in Portsmouth at the time of the murder."

"Maybe that's because you weren't," Sunny pointed out. "Your car—"

"Do you know that he's had people out at Sal DiGillio's checking the repair records on my BMW?" Jane interrupted. "I wouldn't be surprised if he got his hands on the tire, trying to prove that I gave myself a flat to create an alibi." She shook her head. "This guy is relentless, Sunny. Sooner or later, he'll find something he can twist into a reason to bring me back to that station again, and Tobe won't be able to stop him."

She shuddered. "And even if Trumbull doesn't succeed, I still have Dani and Olek busily trying to ruin my life. It's as if everywhere I look, I've got someone coming after me." Jane got out of the chair. "I have to talk to Tobe."

Sunny watched her friend go out the door. *She seems to be seeing a lot of Tobe lately.*

*

Business picked up after Jane left. Sunny spent the afternoon looking at e-mails, answering the phone, and booking several B&B reservations. The shadows were getting pretty long outside when the phone rang and she found Will on the other end. "I'm just on a break," he said quickly. "Would you like to grab a bite this evening? There's a new place that's supposed to be like a New York restaurant."

"Sure," Sunny replied. Since it was a school night, they set an early date. Sunny finished her work, closed up the place, and went home to check in with her dad.

Mike was delighted that she was going out. "I can make myself soup and a sandwich," he assured her. "Have a good time."

Sunny put on a nicer sweater than the one she'd worn to work, a soft wool number in a purplish tweed. Then she put on some makeup and waited for Will.

The place he was talking about turned out to be up in outlet-land, which should have been a warning. When they got there, Sunny realized it had formerly been a burger place that failed. Now it had a new sign, HOLLBECK'S NEW YORK DELI.

Oh yeah, she thought wryly, *very New York.*

The interior hadn't changed very much from the joint's burger-slinging days, a lot of white tile and stainless steel with very bright lights. It was also pretty loud, even though the weeknight diners didn't crowd the place.

A waitress gave them a menu that would have looked more at home in a diner. But there were deli foods that Sunny remembered from her time in New York. "I'll have the brisket platter," she decided. Will went with corned beef and cabbage. When the food arrived, Sunny found that her brisket had been cooked in tomato sauce—not necessarily bad, but definitely not New York style. On the other hand, the beer—Sam Adams—was decent, and cold.

Will took a long pull from his bottle. "I'm worried about Jane and this Phillips guy," he abruptly said.

Sunny tilted her head, a little taken aback by the dinner conversation. "You put them together."

Will winced at her response. "I put them together professionally. But they seem to be hanging out a lot. Ben Semple saw them in a café, acting awfully friendly."

"Well, friendships have been known to come out of professional connections," Sunny pointed out. "They did know each other years ago. They could be catching up from old times."

"Uh-huh." Will took a forkful of corned beef. From the look on his face, Sunny would have thought it was rancid.

"And Jane has been under a lot of stress. It's not surprising she might lean a little on the guy who's helping her out."

Will nodded, conceding the point, but he still looked discontented. "Yeah, but—"

"You know, Will, it's nice to be invited to this real New York experience." Sunny gestured toward the glaring lights and the loud, echoing noise in the restaurant. "But if you're going to take me out and then whine about Jane going around with some other guy, you've got another think coming. This isn't high school. We're adults now—supposedly."

She looked him in the face. He swallowed hard, showing a little embarrassment and a lot of shame.

"It's not that," he began and made a jerky gesture with his hand. "Okay. It probably is a little of that. I'm worried that they're getting a little . . . distracted from what they need to be doing."

"You mean, they're pissing Trumbull off instead of persuading him to look for other suspects?" Sunny said.

Will nodded.

"Well, he certainly did his best to dispose of Christine Venables and her family." She told him about her interrogation and the information that the detectives had dropped.

"I thought they might have been playing me, making up a story to get Jane rattled," she went on. "But it looks as if the information was legit. I talked to Christine's alibi." She gave him a quick recap of her undercover haircut.

Will frowned, toying with his fork. Sunny thought he was going to lecture her about butting into Trumbull's case. Instead, he said, "What they told you could have been only half true. Phillips should definitely check out the husband."

Sunny nodded. "I expect he's doing that."

"As for the daughter, well, that's what we call an unreliable alibi," Will went on slowly. "The girl is out of work, depending on her mom for a place to live, and you say she has a medical condition covered by her parents' insurance?"

"That's right," Sunny said.

"So she's really dependent. Kristi may have given her mother an alibi because she doesn't want to upset the family applecart. Or if she's aware of Christine's relationship with Martin Rigsdale, maybe she's trying to avoid a scandal."

"So you're saying the alibi isn't as strong as it sounds?"

"Yeah." Will speared another slice of corned beef as if he were hunting it rather than eating it. "That's the kind of question a district attorney would consider, trying to decide if he had a strong enough case to bring to court."

"From Trumbull's point of view, it looks as if Jane is guilty until she proves herself innocent."

Will nodded in agreement. "Like it or not, she's a strong suspect. Most murders happen over love or money. Martin humiliated Jane in one and was pestering her about the other. It's a two-fer. No wonder Trumbull likes it."

He dipped his corned beef in a dollop of mustard, brought it to his mouth, and chewed, looking unhappy as he swallowed. "That's why Phillips really has to be on his game."

"No distractions." Sunny had some of her brisket. All of a sudden, it seemed pretty tasteless.

Somehow, they struggled through the rest of the meal on small talk. As a dating experience, Sunny would not list it among her top ten.

As they headed out for Will's pickup, he turned to her. "I'm sorry if I said anything stupid. I like you, Sunny, and I enjoy being with you. I don't want our time together to be a drag."

"You had things on your mind, and so did I," she said. "It's not a big deal—if we don't let it be."

He smiled. "You've got a good way of putting things."

They got into the pickup, and Sunny's phone rang. It was Jane, her voice very shaky. "Could you come over—now? I've got a bit of a situation here."

"On the way," Sunny replied. Jane cut the connection before Sunny could ask any questions.

She turned to Will, who had his cop face on.

"That was Jane," Sunny said. "I hate to ask this, but can you give me a lift to her place?"

"She's in trouble?" Will asked.

"I don't know," Sunny had to admit.

"Well, we'll both find out." Will started up the truck and headed for Jane's house.

Jane answered the door wearing one of her veterinarian's smocks. "Oh, thank God, Sunny."

She broke off when she realized Will was standing there, too. "Why—" Jane began.

"We were out catching a bite to eat," Sunny said, "And we came right over when your call came through."

"If I'd known that, I'd never have bothered you." Jane took Sunny by the arm, lowering her voice. "I don't know how we'll do it with Will around, but I need you to talk some sense into Tobe. He wants to go to the police."

"He's here?" Sunny said.

Jane sighed and led her to the kitchen. Will trailed behind, looking a bit wary.

Tobe Phillips sat at the kitchen counter, holding a bag of frozen corn to his face. He took it away, wincing, and shifted to a new section. In the process, he revealed an ominous swelling below his left eye and a cut on his cheek. Jane quickly put down a tray with a pair of medical gloves, a tube of antiseptic ointment, and a small bandage. She moved the frost-covered bag away from Tobe's face and examined his eye.

"What happened?" Will asked.

"Don't tell him," Jane begged.

"Of course I'm going to tell him," Tobe replied. "I still have to report this to the police."

"This is a police matter?" Will's voice went flat.

"For the Portsmouth police," Tobe explained. "A case of assault."

Will glanced from Tobe to Jane, looking baffled. "You assaulted him, and now you're trying to treat him?"

Is that even kosher for a vet to do? Sunny wondered as Jane whirled around, stung.

"You think I did this to him?" Her voice was way too loud. Jane took a deep breath, and when she spoke again, her voice was quiet and professional. "I'm just trying to make sure he's all right." She turned to look into Tobe's eyes. "Okay. Your pupils are the same size. I don't think we have to worry about a concussion. You didn't vomit or lose any memory."

"I might wish I could forget it," Tobe said. "It was embarrassing. The guy didn't even knock me out—he just landed me on my butt."

"Who did it and where?" Will's cop persona was definitely taking over.

"This big guy," Tobe replied. "And it happened in Portsmouth. Jane called me, pretty concerned about the way the police were taking this case. I took her out to dinner, and we discussed things."

From the look on Will's face, all of a sudden his corned beef wasn't agreeing with him.

"I was walking Jane back to her car," Tobe continued, "when I noticed someone following us, a big guy. When I asked him what he was doing, he sort of blinked, like he wasn't sure what to do. But he made up his mind damn quick. He punched me out and then walked away."

"It was Olek," Jane whispered to Sunny. "I guess Dani told him to keep an eye on me."

Remembering how Olek had to call in when he found

himself being followed, Sunny suspected the big guy was better at following orders than thinking on his feet. Confronted by Tobe and lacking instructions, Olek had done the best he could think of—knocking Tobe down and getting out of there. Simple but efficient in its way.

Unfortunately, Will had overheard. "Olek?" he repeated. "Dani? You mean Olek Linko and Danilo Shostak, the Ukrainian mobsters?"

"I, uh . . ." Jane wilted under Will's interrogation. "I guess so."

"How do you know them?" Will demanded.

"Who is this Olek character?" Tobe said at the same time.

As Jane stumbled through the story, Will pinned Sunny in place with a glare. "I see you left a few facts out when you told me about these guys."

Tobe's face was so pale, his incipient shiner stood out like a blotch on his face. "Ukrainian gangsters? Stolen money? And you didn't even mention it?"

"It's something we don't want to bring attention to." Sunny tried to explain why.

"I don't know if I can just sweep this under the rug," Tobe said. "I'm an officer of the court."

"And I'm an officer of the law," Will added savagely. "You realize that if Martin stole from them, these guys could have killed him? Look what this Olek guy did to Tobe with one shot." He gave the lawyer a condescending smile. "I don't suppose you're used to that kind of rough-and-tumble."

"Don't flatter yourself," Sunny warned Will. "He'd have planted you on the pavement, too. If you want to go up against Olek, I'd suggest hitting him with a truck first. But I don't think they killed Martin."

"Why?" Will ground the word out. "Because they told you nicely?"

"Because they're still looking for the money," Sunny answered.

Will scowled. "So they say." He turned to Jane. "In the meantime, they're trying to extort the same amount from you? Did it occur to you that they're just trying to double their money? They're gangsters, after all."

"If you'd excuse my saying so, I think you're wrong," Tobe said slowly, putting the frozen bag back on his face. "From what you've told me of his history, this Danilo fellow seems to be allergic to trouble. But a murder connected to his operation would bring attention in spades. In my experience—and I have dealt with some organized crime types—if he was guilty, he'd have gotten out of town. If not, there has to be a reason for taking the risk—and that has to be the missing money."

"Fine, fine," Will almost snarled. "So the money is still in play. What are we going to do about these guys?"

Now it was Tobe's turn to go poker-faced—not easy, with vegetables covering half of it. "I think I'm going to play the attorney-client privilege card." He gave Will a hard look with his good eye. "As you said, these guys are gangsters. Can you guarantee Jane and Sunny's safety if you go after them?"

Will stood for a moment with his mouth open, then closed it with a snap. "All right," he said, obviously hating every word. "We'll keep it quiet for now. I hope you're right. Otherwise, I can lose my job."

Hey, I could lose my life, Sunny almost said, but then thought better of it. But one look in Will's eyes showed he was thinking the same thing.

"I'm sorry, Will," Jane said. "We really didn't know what to do."

Will took a deep breath and then let it out forcibly through his nose. "You'd better get to work fixing Tobe's face," he advised. "I think you're going to have a shiner, but let's try to minimize the damage as much as possible."

Jane carefully examined the cut, cleaning the broken skin. Then she covered it with a layer of ointment and topped it with a little bandage. "Try icing it as much as possible," she advised, "just don't rest anything cold on the eye itself. And if you feel sick or dizzy, go see a doctor. A people doctor," she added with a strained smile.

"The other thing—you want to pick someplace where you fell, unless you want to say you walked into a door." Will's eyes were keen as he looked at Tobe. "Did anybody see this happen?"

Tobe shook his head. "It was a quiet street, and Jane bundled me into her car pretty quickly."

"That's good," Will said. "Just decide on your story and stick to it. Now I have to get Sunny home. Then I'll come back and drive you to Portsmouth."

"You don't have to do that," Tobe said. "I can call a cab."

"Sure you can," Will told him, "if you want a witness and a record. Do you have a house or an apartment where people will see you?"

"Nope, I just closed on a house." Tobe shifted the improvised ice pack again. "So that's lucky."

"Yeah." Will looked from Sunny back to the front door. "We'd better get going."

The air outside was getting cold again, but it was even frostier inside Will's pickup. They drove in silence for a while, until Sunny finally cracked. "I didn't want to tell you unless I had to," she said. "I was trying to keep you from falling into this nonsense."

"Uh-huh." Will's voice was toneless "I figured I'd better get you alone in case there were any other surprises you had for me. Stuff that Jane's lawyer shouldn't hear."

"No, that's it, I promise," Sunny assured him. "And from the way you're acting, you can see I did it for your own good."

He made a wordless noise, then glanced over at her. "Well, I guess this trumps taking you out and then—what was the word?—'whining' over an old girlfriend."

Sunny jerked up straight in her seat. "You're keeping score now?"

Will gave her a rueful smile. "Apparently, it's the closest I can come to keeping track of you."

They arrived at Sunny's house, and she gave him an impulsive kiss on the cheek. "I really am sorry."

Will looked at her for a long moment. "I wish you could expand on that." Sunny wasn't sure whether he meant the apology or the kiss. Then he went to open the door. "Got to ferry Tobe home."

Sunny laughed. "There's a ride where I'd like to be a fly on the wall. Don't give him a shiner on the other eye."

Will waited till Sunny was in the doorway. She waved good-bye and came into an empty downstairs. As he always did when Sunny went out, Mike had gone up early, leaving the living room lights on. Lately, though, when she'd come home from a date, Sunny had found a reception committee. Shadow had always greeted her.

Can't think of that now, she thought. *Got to get some sleep.*

*

The next morning, Sunny groaned as she got out of bed. She'd hit the hay early enough, but her mind had kept racing around in circles. And then she'd had weird dreams, where Olek got in a fight with Shadow, and Shadow had knocked him down.

When Sunny came down the stairs, she found that Mike had made breakfast—a good thing. But he obviously hoped to hear something about last night. Sighing, Sunny gave him the whole story.

Mike stared. "You know, I've lived here all my life, and I never met people like you're talking about."

"Well, you were away a lot." Sunny dropped the flip reply when she saw the look on her dad's face. Yeah, thanks to his job Mike hadn't been around for a lot of things . . . like the accident that took his wife's life. "I mean, you've been lucky, Dad. These are people you wouldn't want to run into. Besides, they're Portsmouth people."

The appeal to local pride won out. "Portsmouth," Mike said in dismissive tones, as if that explained everything.

Sunny arrived at the office and settled into the usual Friday routine, where crowds of shoppers and couples called in with last-minute checks or disasters en route, and Sunny did her best to help them.

In a way, it was a comforting routine. Sunny was just sort of puttering mindlessly along when the office door opened and Dani Shostak came in. She sat, gawking, as he came up to her desk.

"The police, they start now to ask questions about the Dr. Rigsdale's money," he said. "Very soon now, I have to go somewhere like Montreal. I'd like to have my money back before I go there. Much less trouble."

He tilted his head a little, his long, thin face contemplating Sunny. "You think whoever it was killed the doctor, they took the money? I keep on thinking it might still be in his house or office, but Olek says no. For a fellow with his size, he is very good at getting into places."

"I'd say Olek is good at a lot of things," Sunny said. "I just wonder if he went a little farther than he intended, asking Martin about the money."

"Olek?" Dani shook his head. "One of the things he's best at is hitting people. Look at that young fellow last night. Olek hits him just enough so it looks like maybe he falls down instead of getting punched. He is professional. He would be very hurt to hear you say these things."

"I'm afraid I'll have to hurt your feelings more," Sunny told him. "I find myself wondering if Martin stole from you, you got your money back and killed him, and now you're trying to double your money by going to Martin's ex-wife."

"That's a smart idea," Dani said. "I wonder if you get it from your cop boyfriend."

Sunny forced herself to keep looking into Dani's eyes, and not show her surprise that he knew about Will. She'd been out with Will often enough; anyone could have spotted them together. It was just a little unsettling that she had missed either the big Ukrainian or his skinny boss.

I guess there are things they're good at.

"Well, I suppose these are things you must wonder. Some people I have done business with, they might do bad things like that. Me, I think that just makes trouble. I think maybe you believe me."

He spread his hands, a man trying to make a point in a language that wasn't his own. Then his face got a little chilly, his manner more direct. "But I got to have that much money. Or *I* end up in trouble."

Dani nodded emphatically and went to the door, to discover Mrs. Martinson standing right outside. Dani opened the door and ushered her in with a little bow.

"Thank you," Mrs. M. said.

She got another bow from Dani, and then he was on his way.

Sunny shook her head. *You've got to appreciate a gangster with manners.*

"So what brings you to this neck of the woods?" Sunny asked. "Are you picking up something at Judson's?"

Helena Martinson shook her head. "I promised you I'd do some more quiet asking around about Christine Venables. Well, I heard something, very much in confidence. A friend of mine had been shopping in some of the Portsmouth art galleries a few weeks ago. She stopped off to have a cup of coffee in a little place in the artsy area. Anyway, she had just finished and was heading for the door when she noticed Christine in a quiet corner."

"She hadn't seen her before?" Sunny asked.

"That's the thing that first struck my friend. She'd been

sitting with her back to Christine, but Christine should have noticed her." Helena cocked her head. "Let's just say my friend is hard to miss. Christine could have stopped by to say hello—if she'd wanted to."

Sunny nodded. "So maybe something was up."

"My friend didn't think about it at the time. She was almost to the door. Why should she go plowing back through this place to get to Christine?" The older woman leaned forward confidentially. "Actually, she was going to. But then her cell phone rang, so she stepped outside to answer it. That should have been the end of the story."

From the lift in Mrs. Martinson's voice, Sunny knew to add, "Except . . ."

"My friend crossed the street, walking back to her car. And who does she see opposite her, going into the café, but Martin Rigsdale?"

Sunny frowned in thought. "Did your friend mention the name of this café?"

Mrs. M. pursed her lips. "From the neighborhood, it had to be something to do with painting . . . or wells."

"Wells?" Sunny echoed blankly.

"Café Artisan," Helena Martinson suddenly said. "Whenever I hear the name, I think of artesian wells."

"As long as it helps you remember," Sunny told her, chuckling.

But her neighbor didn't join in. Instead, Helena looked troubled. "There's something else I should mention. Another friend of mine was up in the outlets last week. She mentioned seeing Carolyn Dowdey at that pet care place with a cat bed and a bag of food."

"Well, we know it wasn't a sale that brought her in,"

Sunny said. "Maybe she's getting an early start on preparing for that replacement cat she discussed with Jane."

"Sunny, that pet adoption class isn't for another month." Mrs. Martinson's voice was troubled as she spoke. "You know that Carolyn isn't exactly what you'd call retiring. Whenever she got a cat, she quoted chapter and verse from this book on how to get the animals to trust you. It was all about setting aside an empty room where the cat was supposed to get acclimated, providing a bed where the cat could be private, and sitting in the room while they ate."

The longer she talked, the blunter Helena became. "This all happened since Shadow got out and went missing."

Sunny blinked. "You think she's trying to forcibly adopt my cat?"

"Carolyn got something else," Mrs. Martinson went on, "one of those wooly pet sweaters."

This revelation almost got a laugh from Sunny. Shadow was about as likely to wear one of those frou-frou outfits as her dad was to don a ballet tutu. "I don't think—" she began.

But her neighbor wasn't finished. "And she asked how it would look on a gray-striped cat."

22

Long after Mrs. Martinson left the office, Sunny sat at her desk, getting nothing done. Her mind kept skittering between the two facts that Mrs. M. had dropped on her.

Maybe I should be glad to hear that Shadow is all right, that he's not freezing out in the woods somewhere. But that thought didn't give her comfort. The image of Shadow locked in a room somewhere kept rising up in her mind's eye. And the idea that he'd be kept there until he started acting like a well-behaved pet . . . Shadow had been part of Sunny's life for months now. She knew him well enough to be sure that he'd never go along with such a plan. He'd try to escape, no matter how dangerous the route. Or by the time this plan was done, he wouldn't be Shadow anymore.

With her elbows on the desk, Sunny leaned her forehead

into her hands. Her head seemed to be pounding with more thoughts than it could hold.

Besides worrying about Shadow, Sunny's brain wouldn't let go of the other story her neighbor had told, about Christine Venables and her secret rendezvous with Martin Rigsdale. Somehow, that had to be useful. Throw it in the pot with motive and an unreliable alibi, and what kind of stew did that make?

The evening shadows came, and so did a few calls from clients with last-minute glitches. Sunny took care of the problems, almost glad for the distraction. But by the time she closed up the office, she felt a strange peace. She'd come to a decision. This plan might end up with her flat on her face, but it was the only way she could test her suspicions. She'd have to try the frontal assault.

So, when she locked up the office, Sunny set off for scenic Piney Brook, as she had always found it described in her tourist information. The area was beautiful, really, even on a chilly Friday evening. The houses out here were mansions in all but name, not merely big like some of the monstrosities going up on the edge of town, but well built and well designed. Like the families who'd lived here for generations, these houses were solid—they belonged.

You could probably lump three homes like mine into one of these, she thought, pulling up at the address she'd gotten from her computer. *And you'd probably still have some room left over.*

She got out of the car and walked to the front door. It was a Friday evening, date night, so there was a good chance Kristi wasn't in. As for the rest . . . Sunny banked everything on the idea that Christine Venables would follow the Kittery Harbor Way, rich folks edition. She'd have cleaning staff, but not actual servants.

Sunny's bet turned out right. She rang the doorbell, and Christine herself answered the door. The woman was dressed in a subdued gray sweater and a darker pair of wool pants. She took in Sunny's parka and jeans and said, "I'm afraid that if you're collecting for something—"

Sunny interrupted her right there. "I'm not here asking for favors, I'm here to do one for you."

That shut Christine up. Standing close to her, Sunny could see that although a little gray had crept into Christine's shoulder-length dark hair, she didn't hide it with dye. Her patrician features still held up well. Maybe a few fine lines had set themselves in around the edges of her large brown eyes. But in general, her picture would go well in any politician's election literature, working in a soup kitchen or helping kids at school.

But instead of the practiced do-gooder campaign expression, Christine looked wide-eyed and wary. "What sort of favor?"

"I'm going to read the minds of the cops who visited you the other day," Sunny told her. "They probably told you that they were checking all the folks who brought patients to Martin Rigsdale. That wasn't really true, although I'm pretty sure you wouldn't be asking around. In your situation, I don't think you'd want to be discussing visits from the police."

That was a shot in the dark, but Sunny had the satisfaction of seeing it hit home. Instead of slamming the door on her, Christine muttered, "Come in."

She led the way into a front parlor with a big fieldstone fireplace and furniture that was older than Sunny—the sort of stuff built to last for generations. "Where's Kristi?" Sunny asked, making Christine stumble slightly as she went to sit in an overstuffed armchair.

"She's out," the dark-haired woman replied stiffly.

"And your husband is in Augusta, helping to run the state," Sunny went on. "Spending a lot of time up there these days. Ah, well, it gives us a chance for a private discussion. I suppose you know that some tongues are wagging about a separation."

That looked to have given Christine a few added gray hairs. "But that's not really what I'm here to talk about. I'm sure you're more interested in what the police know— and what they might suspect. They know you'd been having coffee with Martin Rigsdale at a diner near his office. You've been identified there."

True enough. Between Sunny and Tobe, Mark Trumbull had that fact. Now to mix in a little theory. "They suspect that Kristi's alibi for you isn't as rock solid as it seems. How would Kristi handle her medical expenses without you? For that matter, where would she live? Those are just crass, dollars-and-cents reasons why she might stretch the truth in your favor. There might be more high-minded motives, like avoiding scandal—"

"Stop!" Christine begged.

"But we haven't even gotten to the Café Artisan and how you almost got caught there." After all the buildup, Sunny tried her best shot—and immediately felt terrible as tears began trickling down Christine's cheeks.

"Do you want the money now?" she asked in a choked voice. "I thought I was supposed to deliver it tonight."

"What?" Sunny asked in shock.

"What do you mean, 'What?' " Christine fought to blink her tears away, her eyes getting a bit sharper.

"You let the cat out of the bag," Sunny said. "You're being blackmailed?"

Christine trembled between fear and anger. "Who are you?"

"Someone who's trying to find out who killed Martin Rigsdale," Sunny told her bluntly. "A friend of mine is being accused, and I'd like to clear her. So what are you paying to hide, the affair or Martin's murder?"

A little belatedly, Sunny began looking around to make sure Christine had no weapons close at hand. *Looks as if my reporter's instincts are outrunning my instincts for self-preservation,* she thought ruefully.

But it appeared that she'd gotten a good read on her subject. Christine deflated in her seat. "The affair, of course. Why would I kill Martin? We were in love." She paused for a second. "At least, I thought we were."

"A lot of women come to that conclusion, sooner or later," Sunny said a little grimly. "Usually it happens when they discover they aren't the only woman in a man's life."

"What?" Christine seemed genuinely shocked by that news.

"Maybe the word hasn't made it out here yet, but it's common knowledge in Portsmouth that Martin and his receptionist didn't have a merely professional relationship."

"But she's barely older than Kristi!"

Sunny nodded. "Some people might see that as motive."

"I didn't kill Martin, and don't know who did." Christine's show of spirit quickly fizzled. "Maybe it was the blackmailer. Maybe it's all my fault." The tears began again.

"How is it your fault?"

"The night Martin . . . died"—Christine tripped over the word—"I was supposed to bring money."

"Where?" Sunny asked.

"To his office—he was going to deliver it. I was supposed to come in the secret way—"

"Wait a minute," Sunny said, "you're getting ahead of me. What secret way?"

Christine actually blushed. "It's stupid, really. He had a panel built into his office wall. It led out to the back stairs—and the back door. No one could see me come in, and we—we could go up to his bedroom. And then I could leave again by the back way. He said he'd leave it unlocked so I could bring the money."

She looked down, trembling. "But I couldn't. I could only get my hands on half of what they wanted. When I went to the bank, I found out that my husband had withdrawn most of the money from our joint account. We are separated, and I guess that was the first step toward a real divorce."

"And you lost it," Sunny said, remembering Kristi's story about her mom's out-of-the-ordinary behavior.

Christine nodded. "I didn't know what to do. I got a bottle of wine, trying to work up the nerve to call Martin and tell him. But I had too much. The next thing I remember, I was waking up at one in the morning." Humiliation and guilt added ten years to her face. "If I'd even brought what I could have, maybe the blackmailer—"

"I hate to tell you this, but the blackmailer was Martin." Sunny tried to make her voice gentle. "You have to know he was having money problems."

Christine shook her head violently. When she spoke, she

picked up on the second thing Sunny had said, not the black-mail. "His wife took him to the cleaner's in the divorce."

"He messed up their finances way before the divorce," Sunny told her. "And then he borrowed money from some shady characters to set up his new office. That got him in worse trouble. Martin tried to pressure money out of Jane. When did he tell you about this blackmail?"

"Right before he died," Christine said. "He told me he'd gotten pictures and a demand for fifty thousand dollars. I knew he didn't have that kind of money." Her chin trembled, but she held it high. "And you're wrong about Martin being the blackmailer. Now that he's dead, they've come after me. It's sixty thousand dollars now. That wasn't easy to get. I had to sell some family jewelry."

Sunny blinked, the wheels in her head suddenly spinning into high gear. "And the drop-off is tonight?"

Christine nodded. "I was told to wait for instructions. That's why I thought—"

"Don't take this the wrong way, Christine, but I don't think you're cut out to deal with this," Sunny told the woman, her voice calm and confident. After weeks of stumbling around in the fog, she'd suddenly stepped out into blazing clarity. "I know who's behind this little scheme." She smiled. "And I know a person who can help stop it."

*

"This is crazy," Will said for about the tenth time as they drove to Portsmouth.

"Maybe." Sunny sat with a canvas bag in her lap as she drove, wearing one of Christine's coats—one with a hood. "But if this works out, it will take care of all our problems."

She ran through the instructions from the blackmailer. She—or rather, Christine—was supposed to leave the moneybag in a kid's activity structure in a playground. "It sounds familiar," Sunny said.

"It should," Will told her. "Did you watch the cop show this week where the kid was abducted? This is how they were supposed to pass on the ransom." He looked at the street signs and then ducked down in his seat. "We're getting close. I'm going to bail at the next red light."

That was a block away. As Sunny made the obligatory stop, Will opened the door and slid out. They had already taken the precaution of turning off the Wrangler's dome light. Sunny slowly drove on, as if she were unsure of the neighborhood. *Got to give Will a chance to get into position.*

At last she reached the playground. Pulling up the hood, she got out of the Jeep, moving hesitantly and looking around. *I don't see anyone. Hope nobody else does.*

Her destination was pretty obvious—a structure painted in very primary reds, yellows, and blues. Sunny advanced and put her bag as directed on the corkscrew slide. Then, keeping her head down, she walked back to her Jeep and started the engine.

Sunny drove off, took the first right and then the first parking space she could find, running back to the park on foot. She arrived to find two figures struggling by the play structure. The smaller one had a distinct disadvantage because she was also carrying a large duffel bag.

"Give it up, Dawn!" Sunny called as she came forward.

That apparently took the fight out of Dawn Featherstone. She stopped struggling with Will and swore. "You're always sticking your nose in where it's not wanted," she said. "Getting the cops to ask me a bunch of questions about how things were between Martin and me. Helping that witch who killed him."

"You mean Jane?" Sunny was confused. Why was Dawn still claiming that Jane had killed Martin? She glanced over at Will, who stood with his cop face on, listening to Dawn's confession.

"Yeah. She was always holding Martin back, until he finally had to get rid of her," Dawn accused. "And then she kept trying to get back at him. She had money, but she wouldn't help Martin out. Oh, no. And then, when he finally got hold of some money and we were gonna get outa town, she killed him."

She tapped the duffel bag hanging from her shoulder. "But I was the one holding the money. It was in the trunk of my car when the cops came. It's enough to get me started somewhere else, but I figured I'd get some more from that other old hag that Martin was stringing along. I just had to time it right." Her voice wobbled. "I couldn't be sure when the memorial would be. When we could have the cremation and the urn."

Sunny was still digesting the first part of Dawn's outburst. "Old hag?" she echoed. "Do you mean Christine Venables, the woman who was Martin's age?"

"Martin was always young—always fun," Dawn spat. "And he was smart, too. Look what he got hold of."

She unzipped the bag and dropped it to the ground. Packets of bills spilled out. It was hard not to stare, and Dawn took advantage of the instant's distraction, pulling a gun from her coat pocket.

"And I'm gonna hold on to it!"

23

Shadow carefully hooked his claws into one of the ceiling squares and pulled, peering down into the room below through the opening he'd made. Yes, this was the place where he'd been imprisoned. He pulled the square aside, disentangled his claws, and dropped to the shelf below. For a long moment, he crouched in silence, straining his senses to the fullest. The room was empty.

He glanced toward the window. Good, it was long dark. He'd feared that his wanderings in the dimness above might have thrown off his internal sense of time. But he'd obviously made the right choice about when to scout this area. This was an hour when most humans slept.

He crept down to the floor level, sniffing about. His nose wrinkled at a bad scent, but this was good news. The One Who Reeks had been in here not too long ago. As he came to the wall, he detected a more welcome smell. Shadow quickly stepped forward to eat and drink.

She may smell terrible, but I have to admit, this one is generous.

Shadow ate enough to take the edge off his hunger and drank greedily. It was dry and dusty up beyond the ceiling. Then he took a quick trip to the litter box and started climbing back up again. Humans were supposed to sleep at this time of night, but he couldn't be sure about the One Who Reeks. Best to be gone in case she came in to check the room.

Although she's welcome to all the gifts I left. He hadn't covered up the deposit he'd left in the litter box.

*

Dawn Featherstone told Sunny and Will to back up. "You a cop?" she asked Will, who nodded.

"Okay. Take out the gun, just with the tips of your fingers, and put it on the ground. And then both of you, drop your cell phones," Dawn ordered, following the TV cop show writer's rules of procedure.

Will disarmed himself, and he and Sunny dropped their phones.

"You have handcuffs?" Dawn asked. "Yeah. Toss me the keys. Then take the cuffs and put 'em on your right wrist. Stick that hand over here." Dawn pointed to a sturdy metal ladder on the side of the play structure. "Now, you. Come around and click the other side of the cuffs to your left wrist."

When Sunny complied, they were pretty well attached to the jungle gym. The ladder was kid-sized, the rungs set too closely together to squeeze through. Its base was set in concrete, and the top was welded to one of the metal pipes supporting the structure, *Looks like we're here for the duration,* Sunny thought as the cuff snapped shut.

"Good." Dawn might get most of her ideas from TV, but she seemed to know her way around firearms. She picked up Will's pistol and efficiently removed the magazine. After throwing that and the handcuff keys in one direction into the darkness, she kicked the empty pistol and the phones the opposite way.

Then she checked the bag that Sunny had brought. "Newspaper. It figures. Those rich old broads, they're really cheap."

Dawn shrugged. "Well, I still have what I came with. And by the time anybody finds you, I'll be long gone." She repacked the duffel, slung it over her shoulder, and left.

Sunny tugged against the cuff, wincing as the hard metal cut into her wrist. "What are we going to do?"

"Looks as if Dawn knows lots about TV cops, but not so much about real ones." He twisted around, trying to get his free hand into his right pocket. "For instance, in the real world, it's a good idea to carry a spare set of keys."

He fished the keys out, freed himself and Sunny, then retrieved his pistol. "You also carry a spare magazine or two." He clicked one in place, worked the action, and started after Dawn.

"Stay back," he warned Sunny. "I don't know if that gun she was waving around is loaded, but she seems to know how to use it."

Sunny let him lead, but she was almost on his heels as he ran in the direction Dawn had taken. "Carrying all that cash, Dawn won't want to run far. She must have a car close by."

They exited the darkness of the park and looked up and down the street ahead. It was empty. Keeping his pistol down by his side, Will ran to the first intersection, looking first right, then left.

Halfway down the block, Sunny spotted Dawn dangling from a big figure's right hand. His left hand held out her gun. Olek gave the girl a shake and then deposited her in the street. Beside him, Dani was shouldering the duffel bag as Will and Sunny came up. "It was just as well we give you the backing," Dani said. "She was a trickier one than you thought."

Olek kept a cold eye on the pistol in Will's hand, Dawn's gun ready in his.

"Okay, you got what you wanted." Will's voice went into tough cop mode. "You'll be heading out of town now?"

"Right now," Dani promised. "We finish with the doctor's business, so you tell the other cops to check his bank. Not so good. I don't know if I come back." He sighed. "More trouble."

Then he looked at Sunny. "But remember this. I owe you a favor."

She watched the Ukrainian odd couple head off for their car. "Guess we'd better start looking for our phones so we can call Trumbull," she said. "I bet he's going to love this."

*

Detective Trumbull was definitely not in a good mood. Even Fitch was staying out of his way. "You've got a hell of a nerve," the big man rumbled at Sunny. Then he glared at Will. "And why in God's name did you help her?"

"We were trying to break up an extortion attempt," Will

said. "Preferably in a way that wouldn't cause any embarrassment for an elected official."

"Yeah? Well, you'll find that Maine officials don't have much pull on this side of the river," Trumbull said, but that was mostly bluff. One thing that Sunny had learned from her dad was that politics was definitely the art of the possible.

Trumbull regarded them sourly for a moment. "So you thought that you could talk this girl out of blackmail, and she turns up with a duffel full of money—money that Rigsdale had gotten his hands on."

"Money that these two foreign guys turned up and claimed," Sunny said.

"They're some sort of Ukrainian loan sharks," Will said. "I thought things were going to get hairy, but they had paperwork proving that the money belonged to them."

"You can check with Martin's bank," Sunny added.

"Right," the detective said with heavy irony. "Everything nice and neat. I know when I'm being handed a package. And don't keep smiling at me like a nine-year-old, young woman. I should rat your boyfriend here out to Sheriff Nesbit and get his butt roasted but good."

Sunny continued to give him a bright smile. *But you've got other things to worry about, like a murder investigation circus that's just gained two more rings. And I've done some checking. As annoyed as you might be with Will, you really don't like Frank Nesbit.*

Finally, Trumbull made a cutting gesture with his hand. "All right. Thanks very much for your statements. I'll be questioning Ms. Featherstone. Good-bye."

As they got back into Sunny's Wrangler, she was still

in a good mood. "Well, that could have gone much worse. Feel like having a very early breakfast?"

Will shook his head, frowning in thought. "We've dumped a lot on Trumbull's plate, but it still doesn't clear Jane. And even worse, we're clean out of murder suspects."

"Then we'll have to look for more," Sunny replied. "And considering the way Martin liked to spend his time, I expect that they'll be female." She drove for a moment in silence. "In fact, I'm pretty sure there must be another lover in the underbrush."

"What leads you to that conclusion, Sherlock?" Will asked.

"Martin's secret doorway to paradise," Sunny replied. "It has to be the way the killer got in. I expect Dawn didn't know about it—after all, that was how Martin was sneaking Christine in, literally behind her back. Dawn was on the front desk, and we were the only people who came in that way—that's why she keeps insisting that Jane did Martin in."

Will nodded slowly. "We know the back door was unlocked for Christine. Now we just have to find out who used it instead."

"At least we've gotten Jane and Tobe some breathing space." The conversation lapsed for a moment as Sunny negotiated the bridge crossing. "In the meantime, I'd like to suggest a new project."

"It doesn't have anything to do with blackmail and foreign money launderers, does it?" Will asked warily.

"No," Sunny told him, "it's a lot farther down the scale—catnapping."

As they got off the interstate and began negotiating the winding country roads, Sunny related the other story that Mrs. Martinson had passed along.

"So you think this Dowdey woman might be holding Shadow against his will?" The skeptical, tough-cop tone crept into Will's voice.

"Shadow is a wanderer," Sunny said. "That's the first thing Ada Spruance told me about him. And I guess he proved it when he wandered off from my house. If someone is locking him up in the hopes of turning him into a house cat, I don't think that's going to turn out well."

Will sighed. "So what do you want to do?"

"Tomorrow—or later this morning—"

"Try 'early this afternoon,'" Will suggested.

"Whenever," Sunny said impatiently. "I'll print out some more posters. Then we'll visit Mrs. Dowdey, pretending we're going door to door."

"Try to shame her into giving up Shadow if she's got him?" Will nodded. "Sounds like a workable plan."

"And if that doesn't do it, we'll try some old-fashioned snooping," Sunny added. "I'll mention this system for getting cats acclimated, and ask to see what sort of setup she uses."

"I'm glad you started using 'I' instead of 'we,'" Will said.

"Well, of course you're coming along," Sunny told him. "I'll have a lot more clout if I come knocking at her door with a town constable at my side."

*

The weather was chill and blustery that afternoon as they made their way up Carolyn Dowdey's walk. But that wasn't the reason that Will looked so very ill at ease. "After last night, I'm going to be on pretty thin ice with the sheriff," he muttered. "This could be considered a misuse of authority."

"You're helping to look for a lost kitty," Sunny said. "What could be more innocent?"

She gave the bell a healthy ring and held her lost cat posters up. After a moment, Mrs. Dowdey opened the door a crack, peering doubtfully out at them. "Can I help you?"

"Oh, I hope so." Sunny tried to put a little excess enthusiasm into her voice. "Have you seen this cat in the neighborhood?" She went to hand over a poster and then brightened. "Wait a minute, you've actually met Shadow. It's Mrs. O'Dowd, right?"

The woman stiffened at having her name mistaken for that of the town's worst dive bar. "It's Dowdey," she corrected.

"I'm so sorry." Sunny went for her best contrite look. "It's just that I'm nearly out of my mind with worry over this little guy. He went off wandering in this horrible weather."

Mrs. Dowdey nodded, an odd expression on her face. "Some cats do that, I'm told."

"Even if he's adopted another family, I just want to know that he's safe," Sunny implored. She turned to Will. "Constable Price here has been kind enough to volunteer his time to help me search."

"Constable," the older woman repeated, giving Will a sidelong look. Will nodded, looking a little at a loss for words when confronted with the stink of spoiled perfume that wafted out the door.

"Yes, ma'am," he finally managed in his best good-cop voice. "Any help would be appreciated."

"I don't know what help I can offer," Mrs. Dowdey said dismissively. Then the Kittery Harbor Way kicked in as she added, "Other, perhaps, than inviting you in for a warm drink." Will turned to Sunny, giving her a you're-going-to-owe-me look.

Mrs. Dowdey led them into what had been a large, graceful center hall in the home's original incarnation. A formal parlor stood off on the left, but the woman led to the right, down a short hallway with a drop ceiling, and into what would have been the family room if a family had been living there. Large glass windows let in pale daylight—and probably let out a lot of heat. No wonder Carolyn Dowdey was wearing a heavy sweater. And she had a large, high-end brocade reclining chair pulled right up in front of a built-in fireplace that seemed a little small for the room.

"How lovely," Sunny lied through her teeth. "This looks like something Mr. Allerton would do."

"That's right." Her hostess smiled, obviously pleased.

"A friend of my dad's is considering some renovations, and that's one of the contractors he's considering. I understand he did a lovely job on Dr. Rigsdale's office—the one in Portsmouth."

"That's true," Mrs. Dowdey said, a bit less pleased at the turn in the conversation.

I wonder how much Allerton talked about that project? Sunny asked herself. *Who might know about the secret panel?*

"I heard he installed several exotic built-ins," Sunny

went on, keeping an eye on the other woman. Something was going on there, but she wasn't sure what. "But there were some cost overruns. I guess you have to expect that with construction."

"And with other things." Mrs. Dowdey went to the fireplace, opening the glass doors that protected the hearth. She picked up the poker and turned to Will. "Would you mind, Constable?"

"Certainly not," Will replied, stepping forward and reaching for the fireplace tool.

As he did, Carolyn Dowdey used it to whack him on the side of the head. Will went down in a heap.

"Overruns are all right when you're adding on to a house," the woman said to Sunny as if nothing had happened. "It's a different thing when your pet's life is at stake. Dr. Rigsdale deserved what I did to him."

In the dimness beyond the ceiling, Shadow crouched, trying to sleep. Every movement he made raised a cloud of dust. How much longer could he stay up here? He'd explored every place he could get to and hadn't found a way out.

Sooner or later, he'd come down for food or a drink, and the One Who Reeks would appear from behind the door. She'd find his hiding place and ensure he wouldn't even have that empty escape.

Sunny, why did I leave you? For the thousandth time, he asked himself the question. And as he did, his ears suddenly flicked forward. He was wishing so hard, he thought he heard Sunny. Her voice seemed to come from the big room. Shadow charged along the metal path and squashed himself through the hole in the wall. Could it be? Had she found him?

As he came through, he heard a crash. Yes, that was definitely Sunny's voice, getting louder.

*

"Excuse me?" Sunny popped out of her chair as Carolyn Dowdey advanced on her. "What are you doing?"

"Making sure I get to stay with my new cat," Mrs. Dowdey said, hefting the poker. "Mrs. Purrley got sick, and everything that so-called doctor recommended just made her sicker—and cost more money. Intravenous this, surgical that, and in the end I was giving daily doses of something to keep her going from a syringe. And finally, when my poor cat just couldn't keep going anymore, he suggested that she be put to sleep. Of course, he charged for that, too."

"I'm sorry." Sunny maneuvered to keep the chair between her and this crazy lady.

"And then, when Mrs. Purrley was gone, he gave me a movie disc that was supposed to make me feel better." Mrs. Dowdey's cat face wasn't quivering; it was twitching. "It didn't. And then he had the nerve to charge me for it! That was when I decided it was time to give Dr. Rigsdale some of his own medicine."

Okay, that's enough, Sunny decided. *You're younger and faster than this old woman. Just dodge around her, get out the door . . .*

Before Sunny could try, Mrs. Dowdey launched a wild swing that struck the chair Sunny was sheltering behind. It toppled over.

Don't know that I'm stronger. Sunny backpedaled, darting behind an occasional table. Mrs. Dowdey shattered the thing, knickknacks and all. "It was easy enough. Joe Allerton had mentioned that silly secret door. Dr. Rigsdale was at his desk, with his back to me. The first thing he said was, 'Did you bring the money?' " She laughed, an ugly, rasping sound. "It was the last thing he said, too."

She waved the poker. "I came prepared, you see, and I was lucky, too. It was easy enough use his chair to roll him into the examination room after I hit him. Getting him onto the table was a little more work, but I managed in the end. Then it was just a question of finding the right drug among his supplies. He'd already taught me how to do the injections for Mrs. Purrley."

Her face crumpled a little at the memory of her cat but then brightened as she returned to her story. "I found a vein and emptied the hypodermic into it. His arm jerked, breaking off the tip, but he was well on his way by then. It's remarkable, really, how easy it is to kill someone when you put your mind to it."

Or when you lose your mind, Sunny thought. *Got to get to the door. Can't turn my back on her.* She faked left, dodged right, and took cover for a moment behind another table. Her pursuer destroyed that one, too.

An irrelevant thought popped into Sunny's head. *This is going to cost a fortune to redecorate. After they clean up all the blood.*

She tried to grab the poker from Carolyn's grasp and nearly got her wrist broken for her trouble. Shaking her hand, Sunny ducked behind another chair. She was running out of furniture. This time when Mrs. Dowdey came at her, Sunny shoved the chair so it fell onto the woman. Carolyn stumbled back, and Sunny ran for the door. She got as far as the fireplace before a reflection in the glass door gave her a second's warning.

Sunny ducked and rolled as that damned poker swooped through the spot where her head had been a moment before. She scrabbled back on her hands, knees, and butt. Carolyn Dowdey came straight at her, the poker raised in both hands to bring it down in a death stroke.

She paused for a second as a weird noise came from above—a keening, guttural, coughing and sneezing noise.

And then one of the ceiling panels gave way, and a furious, dusty cat came flying down.

Carolyn had twisted round to see what was going on. Shadow landed against her shoulder. He bounced one way, she went the other, crashing into the oversized recliner. It rocked back and flew open as Carolyn landed face-first against the back.

The woman recovered quickly, swarming over the arm of the chair as Sunny regained her feet.

"Enough!" Carolyn shouted, coming at Sunny again.

Then she let out a scream and lurched back. Shadow circled her legs, darting in to claw again. Carolyn swung low with the poker as Shadow danced away.

She's right, Sunny decided. *This is enough!* She leaped onto Carolyn before the woman could swing at Shadow again. They rolled around in a confused and nasty struggle, Sunny choking and half-blinded by the stink of rancid perfume. And then Carolyn was over her again, teeth bared, her cat face murderous.

Is this the last thing a mouse sees? Sunny found herself wondering.

Then Shadow came whirling up, going for Carolyn's

face. She reared back, Sunny bucked, the woman flopped on the floor . . .

And a foot came down on the poker.

Will weaved a little, but he had his gun out and pointed at Carolyn Dowdey.

"Get out of this house!" she screeched at him. "I'll say you came in here and tried to rob me! Whatever you think you know, it's not enough to prove anything!"

Sunny was using the opened recliner to pull herself to her feet when she suddenly stopped. "Or maybe not," she said. "My dad had a chair like this in our living room. He and my mom got into an awful fight because she said he'd lost one of her silver spoons. Went on for months, until one day he pushed back to recline, and I saw something shiny in the piece of fabric that connects the footrest to the seat."

On her feet now, she pointed to the hammocklike piece of brocade fabric. Nestled in it was a hypodermic syringe— a syringe with a broken needle.

Still on her knees, Carolyn Dowdey looked down, a dazed expression on her face. "I thought I brought it home, but I couldn't find it. So I figured I must have lost it on the way."

"Call 911," Will told Sunny. "The sheriff's going to be happy about one thing. This woman is going to another jurisdiction."

*

Even with the fatal hypodermic turning up, Carolyn Dowdey might have made a long, drawn-out legal fight of it. But now that the cat was out of the bag—or the ceiling— she told the whole story to the officer who arrived, to

Sheriff Nesbit, Detectives Trumbull and Fitch . . . and even to the news crews that quickly gathered. It was as if, after years of being alone, Mrs. Dowdey relished being the center of attention. As for Sunny, she just wanted to get done with the formalities of giving a statement and dealing with the media as quickly as possible. The big thing was to get Shadow safely home. Besides, he didn't like the bright lights from the cameras.

It was a pretty odd-looking party that convened the next day. Both Will Price and Tobe Phillips sported shiners. Will also had a bandage over his cheekbone. Mike and Mrs. Martinson shared half the couch. Will sat on the other side, with Sunny on the floor at his feet. Across the room, Tobe had an armchair, and Jane sat on the floor.

Shadow occupied Sunny's lap, purring away. He'd been very attached to her since coming home—sometimes literally. She had pulls in several sweaters from his attempts to climb on her.

"Are you ready?" Jane asked. "Start petting Shadow and making much of him. Let him know you love him."

While Sunny did that, Jane reached into the bag at her side and took out Toby the pup. He had grown noticeably bigger already, but showed the same bumbling eagerness as before when Jane put his paws on the floor.

Toby spotted Shadow and, yipping like a nut, came toward him. Under Sunny's hands, she could feel the cat's muscles tense. But with Sunny holding him, Shadow held his ground until Toby came nose to nose with him.

The cat gave a deep sigh. Sunny wasn't sure if that was annoyance or resignation. But he stayed there . . . until Toby suddenly came at him with a large, pink tongue.

Shadow tried to jump back, and Sunny lifted him to her shoulders. "Okay, that's enough for a first try," she said. "And for the time being, the new house rule is no licking."

The others laughed and raised glasses. "No licking!"

"At least," Will leaned forward to mutter, "not on the first date."